YOU NEVEI
THE NEXT PAGE WILL TAKE
YOU...

You hold in your hand Armchair Fiction's twelfth volume of Science Fiction Gems, a collection full of first-rate stories from the most imaginative minds ever to take up the speculative fiction pen.

You'll wander through time & space; be inspired by weird and wonderful creatures, or fight seemingly insurmountable intergalactic problems. Or perhaps you'll set foot on distant worlds, where time and space shift back and forth or deadly seas threaten your very survival.

If old fashioned space opera is your cup of tea, you'll find yourself fighting for your life against an interplanetary race of deranged aliens who are hell bent on destroying the Earth!

All these and more will usher you on a thought-provoking journey, guided by the most exciting authors of yesteryear.

TABLE OF CONTENTS

SCIENCE FICTION GEMS

Volume 12

THEODORE STURGEON
and others

**Edited and Compiled by
Gregory Luce**

ARMCHAIR FICTION
PO Box 4369, Medford, Oregon 97504

The original text of these stories first appeared in Amazing Stories, Fantastic, Super Science Stories, Orbit Science Fiction, *and* Space Science Fiction.

Copyright 2016 by Gregory J. Luce
All Rights Reserved

For more information about Armchair Books and products, visit our website at…

www.armchairfiction.com

Or email us at…

armchairfiction@yahoo.com

Beware the Fury

By THEODORE STURGEON

Meet Wolf Reger—traitor. Compared to him Benedict Arnold was a national hero and Judas Iscariot a paragon of virtue. At least that's the way it showed in the Major's notes... But traitors aren't born that way. Something has to happen to them long before they turn against society. That's why, when you dig deep enough, you may find that the word traitor can be one hell of a misnomer...

READ it for yourself," said the Major.

She took the sheaf of flimsies from him and for a moment gave him that strange dry gaze. *The woman's in shock,* he thought, and did what he could to put down the other two memories he had of eyes like that: an injured starling, which had died in his hand; his four-year-old niece, the time he struck her, and the long unbearable moment between the impact and her tears. Mrs. Reger read carefully and slowly.

Department of Defense
Bureau of Astronautics
Division of Planetary Exploration
Personnel Office
TOP SECRET

She said, at last, "That is the foulest thing a human being has ever done." Then her mouth slept again.

"I'm glad you agree," he said gratefully. "I was afraid that—"

"I don't think I understand you," she said tonelessly.

"That's what I was afraid of," he said miserably. "You meant the report. I thought you meant Wolf Reger."

She glanced down at the report. "That isn't Wolf. Wolf might be a lot of things...things that are...hard to understand. But he isn't a traitor." The Major saw her face lifting and turned his head to avoid those hurt eyes. "I think," she said quietly, "that you'd better go, Major, and take those lies with you."

He made no move toward the report. "Mrs. Reger," he suddenly shouted, "do you think I'm enjoying this? Do you think I volunteered for this job?"

"I hadn't thought about you at all."

"Try it," he said bitterly. Then, "Sorry. I'm sorry. This whole thing…" He pulled himself together. "I wish I could believe you. But you've got to realize that a man died to make that report and get it back to us. We have no choice but to take it for the truth and act accordingly. What else can we do?"

"Do what you like. But don't ask me to believe things about my husband that just aren't so."

God, he thought, *where did a rat like Reger ever find such a woman?* As gently as he could, he said, "Very well, Mrs. Reger. You needn't believe it… May I tell you exactly what my assignment is?"

She did not answer.

He said, "I was detailed to get from you everything which might have any bearing on—on this report." He pointed. "Whether I believe it or not is immaterial. Perhaps if you can tell me enough about the man, I won't believe it. Perhaps," he said, knowing his voice lacked conviction, "we can clear him. Wouldn't you help clear him?"

"He doesn't need clearing," she said impatiently. Then, when he made a tiny, exasperated sound, she said, "I'll help you. What do you want to know?"

All the relief, all the gratitude, and all the continuing distaste for this kind of work were in his voice. "Everything. Why he might do a thing like that." And, quickly, "Or why he wouldn't."

BEWARE
THE FURY

By
THEODORE STURGEON

Illustrated by
Louis Priscilla

7

She told him about Wolf Reger, the most hated man on Earth.

Beware the fury of a patient man.

Wolf Reger had so many talents that they were past enumerating. With them he had two characteristics that were extreme. One was defenselessness. The other was an explosive anger, which struck without warning, even to Reger himself.

His defenselessness sprang from his excess of ability. When blocked, it was all too easy for him to excel in some other field. It was hard to make him care much for anything. Rob him, turn him, use him—it didn't matter. In a day, a week, he could find something better. For this he was robbed, and turned, and used.

His anger was his only terror. Perhaps this was innate; more likely it was the result of his guardian's cold theory of discipline, and a conviction that anger is a destructive habit and must be crushed the instant it shows itself. When he was two, when he was three, and twice when he was five, Wolf Reger was knocked unconscious by single, instant blows when he showed anger. Direct punishment was never necessary again.

When he was eight he was chasing another boy—it was fun; they ran and laughed and dodged through the boy's large old house. And at the very peak of hilarity, the other boy ran outside and slammed the french doors in Wolf's face and stood grinning through the glass. Wolf instantly hit the face with his fist. The double-thick glass shattered. Wolf severed two tendons and an artery in his wrist, and the other boy fell gasping, blood from his carotid spurting between his futile fingers. The boy was saved, but the effect on Wolf was worse than if he had died.

He never ran and shouted again. He lived every moment of the next four years under the pressure of his own will, holding down what he felt was an internal devil, analyzing every situation he met for the most remote possibility of its coming to life again.

When he was twelve he met a situation he could not avoid. He was in his second year of high school then, and every day for three weeks a bulky sophomore twice his size would catch him on his way from English to Geometry II, wrap a thick arm around his neck, and grind a set of knuckles into his scalp. Wolf took it and took it, and one day he tore himself free and struck. He was small and thin, and the chances are that the surprise of the attack was more effective than its power. Their legs were entangled and the bigger boy was off balance. He hit the tile floor with his head and lay quite still with his lips white and blood trickling from his ear. For six weeks they did not know if he would live or not. Wolf was expelled from school the day it happened, and never went to another. From that point on he never dared be angry.

It was easy to hate Wolf Reger. He surpassed anyone he worked with and was disliked for it. He retreated from anyone who wanted what he had, and was despised for it.

He had two great successes—one a chemical process and one an airfoil design. They taught him enough about fame to frighten him away from it. Fame meant people, meetings, associates. After that he let others take the credit for the work he did, and if he hated them, he dared not show it.

At thirty he was married.

"Why?"

The question hung offensively in the air between them for an appreciable time before the Major realized that he had spoken it aloud and incredulously.

She said, carefully, "Major, what have you in your notebook so far?"

He looked down at the neat rows of symbols. "A few facts. A few conjectures."

With an accuracy that shook him in his chair, she said coldly, "You have him down as a warped little genius with every reason to hate humanity. If I weren't sure of that, I wouldn't go on with this. Major," she said suddenly in a different voice, "suppose I told you that I was walking down the street and a man I had never seen before suddenly roared at me, leapt on my back, knocked me down, beat me and rolled me in the gutter. Suppose you had fifty eyewitnesses who would swear it happened. What would you think of the man?"

He looked at her sleek hair, her strong, obedient features. Despite himself he felt a quixotic anger toward her attacker, even in hypothesis. "Isn't it obvious? The man would have to be a drunk, a psychopath. At the very least he would have to be deluded, think you were someone else. Even if he did, only a real skunk would do a thing like that to a woman." He suddenly realized how easily she had pulled him away from his subject, and was annoyed. "What has this to do—"

"I hope you'll soon see," she said thoughtfully. Then, "You wanted to know why he married me."

The army wants to know that, he corrected silently. *I'd like to know why you married him.*

She committed suicide.

Relentlessly she told the Major why, and he put his pencil down until she had finished with that part of the story. This was a report on Reger, not on his wife. Her reasons were good, at the time, and they constituted a tale of disillusion and defeat, which has been, and will be, told again and again.

She stumbled out into the desert and walked until she dropped; until she was sure there could be no rescue; until she had barely strength to lift the phial and drink its contents. She regained consciousness eight months later, in civilian married quarters at Space Base Two. She had been dead twice.

It was a long time before she found out what had happened. Reger, who would not permit himself to move about among people, took his exercise at night, and found her.

How he saved her, no one but Reger could know. He knew she was drugged or poisoned, and exhausted. He found the right medication to keep her from slipping further away, but for weeks he could not bring her back.

Her autonomic nervous system was damaged. When she began to convalesce, he started drug therapy.

And still he kept his job, and no one knew.

And then one day there was a knock on his door. One room and bath; to open the door was to open the whole room to an outsider. He ignored the knock and it came again, and then again, timidly but insistently. He extrapolated, as always, and disliked his conclusion. A woman in his bachelor quarters created a situation which could only mean people and people talk, and talk—and the repeated, attenuated annoyance which, of all things, he feared most.

He picked her up and carried her into the bathroom and shut the door. Then he answered the knock. It was nothing important—a chirping little bird of a woman who was taking up a collection for a Thanksgiving party for the orphans in town. He wrote her a check and got rid of her, snarling suddenly that she must never bother him again—and pass the word. That, and the size of the check, took care of her and anyone like her.

He nearly collapsed from reaction after she had gone. He knew he could not possibly outguess the exigencies that might arise to bring other people on errands. She had been with him for four months now. How could he explain her? Doctors would know she had been under treatment for some time; the Air Force people at the Base, and their cackling wives would make God only knew what sort of racket about it.

So he married her.

It took another six weeks to build her up sufficiently to be moved. He drove her to a town a hundred and fifty miles away and married her in a hotel room. She was under a skillfully applied hypnotic, and carefully instructed. She knew nothing about it at the time and remembered nothing afterward. Reger then applied for married quarters, moved her back to the Base, and continued her therapy. Let them pry.

"There's your androphobe," said Mrs. Reger. "He could have let me die. He could have turned me over to the doctors."

"You're a very attractive woman," he pointed out. "You were that, plus a challenge...two kinds of challenge. Could he keep you alive? Could he do it while doing his job? A man who won't compete with people generally finds something else to pit himself against."

"You're quite impartial while you wait for all the facts," she said bitterly.

"No I'm not," he said, and quite astonished himself by adding, "It's just that I can't lie to you." There was a slight emphasis on the last word, which he wished he could go back and erase.

She let it pass and went on with her story.

She must have had consciousness of a sort long before he was aware of it. She was born again, slowly, aware of comfort and safety, an alternation of light and dark, a dim appreciation of the ways in which her needs were met, a half-conscious anticipation of his return when she found herself alone.

He told her, with terror in his eyes, of their marriage, and he begged her pardon for it. It was as if a harsh word from her would destroy him. And she smiled and thanked him.

She convalesced very quickly after that. She tried her very best to understand him. She succeeded in making him talk about himself, and was careful not to help him, ever, nor to work with him at anything.

At the time the *Starscout* was in the ways, and they were running final tests on it. Reger was forced to spend more and more time out at the gantry area.

His extrapolations never ceased, and he was aware before she was that, not being a Wolf Reger, her needs were different from his. He suggested that she walk in the sun when he was away. He told her where the commissary was, and left money for shopping. She did as he expected her to do.

Then he didn't come back from the gantry area any more, and when the fifty or sixty hours got to be seventy and eighty, she made up her mind to find him. She knew quite a few people at the Base by that time. She walked in, stopping at the post office on the way. The divorce papers were waiting for her there.

The Major dropped his pencil.

"You didn't know about that."

"Not yet. We'd have found out anyway." He stooped blindly for the pencil and cracked his head noisily on the coffee table. He demanded, "Why? Why did he divorce you?"

"He didn't. He filed suit. It has to be put on the court calendar and then heard, and then adjudicated, and then there's a ninety day wait...you know. I went to a dance."

"A—oh." He understood that this was in answer to his question. "He divorced you because you went to a dance?"

"No! ...well, yes." She closed her eyes. "I used to go to the Base movie once in a while when Wolf was working. I went down there and there was a dance going on instead. I sat with one of the women from the commissary and watched, and after a while her husband asked me to dance. I did. I knew Wolf would have let me if he'd been there—not that he ever would.

"And I happened to glance through the door as we danced past, and Wolf was standing just outside. His face…"

She rose and went to the mantel. She put out her hand very slowly, watching it move, and trailed the tips of her fingers along the polished wood. "All twisted. All…

"As soon as the music stopped," she whispered, "I ran out to him. He was still there."

The Major thought: *Don't break, for God's sake don't. Not while I'm here.*

"Extrapolation," she said. "Everything he saw, he computed and projected. I was dancing. I suppose I was smiling. Wolf never learned to dance, Major. Can you imagine how important that can be to a man who can do anything?

"When I got outside he was just the same as always, quiet and controlled. What he was going through inside, I hate to think. We walked home and the only thing that was said was when I told him I was sorry. He looked at me with such astonishment that I didn't dare say anything else. Two days later he left."

"On the *Starscout*. Didn't you know he was a crewmember?"

"No. I found out later. Wolf had so many skills that he was nine-tenths of a crew all by himself. They'd wanted him for the longest time, but he'd always refused. I guess because he couldn't bear sharing quarters with someone."

"He did, with you."

"Did he?"

The Major did not answer. She said, "That was going to end. He was sure of that. It could end any time. But space flight's something else again."

"Why did he divorce you?"

She seemed to shake herself awake. "Have I been talking out loud?" she asked.

"What? Yes!"

"Then I've told you."

"Perhaps you have," he conceded. He poised his pencil.

"What are you going to write?" When he would not answer, she said, "Not telling the truth any more, Major?"

"Not now," he said firmly.

For the second time she gave him that searching inspection, really seeing him. "I wonder what you're thinking," she murmured.

He wrote, closed the book and rose. "Thank you very much for cooperating like this," he said stiffly.

She nodded. He picked up his hat and went to the door. He opened it, hesitated, closed it again. "Mrs. Reger —"

She waited, unbelievably still—her body, her mouth.

"In your own words—why did he file suit?"

She almost smiled. "You think my words are better than what you wrote?" Then, soberly, "He saw me dancing and it hurt him. He was shocked to the core. He hadn't known it would hurt. He hadn't realized until then that he loved me. He couldn't face that he was afraid we might be close. And one day he'd lose his temper, and I'd be dead. So he went out into space."

"Because he loved you."

"Because he loved me enough," she said quietly.

He looked away from her because he must, and saw the report still lying on the coffee table. "I'd better take this along."

"Oh yes, do." She picked it up, handed it to him. "It's the same thing as that story I told you—about the man knocking me down."

"Man—oh. Yes, that one. What was that about?"

"It really happened," she said. "He knocked me down and beat me, right in broad daylight, in front of witnesses, and everything I said about it is true."

"Bastard," growled the Major, and then blushed like a girl. "I'm sorry."

She did smile, this time. "There was a loading-dock there, in front of a warehouse. A piece of machinery in a crate got loose and slid down a chute toward the street. It hit a drum of gasoline and struck a spark. The first thing I knew, I was all over flames. That man knocked me down and beat them out with his bare hands. He saved my life."

Slowly, his jaw dropped. She said, "It makes a difference, when you know all the facts, doesn't it? Even when the first facts you got are all true?" She rapped the TOP SECRET stamp with her fingernails. "I said this was all a lie. Well, maybe it's all true. But if it is, it's like the first part of that little story. You need the rest of it. I don't. You don't know Wolf Reger. I do. Goodbye, Major."

He sat in his office at Headquarters and slowly pounded the fresh copy of his transcribed notes: *I have to send them the way they are,* he thought, and *but I can't. I can't.*

He swore violently and got up. He went to the water-cooler, punched out a paper cup, filled it, and hurled it into the wastebasket. *All I have is facts. She has faith.*

He cursed again and snatched up his briefcase, unlocked it, and took out the secret report. He slammed it down on top of his transcript. *One more look. One more look at the facts.*

He read:

This is the fourth time I've erased this tape and now I got no time for officialese if I'm going to get it all on here. A tape designed for hull inspection reports in space wasn't designed for a description of a planetary invasion. But that's what it's got to be. So, for the record, this is Jerry Wain, Starscout *navigator, captive on one of the cruisers that's going to invade Earth. First contact with extraterrestrials. Supposed to be a great moment in human history. Likely to be one of the last moments too.*

The Starscout's *gone and Minelli, Joe Cook, and the Captain are dead. That leaves me and that bastard Reger. The aliens had us bracketed before we knew it, out past Jupiter. They cut up the scout with some sort of field or something that powdered the hull in lines as broad as your hand. No heat, no impact. Just fine powder, and she fell apart. Joe never got to a suit. The Captain went forward to stay with the ship, I guess, and couldn't have lived long after they sliced the dome off the control room. The three of us got clear and they took us in. They cut Minelli up to see what his guts looked like. I haven't seen Reger but he's alive, all right. Reger, he can take care of himself.*

I've only seen two of the aliens, or maybe I saw one of 'em twice. If you can imagine a horseshoe crab made out of blue air foam, with a wide skirt all the way around it, the whole works about four and a half meters across, that's close. I'm not a biologist, so I guess I can't be much help on the details. That skirt sort of undulates front to back when it moves. I'd say it swims through

*the air—hop and glide, hop and glide. It can crawl too. First I thought it slid
along like a snail but once I saw a whole mess of little legs, some with pincers
on them. I don't know how many. Too many, anyhow. No eyes that I could
spot, although it must have 'em; it's light in here, grayish, like on a snowfield
on an overcast day. It comes from the bulkhead. Floor, too – everywhere.*

*Gravity, on a guess, is about one-sixth Earth. The atmosphere's hot, and
seems to be light gases. I cracked my oxy relief valve and struck a spark on it
with the back of my glove, and that was pretty spectacular. Hydrogen for sure.
Something else that gives an orange cast to the flame. You figure it.*

*The compartment I'm in is altogether bare. There's a transparent oval port
on one bulkhead. They can take off like a bullet and stop as if they'd hit a
wall. They have some way of cancelling inertia. Or most of it. Riding inside is
pretty rough, but coming to a dead stop in two seconds from a thousand k.p.h.
or better should butter you all over the walls instead of just slamming you into
the bulkhead like it does. They can't operate this inertia field close to a
planet—they use wings, and they don't have the right wings. Not for Earth.
Not yet.*

*I counted twenty-six ships—sixteen big ones, cruisers I guess you'd call
them; two-fifty to three hundred meters long, perfect cylinders. And ten small
ones, oblate spheres, thirty meters in diameter.*

*When they brought us in first they slung me in here and nothing happened
that I knew about, for sixteen hours. Then that first bug came in through a
sort of pucker in the wall that got transparent and spread out and let him
through and then bing! The wall was solid again.*

*I guess I went a little crazy. I had my antenna-wrench off the belt-rack
and was throwing it almost before I knew what I was doing. I missed. Didn't
allow for the gravity, I guess. It went high. The bug sort of humped itself and
next thing I knew I couldn't move. I could, inside the spacesuit, but the suit
was like a single iron casting. It toppled slowly and lay there.*

*The bug slid over to me and hitched up a little—that's when I saw all those
little legs—and got everything off my belt—torch, stillson, antenna-reel,
everything that would move. It didn't touch my tanks—I guess it knew
already about the tanks. From Reger, busy-boy Reger. It took the whole
bundle over to the outer bulkhead and all of a sudden there was a square hole
there. It dropped my stuff in and the hole went away, and out through the port
I could see my stuff flash away from the ship, going like hell. So that's how I
found out about the disposal chute.*

The bug slid away to the other wall and I was going to give it a shot from my heel-jets, but somehow I had sense enough not to. I didn't know what damage they'd do, and I might be able to use 'em later. If anyone's reading this, I did.

They don't feed me, and my converters are pretty low. I've rationed my air and water all I could, but it's past conversion now, without a complete recharge, and I'm not likely to get that.

This whole time, the ships have been busy. We're in the Belt. I'd guess, without instruments, around 270-20-95. Check those coordinates and hunt a spiral from that center—I'm pretty sure we're near that position. Put infrared on it; even if they've gone by then, there should be residual heat in these rocks out here. They've leeched onto a big one and it's practically gone now. They make long fast passes back and forth like a metal-planer. I can't see a ray or beam or anything, but the surface flows molten as the ships pass. Mining. I guess they filter the slag some way and distill the metals out. I wouldn't know. I'm a navigator. All I can think of is those ships making passes like that over the Golden Gate and Budapest and LaCrosse, Wisconsin.

I found out how to work the disposal chute. Just lean against it. It was a lock with some sort of heavy coils around it, inside, I guess to project refuse away from the ship so it wouldn't orbit.

Well, six hours ago a sort of dark spot began to show on the inboard bulkhead. It swelled up until it was a knob about the size of your two fists, shiny black, with some kind of distortion field around it so it was muzzy around the edges. For a while I couldn't figure it at all. I touched it and then took hold of it, and I realized it was vibrating around five hundred cycles, filling my suit with the note. I got my helmet onto it right away.

The note went on and then changed pitch some and finally spread out into a noise like a forty-cycle carrier, and something started modulating it, and next thing it was saying my name, flat and raspy, no inflection. An artificial voice, for sure. "Wain," it said, clearing itself up as it went along. "Wain, Wain."

So I kept my head tight against it and yelled, "Wain here."

It was quiet for a while, just the carrier, and then the voice came in again. I won't bother you with exactly what it sounded like. The language was rugged but clear, like "Wain we no have planet you have planet we take you help."

There was a lot of yelling back and forth until I got the picture. And what I want to tell you most is this: once in a while when I listened real carefully, I heard another voice, murmuring away. Reger—that I'll swear. It was if this voder, or voice machine, was being run by one of the bugs and Reger was telling it what to say but they wouldn't trust him to talk directly to me.

So damn cold-blooded, it wasn't us they were after. You clear a patch of wood, you're not trying especially to dispossess the squirrels and the termites. That just happens while you work.

For a while I hoped we could maybe do something, but item by item they knocked that out of my head. Reger'd told 'em everything.

We're done, that's all.

So I asked what's the proposition, and they said they could use me. They didn't really need me, but they could use me. They said I could have anything I wanted on Earth, and all the slaves I could put to work. Slaves.

Maybe I shouldn't even try to warn you. Maybe it'll be better if you never know what hit you...

Reger, he...he's...ah stick to facts, Wain. Something makes him hate Earth enough to...I don't see even a coward doing a thing like this just to save his skin. He has to have some other reason.

The bump on the wall said, Reger work with him, you can trust.

Yeah, I can trust. I told them what to do with their proposition and shove Reger along after it.

Now this is what I am going to do. Try, anyhow. My suit's the only one with a tape recorder, and it's internal. Could be Reger doesn't even know about it. What I'm going to do is wait until this ship starts paring away at the asteroid. It gets up quite a hell of a speed at each pass, more than you'd think, because of the inertialess field. At the sunward end of one pass, I'll go out the chute. I'll have the ship's speed plus the throw-out coils in the chute.

I'll gyro around to head for the sun. I've wired the heel-jet starter to my oxy supply. When the oxy stops flowing the jets'll cut in.

And I've wired the jets to my distress squealer. When the fuel's all gone the squealer'll cut in.

We're positioning over the rock.

Don't anybody call me a hero for doing this. I'm not doing it for you. I'm doing it to Reger. That bastard Reger...

Jimmy Wain here, over and out.

The Major lifted the flimsies to uncover his own transcript. Coldly it listed the pertinent facts of his interview with the traitor's wife. He read them through again slowly, right through the last paragraph, which said:

SUMMATION: *It is indicated that the subject is a brilliant but twisted individual, and that early influences as noted, plus his mode of life, have induced a morbid fear of himself and a deep distrust of every human being, including his wife. His extrapolative ability plus his vivid imagination seem to have created a certainty in him that he had been betrayed, or that he certainly would be. His actions as reported by Signalman Wain are apparently motivated by a conviction that all his life humanity has tried to anger him so that he will be punished for his anger. This is his opportunity for vengeance without punishment.*

The talker hissed, and a voice said, "Major, the Colonel would like your report on the Reger interview."

"Roger," He caught it up, held it, then slid it into his auto-writer and rapidly tapped out:

The undersigned wishes to stress the partial nature of the above report, based as it is on the statement of a man under serious strain. Further evidence might conceivably alter the conclusions as stated.

He signed it and added his rank and section, rolled it, canned it and slapped it into the pneumatic tube.

"Now what the hell did I do that for?" he asked himself. He knew what the answer was. He rose and went to the mirror in the corner by the water-cooler, and peered into it. He shook his head in disgust.

When the ships were sighted, Wain's recording came out of the files and went straight to the wire services. One of the columnists said later that the ensuing roar from Earth all but moved the moon out of its orbit.

Without Wain's recording, the alien might have slipped close, or even landed, before the world was alerted.

The ships came single file, faster than any man-made object had ever travelled. They were exactly what Wain had described.

They bore straight in for Earth, their single file presenting the smallest possible profile to Earth radar, (Reger knew radar.) When every known law of spatial ballistics dictated that with that course, at that velocity, they must plunge straight into the planet, they decelerated and swung to take up an orbit—rather, a powered course—around the planet, just out of rocket interceptor range (which Reger knew).

And now their wings could be seen. Telefax and television, newspapers and government agencies researched their contours in minutes. They were familiar enough—a gull-wing design which one aeronautical engineer described as having every characteristic that could be built into a wing. Each wing, from root to tip, had its own reverse dihedral. Each was sharply tapered, and sharply swept back. Even the little spherical destroyer had them, along with a boom to support the butterfly tail. There was one Earth design almost exactly like it—an extremely stable large-plane airfoil for subsonic use. The designer: Wolf Reger.

The space scouts roared up to challenge them, heavy with armament and anger. They sent a cloud of missiles ahead of them. There was H. E. and atomics, solid-shot and a whole spectrum of random-frequency radio, just in case.

The radio waves affected the aliens precisely as much—as little as the fusion warheads. Telescopic lenses watched the missiles race to their targets and simply stop there, to slide around the shining hulls and hang there until, one by one, they were brought aboard.

And then the little scouts tried to ram, and were deflected like angling guppies from the sides of an aquarium, to go screaming off into space and a laborious turn.

For three days the enemy circled outside the atmosphere, holding their formation, absorbing or ignoring everything Earth could throw at them.

The Major telephoned Reger's wife to ask if she had removed the name from her mailbox and doorbell. She said indignantly that she had not, would not, and need not. The Major sighed and sent a squad down late that night to arrest her. She was furious. Yet she conceded his point fairly the next morning when she saw the newspaper photographs of her apartment. Even the window frames were gone. The mob had chopped right through the floor in places, had even heaved the bathtub twelve floors down to the street. "You should know as much about people as you think you know about Wolf Reger," he said.

"You should know as much about Wolf as you do about people," she countered. There was, with her composure, a light he had not seen before.

He kept her in his office. She seemed not to mind. He let her read all the invasion reports as they came in, and he watched every flicker of expression in her face. "When are you going to admit that enough facts are in to show that there's no hero in this story, no one beating out flames?"

"Never. Have you ever been married, Major?"

Sourly, he thought, *Have you?* "No," he said.

"You've loved someone, though?"

He wondered how she kept her features so controlled under stress. He would like to learn that trick.

He said, "Yes."

"Well, then. You only need a few facts about the one you love. Just enough to point the way."

"Three points on a graph to give you a curve, so you can know its characteristics and extend it. Is that what you mean?"

"That's one of the things I mean."

"They call that extrapolation. Your boy's specialty."

"I like that," she said softly. "I like that very much." She detached her eyes from him, from the room, and smiled at what she saw.

"God!" he exploded.

"Major!"

"You're going to get clobbered," he said hoarsely. "You're going to get such a kick in the teeth...and there isn't a thing in the world I can do about it."

"Poor Major," she said, looking at him as if he were a memory.

There was a click, and electronic noise filled the room. The talker barked, "Enemy spiraling in. Stand by for trajectory."

"Now you'll see." They realized that they had spoken in unison, but it was the wrong time to exchange a smile.

"Arizona!" said the speaker, and "Stand by."

"Stand by hell," growled the Major. "We'll get the fine points by radio. Come on."

"You'll take me?"

"Wouldn't let you out of my sight."

21

They ran to the elevators, shot to the roof. A helicopter whisked them to the field, and a jet took them in and tore up and out to the lowering sun.

An unbroken cordon can be thrown about a hundred square miles in less than an hour and a half. This is true, because it was done immediately after the alien fleet touched Earth. Once the landing site was determined, the roads writhed with traffic, the desert crawled with men and machines, the air shook with transports, blossomed with parachutes. The ring had not quite closed when the enemy formation came down almost exactly in the predicted center. No longer a single file, the formation was nearly spherical. It arrived on Earth with two thunders—one, the terrible crack as the cloven air smashed back to heal itself, and rebounded and smashed again; the other, a shaking of the Earth itself.

And the cordon stopped, flattened, lay still as a stain while the furious globe built itself in the desert, flung its coat of many colors about itself, mounted the sky, and donned its roiling plumes.

And there were no ships, no aliens, no devils there in the desert, but hell itself.

They saw it from the jet, because they were keeping close radio contact with the landing, and straining their eyes into the sunset for a glimpse of the fleet. Their pilot said he saw them, coming in at an impossible speed. The Major missed them as they blinked by, but he did see their wings, like a flurry of paper over a windy corner, drifting brokenly down. And then the fireball fought the sun and, for a while, defeated it, until it became a leaning ghost in a broad, torn hat.

It seemed a long, long time after that when the Major, his palms tight to his eyes, whispered, "You knew that would happen."

"No I didn't," she whispered back, cathedral-awed. "I only knew *something* would happen."

"Reger did this?"

"Of course." She stirred, glanced at the tower of smoke, and shuddered.

"How?" he murmured. "How?"

He closed his eyes against the lingering glitter of the atom blast, and in his memory saw again those broken, fluttering pieces of wing.

"The wings tore off." To the pilot he said, "Isn't that what happened, Captain?"

"It sure is," said the young man. "And no wonder, sir, the way they flashed in. I've seen that happen before. You can fly under the speed of sound or over it, but you better not stay just at it. Looked to me as if they hung on the barrier all the way in."

"All flown from one set of controls...probably an automatic pilot, with the course and speed all set up." He looked at the woman. "Reger set it up." Suddenly he shook his head impatiently. "Oh no! They wouldn't let him get away with it. Why would they let him deploy their ships?"

"I guess," said the pilot reflectively, "because he made the wings for them, they thought he would know best how to use them."

Mrs. Reger said, "Everything else he told them was true."

"But they'd have known about the barrier. Captain, just what is the speed of sound up in the stratosphere?"

"Depends, sir. At sea level it's around 340 meters per second. Up at 30 kilometers or so it's around 300, depending on the temperature."

"The density?"

"No sir. Most people think that, but it isn't so. The higher the temperature, the higher the speed of sound. Anyway, the sound barrier they talk about is just a convenient term. It happens that shock waves form around a ship anywhere from 85% to 115% of the speed of sound, because some airflow around it is supersonic and some still subsonic and you get real weird flow patterns."

"I see. Captain, could you set up a flight-plan which would keep an aircraft at the buffeting stage from the top of the atmosphere down to the bottom?"

"Imagine I could, sir. Though you wouldn't get much buffeting above 35 kilometers or so. No matter what the sonic speed, the air's too thin for shock wave formation."

"Tell you what. You work out a plan like that. Then radio Radar at Prescott and get the dope on Reger's approach."

"Yes sir." The young man went to work at his chart table.

"It's so *hard* for you," Mrs. Reger said.

"What is?"

"You won't believe it until your little graph's all plotted, with every fact and figure in place. Me, I *know*. I've known all along. It's so easy."

"Hating is easy too," said the Major. "You've probably never done much of that. But *un*hating's a pretty involved process. There's no way of doing it but to learn the facts. The truth."

They were five minutes away from the mushroom when the Captain finished his calculations. "That's it, sir, that's what happened. It couldn't have been an accident. All the way down, under power, those ships stayed within four percent of sonic speed, and tore themselves to pieces. You really think Reger planned that approach, that way, sir?"

"Looks like it. From thirty kilometers to the ground, at that speed...it was all over in fifteen seconds."

"Reger," muttered the pilot. He went back to the controls and switched off the automatics. "One of the radar pix showed Reger's spacesuit, Major," he said. "Looks like he bailed out same as Wain did—through a disposal chute."

"He's alive!"

"Depends." The young man looked up at the Major. "You think that mob down there is going to wait while we compute velocities for 'em?"

"That's a military setup, Captain. They'll do what they're told."

"About *Reger*, sir?"

He turned his attention to the controls, and the Major went thoughtfully back to his seat. As they whistled down to the airstrip behind the cordon, he suddenly thumped his knee. "Light gases, high temperature—of *course* those bugs never heard of a shock-wave at what we call sonic speed! You see? You see?"

"No," she said. He understood that she did not need to see. She knew.

No ships, no aliens, no invasion. That, apparently, changed nothing. Reger's spacesuit had been found—empty. Reger was holed up in the brush, or mingling with the service men and refugees inside the cordon. They were closing the cordon and they would get him. A matter of time, they told him at the command post.

The Major pounded the calculations he had brought. "Damn it, he's innocent, can't you see that?"

The young non-com from Psych Warfare—all the brass was inside the cordon, joining the search—said gently, "Yes, sir. I see it. But you don't know what's going on in there. Too many people have hated that man for too long. You can't stop 'em with a 'now-hear-this' on the speakers. Even if the soldiers held off, the place is full of civilians and they're foaming at the mouth."

"Nonsense! Orders are orders! By God I'll—"

"Please," said the non-com, "will you go inside and see for yourself?"

The Major glanced back toward the airstrip and the dark jet, where the young pilot stood guard over the woman. "I will," he said. He handed over the tablet. "Take these and do what you can to spread the word."

"Yes *sir.*" He walked briskly out into the darkness until the Major was out of sight. *"Me* say anything good about Reger—in *there?"* he murmured. "Not this boy. Some other time." He shoved the papers into his tunic and returned to the CP.

The Major walked quietly through the mob, listening. There were soldiers and Air Force men, security officers and civilians. Behind him, the cordon, tightening, reducing the strip between themselves and the radioactive area. In the cordon, a human gateway: FBI, CIA, G-2, screening. The Major listened.

"He got to be inside somewhere."

"Don't worry, we'll get the—"

"Hey George, tell you what. We get our hands on him, let's keep our mouth shut. Army gets him; it's a trial and all kind of foofaraw. This bunch gets him, they'll tear him to pieces right *now.*"

"So?"

"Too quick. You and me, one or two other guys from around here—"

"I hear you."

From somewhere back of the cordon, a tremendous huffing and puffing, and a casual, enormous voice, "Mike hot, Lieutenant," and then the Psycho Warfare officer: "All right, Reger. We know you didn't mean it. No one here will hurt you. You'll get fair treatment all down the line. We understand why you did it. You'll be safe. We'll take care of you. Just step right up."

The spacesuit hung grotesquely by its neck against a shattered barn wall. A scraggly man in filthy coveralls stood by a pile of rocks and chunks of four-by-four. "Just three for a dime, gents, and the ladies free. Step right up and clobber the son. Limber up for the real thing. I thank you sir. Hit him hard." A corporal hefted a round stone and let fly. It hit the spacesuit in the groin and the crowd roared. The scraggly man chittered, "One on the house, one on the house!" and handed over another stone.

The Major touched a smooth-faced lieutenant on the arm. "What goes on?"

"Huh? The suit, sir? Oh, it's all right. G-2's been and gone. His, all right. He's got to be around some place. Well, it's us or the hot stuff—he can take his choice. The cordon's getting radiation armor."

"There'll be hell to pay over this caper."

A soft voice said, "One look around here, I wish Reger'd gotten away with it."

The Major said warmly, "You're a regular freak around here, mister," and was completely misunderstood. The man ran away, and the Major could have bitten his tongue in two.

I want to be in a place, the Major thought suddenly, passionately, *where the truth makes a difference.* And: *If I were a genius at extrapolation, where would I hide?*

"Mr. Reger, you're a reasonable man," bellowed the speaker.

"Three for a dime. For a quarter you can throw a second lootenant."

"He should hold out. He should go back into the bald-spot and fry slowly."

The cordon moved in a foot. *I just thought of the funniest gag,* thought the Major. You *pour vinegar on this sponge, see, and hold it up on this stick...*

Slowly he walked back toward the cordon, and then like a warm, growing light, it came to him what he would do if he were a genius at extrapolation, trapped between the advancing wolves and the leaping flames. He'd be a flame, or a wolf. But he couldn't be this kind of a flame. He couldn't be an advancing wolf. He'd have to be a wolf that stayed in one spot and let the advance pass him.

He went and stood by the man.

This wasn't the notorious Reger face, hollowed, slender, with the arched nose.

He realized abruptly that the man's nose was broken and not bruised. A man could do that with his own hands if he had to. And a man would have to wear coveralls for weeks to get them that filthy. Say, in a spacesuit.

"I'll take three," he said, and handed the man a dime.

"Atta boy, Maje." He handed over two rocks and a billet. The Major aimed carefully, and said from the side of his mouth, "Okay, Reger. We've got to get you out of here."

And I could be wrong, too, thought the Major. *Even if he isn't Reger, this mob would tear him to pieces if I so much as pointed my finger.* He hurled his rock at the spacesuit. From the side of his mouth, hardly moving his lips, he said, "High temperature, light gases, no barrier, I know what you did. Let me get you out of here."

"One on the house!" bellowed the barker. "You sure can throw it, Major."

The Major said, softly, "One thing you never extrapolated, genius. Your wife never lost faith. Two billion people hated your guts, but she wouldn't break."

"I can't hear a word you say," said the barker, and yelled, "Each man kills the thing he loves, and we all love Reger! Come on, lovers!"

He wants to live, thought the Major, *but not with her; he thinks he might kill her with that temper. That's why he shipped out in the first place.*

That temper...

He hefted the billet of wood. Aiming apparently at the space-suit, but speaking into and over his shoulder, he said, "Fine hunk o' flesh, that woman. I'll have 'er one way or another, but it'll be easier with you out of the way. Come on, damn you, make a break." He started to swing as he spoke.

As long as he lived, he would not forget his microsecond of terror. For the barker sprang at him so fast that he seemed to disappear from where he stood and reappear in midair, teeth bared, claws out. The billet landed heavily on the man's temple, and the Major knew it was a solid blow, knew that consciousness was gone. And the terror existed in that instant before the man's body struck him, for even through unconsciousness the hate went on, twisting the corpse-like features and finishing the animal attack even while the eyeballs were rolling up, the mind darkening.

He let the flailing claws strike him and fall limp, concentrating only on bracing himself so he would not fall, so there would be no scuffle to draw attention. He threw a thick arm around the man's chest and held him upright, walked with him so quickly to the gate in the cordon that the crowd around the spacesuit barely had time to turn their heads.

To the FBI man he said, "If it's all the same to you, I'm curtailing this enterprise."

A G-2 lieutenant opened his mouth to protest, glanced at the Major's leaves, and shut his mouth. The FBI man said, "Good idea, Major. That sideshow was pretty sickening. Who is he?"

Recalling the running feud between the Army and his own branch of the Service, the Major glanced at and away from the G-2 man. "One of my own men acting above and beyond the call of duty," he said disgustedly, and shouldered through the opening. The G-2 shavetail ineptly covered up a snicker, and then they were through.

The Major commandeered a jeep and dismissed the driver. They hummed off through the darkness toward the airstrip.

Halfway there, the Major pulled off the road into the thick shadows of a yucca forest. He fumbled in the catch-all and found a length of tow-chain. He drew it around the unconscious man's biceps and knotted it behind him. Then he began to roll the head and slap the hot cheeks. The man moaned.

"You're safe, Reger," the Major said. "Safe now, Reger, you're safe." He felt, rather than saw, the sudden tension that came with consciousness.

"I'm taking you back to your wife. You're safe now."

"I'll kill her. Someday I'll kill her," he mumbled. "Let me go. Why not let them get me?"

Why? Instead, he said, "You'll never kill her, Reger. And if you did, it would be all right. She'd rather die that way than live without you... But we're going to fix that. We're going to make it so you can get mad at anyone, any time, and no one will get hurt. No matter what it takes. We owe you a lot."

Reger sat up dizzily and looked back toward the pool of light, the growls of hate at the cordon. "Everybody owes me. Why *that?*"

"Wain got a report through. Everyone on Earth thought you had turned Earth over to the aliens."

"Wain's all right?"

"Dead."

"Poor Wain," Reger said gently. "He got mad. Man doesn't think right, when he gets mad."

"That's what they thought about you."

He snorted, bitterly. "I didn't *dare* get mad! That's how I could think. Didn't anyone figure that out?" He hung his head and said, "All my life I've been protecting human beings—why should I stop?" He tugged at his bonds. "You can turn me loose. I never *stay* mad."

The Major freed him, started the jeep, and pulled back to the road. Reger was quite quiet until they were on the strip, when he said hoarsely, "You didn't love her enough to turn me over to that mob. You'll never have a better chance."

"Did I say I loved her?"

"One way or another."

They approached the dark jet plane. "So I didn't love her enough," growled the Major. He reached up and slapped the side of the plane. *I just loved her enough to do this,* "I brought him back," he called.

The door opened, and from the shadows she said, "I knew you would."

They helped Reger in. The Major climbed in beside the pilot. "Fly," he said.

The Major thought: *She knew I would. She had faith in me, too.*

A long time later he thought. *That's something, anyway.*

THE END

29

The Last Night of Summer

By ALFRED COPPEL

*When the end comes, it will be different from anything man has imagined—
and it will also be different for each of us who must face it alone.*

THERE were fires burning in the city. With the house dark—
the power station was deserted by this time—Tom Henderson
could see the fires clearly. They reflected like bonfires against the
pall of smoke.

He sat in the dark, smoking and listening to the reedy voice of
the announcer that came out of the battery-powered portable radio.

"—mean temperatures are rising to abnormal heights all over
the world. Paris reports a high yesterday of 110 degrees...Naples
was 115...astronomers predict...the government requests that the
civil population remain calm. Martial law has been declared in Los
Angeles—"

The voice was faint. The batteries were low. Not that it
mattered. *With all our bickering,* Henderson thought, *this is the finish.
And we haven't got what it takes to face it.* It was so simple, really. No
war of the worlds, no collision with another planet. A slight rise in
temperature. Just that. The astronomers had discovered it first, of
course. And there had been reassuring statements to the press.
The rise in temperature would be small. Ten percent—give or take
a few million degrees. They spoke of surface tensions, internal
stresses and used all the astrophysical terms not one man in two
million had ever taken the trouble to understand. And what they
said to the world was that on the last night of summer it would die.

It would be gradual at first. Temperatures had been high all
summer. Then on September 22nd, there would be a sudden surge
of heat from that familiar red ball in the sky. The surface
temperature of the Earth would be raised to 2000 centigrade for
seventeen hours. Then everything would be back to normal.

Henderson grinned vacuously at the empty air. *Back to normal.*
The seas, which would have boiled away, would condense and fall

THE LAST NIGHT OF SUMMER

By
Alfred Coppel

Illustration by
Jack Faragasso

as hot rain for a month or so, flooding the land, washing away all traces of man's occupation—those that hadn't burned. And in two months, the temperature would be down to where a man could walk on the surface without protective clothing.

Only there would not be very many men left. There would only be the lucky ones with the talismans of survivals, the metal disks that gave access to the Burrows. Out of a population of two billions, less than a million would survive.

The announcer sounded bone-weary. *He should,* Henderson thought. *He's been on the air for ten hours or more without relief. We all do what we can. But it isn't much.* "—no more applicants are being taken for the Burrows—"

I should hope not, Henderson thought. There had been so little time. Three months. That they had been able to build the ten Burrows was tribute enough. But then money hadn't mattered, had it? He had to keep reminding himself that the old values didn't apply. Not money, or materials, or even labor—that standby of commerce. Only time. And there hadn't been any of that.

"—population of Las Vegas has been evacuated into several mines in the area—"

Nice try, but it wouldn't work, Henderson thought languidly. If the heat didn't kill, the overcrowding would. And if that failed, then the floods would succeed. And of course there would be earthquakes. *We can't accept catastrophe on this scale,* he told himself. *We aren't equipped mentally for it any better than we are physically.* The only things a man could understand were his own problems. And this last night of summer made them seem pretty small, as though they were being viewed through the wrong end of a telescope.

I'm sorry for the girls, he thought. Lorrie and Pam. They should have had a chance to grow up. He felt a tightness in his throat as he thought of his daughters. Eight and ten are sad ages to die.

But he hadn't thought of them before, why should the end of the world make it any different? He had left them and Laura, too. For what? For Kay and money and a kind of life that would go out in a bright flash with the coming of dawn. They all danced their minuscule ballet on the rim of the world while he sat, drained of purpose or feeling, watching them through that reversed telescope.

He wondered where Kay was now. All over the city there were Star Parties going on. The sky was the limit tonight! Anything you want. Tomorrow—*bang!* Nothing denied, nothing forbidden. This is the last night of the world, kiddo!

Kay had dressed—if that was the word—and gone out at seven. "I'm not going to sit here and just wait!" He remembered the hysteria in her voice, the drugged stupor in her eyes. And then Trina and those others coming in, some drunk, others merely giddy with terror, Trina wrapped in her mink coat, and dancing around the room singing in a shrill, cracked voice. And the other girl— Henderson never could remember her name, but he'd remember her now for all the time there was left—naked except for her jewels. Diamonds, rubies, emeralds—all glittering and sparkling in the last rays on the swollen sun. And the tears streamed down her cheeks as she begged him to make love to her—

It was a nightmare. But it was real. The red sun that slipped into the Pacific was real. The fires and looting in the city were not dreams. This was the way the world was ending. Star Parties and murder in the streets, and women dressed in gems, and tears—a million gallons of tears.

Outside there was the squeal of tires and a crash, then the tinkling of broken glass and silence. A shot came from down the street. There was a cry that was part laughter and part scream.

I'm without purpose, Henderson thought. *I sit and watch and wait for nothing.* And the radio's voice grew fainter still.

"—those in the Burrows will survive...in mines and caves...geologists promise a forty percent survival...behind the iron curtain—"

Behind the iron curtain, surely nothing. Or perhaps it would be instantaneous, not sweeping across the world with dawn. Of course, it would be instantaneous. The sun would swell—oh, so slightly—and eight minutes later, rivers, lakes, streams, the oceans—everything wet—would boil up into the sky...

From the street came a rasping repetitive cry. Not a woman. A man. He was burning. A street gang had soaked him with gasoline and touched him with a match. They followed him shrieking: preview, preview! Henderson watched him through the window as he ran with that *uuuh uuuh uuuh* noise seemingly ripped from his throat. He vanished around the corner of the next house, closely pursued by his tormentors.

I hope the girls and Laura are safe, Henderson thought. And then he almost laughed aloud. Safe. What was safety now? *Maybe,* he thought, *I should have gone with Kay.* Was there anything left he wanted to do that he had never done? Kill? Rape? Any sensation left untasted? The night before, at the Gilmans', there had been a ludicrous Black Mass full of horror and asininity: pretty Louise Gilman taking the guests one after another amid the broken china and sterling silver on the dining table while her husband lay half dead of self-administered morphine.

Our set, Henderson thought. *Brokers, bankers, people who matter.* God, it was bad enough to die. But to die without dignity was worse yet. And to die without purpose was abysmal.

Someone was banging at the door, scratching at it, shrieking. He sat still.

"Tom—Tom—it's Kay! Let me in, for God's sake!"

Maybe it was Kay. Maybe it was and he should let her stay outside. *I should keep what shreds of dignity I have,* he thought, *and die alone, at least.* How would it have been to face this thing with Laura? Any different? Or was there anything to choose? *I married Laura,* he thought. *And I married Kay, too.* It was easy. If a man could get a divorce every two years, say, and he lived to be sixty-five, say—then how many women could he marry? And if you assumed there were a billion women in the world, what percentage would it be?

"Let me in, Tom, damn you! I know you're there!"

Eight and ten isn't very old, he thought. *Not very old, really.* They might have been wonderful women...to lay amid the crockery and cohabit like animals while the Sun got ready to blow up?

"Tom...!"

He shook his head sharply and snapped off the radio. The fires in the city were brighter and bigger. Not sunfires, those. Someone had set them. He got up and went to the door. He opened it. Kay stumbled in, sobbing. "Shut the door, oh, God, shut it!"

He stood looking at her torn clothes—what there was of them—and her hands. They were sticky red with blood. He felt no horror, no curiosity. He experienced nothing but a dead feeling of loss. *I never loved her,* he thought suddenly. *That's why.*

She reeked of liquor and her lipstick was smeared all over her face. "I gave him what he wanted," she said shrilly. "The filthy swine coming to mix with the dead ones and then run back to the Burrow—" Suddenly she laughed. "Look, Tom—look!" She held out one bloody hand. Two disks gleamed dully in her palm.

"We're safe, safe—" She said it again and again, bending over the disks and crooning to them.

Henderson stood in the dim hallway, slowly letting his mind understand what he was seeing. Kay had killed a man for those tickets into the Burrow.

"Give them to me," he said.

She snatched them away. "No."

"I want them, Kay."

"No, nononono—" She thrust them into the torn bosom of her dress. "I came back. I came back for you. That's true, isn't it?"

"Yes," Henderson said. And it was also true that she couldn't have hoped to reach a Burrow alone. She would need a car and a man with a gun. "I understand, Kay," he said softly, hating her.

"If I gave them to you, you'd take Laura," she said. "Wouldn't you? *Wouldn't you?* Oh, I know you, Tom. I know you so well. You'd never gotten free of her or those two sniveling brats of yours—"

He struck her sharply across the face, surprised at the rage that shook him.

"Don't do that again," she said, glaring hatred at him. "I need you right now, but you need me more. You don't know where the Burrow is. I do."

It was true, of course. The entrances to the Burrows would have to be secret, known only to those chosen to survive. Mobs would storm them otherwise. And Kay had found out from the man—that man who had paid with his life for forgetting that there were only potential survivors now and animals.

"All right, Kay," Henderson said. "I'll make a bargain with you."

"What?" she asked suspiciously.

"I'll tell you in the car. Get ready. Take light things." He went into the bedroom and took his Luger from the bedside table drawer. Kay was busy stuffing her jewelry into a handbag. "Come on," he said. "That's enough. Plenty. There isn't much time."

They went down into the garage and got into the car. "Roll up the windows," he said. "And lock the doors."

"All right."

He started the engine and backed onto the street.

"What's the bargain?" Kay asked.

"Later," he said.

He put the car in gear and started down out of the residential district, going through the winding, wooded drives. There were dark shapes running in the shadows. A man appeared in the headlights' beam and Henderson swerved swiftly by him. He heard shots behind. "Keep down," he said.

"Where are we going? This isn't the way."

"I'm taking the girls with me," he said. "With us."

"They won't let them in."

"We can try."

"You fool, Tom! They won't let them in, I say!"

He stopped the car and twisted around to look at her. "Would you rather try to make it on foot?"

Her face grew ugly with a renaissance of fear. She could see her escape misting away. "All right. But I tell you they won't let them in. No one gets into a Burrow without a disk."

"We can try." He started the car again, driving fast along the littered streets toward Laura's apartment.

At several points the street was blocked with burning debris, and once a gang of men and women almost surrounded them, throwing rocks and bits of wreckage at the car as he backed it around.

"You'll get us both killed for nothing," Kay said wildly.

Tom Henderson looked at his wife and felt sick for the wasted years. "We'll be all right," he said.

He stopped the car in front of Laura's. There were two overturned cars on the sidewalk. He unlocked the door and got out, taking the keys with him. "I won't be long," he said.

"Say goodbye to Laura for me," Kay said, her eyes glittering.

"Yes," he said. "I will."

A shadow moved menacingly out of the dark doorway. Without hesitation, Tom Henderson lifted the Luger and fired. The man fell and did not move. *I've just killed a man,* Henderson thought. And then: *But what does it matter on the last night of summer?*

He shot away the lock and walked swiftly up the dark hallway, up the two flights of stairs he remembered so well. At Laura's door, he knocked. There was movement within. The door opened slowly.

"I've come for the girls," he said.

Laura stepped back. "Come in," she said.

The scent she wore began to prod memories. His eyes felt unaccountably hot and wet. "There's very little time," he said.

Laura's hand was on his in the dark. "You can get them into a Burrow?" she asked. And then faintly, "I put them to bed. I didn't know what else to do."

He couldn't see her, but he knew how she would look: the close-cropped sandy hair; the eyes the color of rich chocolates; her so familiar body supple and warm under the wrapper; the smell and taste of her. It didn't matter now, nothing mattered on this last crazy night of the world.

"Get them," he said. "Quickly."

She did as she was told. Pam and Lorrie—he could hear them complaining softly about being awakened in the middle of the night—soft little bodies, with the musty-childish odor of sleep and safety. Then Laura was kneeling, holding them against her, each in turn. And he knew the tears must be wet on her cheeks. He thought: *say goodbye and make it quick. Kiss your children goodbye and watch them go out while you remain alone in the dark that isn't ever going to end. Ah, Laura, Laura—*

"Take them quickly, Tom," Laura said. And then she pressed herself against him just for an instant. "I love you, Tom. I never stopped."

He lifted Pam into his arms and took Lorrie's hand. He didn't trust himself to speak.

"Goodbye, Tom," Laura said, and closed the door behind him.

"Isn't Mommy coming?" Pam asked sleepily.

"Another time, baby," Tom said softly.

He took them out to the waiting car and Kay.

"They won't take them," she said. "You'll see."

"Where is it, Kay?"

She remained sullenly silent and Henderson felt his nerves cracking. "Kay—"

"All right." She gave him directions grudgingly, as though she hated to share her survival with him. She wouldn't look at the girls, already asleep in the back of the car.

They drove through the city, the looted, tortured city that burned and echoed to the shrill gaiety of Star Parties and already stank of death.

Twice, they were almost struck by careening cars, filled with drunken, naked, insane people, all with the desperate desire to make this last night more vivid than all the others back to the very beginning of time.

The headlights illuminated tableaus from some wild inferno as the car swung around through the concrete cemetery the city had become.

A woman hung by the ankles, her skirt shrouding her face and upper body, her legs and buttocks flayed...

Psalm singers kneeling in the street, not moving as a truck cut a swath through their midst. And the hymn, thin and weak, heard over the moans of the dying: *Rock of Ages, cleft for me, let me hide myself in thee...*

Sudden sun-worshippers and troglodytes dancing round a fire of burning books...

The death throes of a world, Henderson thought. *What survives the fire and flood will have to be better.*

And then they had reached the silent hill that was the entrance to the Burrow, the miles-deep warren clothed in refrigerator pipes and cooling earth. "There," Kay said. "Where you see the light. There'll be a guard."

Behind them, the fires burned in the city. The night was growing lighter, lit by a rising moon, a moon too red, too large. *Four hours left, perhaps,* Tom thought. *Or less.*

"You can't take them," Kay was whispering harshly. "If you try they might not let us in. It's kinder to let them stay here—asleep. They'll never know."

"That's right," Tom said.

Kay got out of the car and started up the grassy slope. "Then come on!"

Halfway up the hill, Henderson could make out the pacing figure of the guard: deathwatch on a world. "Wait a minute," he said.

"What is it?"

"Are you sure we can get in?"

"Of course."

"No questions asked?"

"All we need are the disks. They can't know everybody who belongs."

"No," Tom said quietly. "Of course not." He stood looking at Kay under the light of the red moon.

"Tom—"

He took Kay's hand. "We weren't worth much, were we, Kay."

Her eyes were bright, wide, staring.

"You didn't really expect anything else, did you?"

"Tom—Tom!"

The pistol felt light in his hand.

"I'm your wife—" she said hoarsely.

"Let's pretend you're not. Let's pretend it's a Star Party."

"My God—please—nonono—"

The Luger bucked in his hand. Kay sank to the grass awkwardly and lay there, eyes glazed and open in horrified surprise. Henderson opened her dress and took the two disks from between her breasts. Then he covered her carefully and shut her eyes with his forefinger. "You didn't miss much, Kay," he said looking down at her. "Just more of the same."

He went back to the car and woke up the girls.

"Where are we going now, Daddy?" Pam asked.

"Up there on the hill, dear. Where the light is."

"Carry me?"

"Both of you," he said, and dropped the Luger into the grass. He picked them up and carried them up the hill to within a hundred feet of the bunker entrance. Then he put them down and gave them each a disk. "Go to the light and give the man there these," he said, and kissed them both.

"You're not coming?"

"No, babies."

Lorrie looked as though she might start crying.

"I'm afraid."

"There's nothing to be afraid of," Tom said.

"Nothing at all," Pam said.

Tom watched them go. He saw the guard kneel and hug them both. *There is some kindness in this stripping of inhibitions,* Henderson thought, *something is left after all.* They disappeared into the Burrow and the guard stood up saluting the darkness with a wave. Henderson turned and walked back down the hill, skirting the place where Kay lay face to the sky. A warm dry wind touched his face. *Time running out quickly now,* he thought. He got into the car and started back toward the city. There were still a few hours left of this last night of summer, and Laura and he could watch the red dawn together…

THE END

Moon-blind

By LESTER DEL REY

Either Soames or all of Earth was crazy. He knew he'd landed on the Moon in 1948. They knew no ship had left Earth and that he had died in World War II. And all the proof was on their side.

After four years, the clouds looked good. From up there, they had been blurs on the white and green ball that hung in the sky to mock him. Now, as they seemed to rush up towards him they spelled home—or death. There were worse things than death.

For the moment, the sight of the Earth swelling below him brought a lump in Bill Soames' throat. He'd hated it, cursed it, and screamed at it during the long Lunar days. He'd loathed the smug fools on it who had deserted him after calling him a hero and had left him to die or get back by himself. But now the call of his kind washed all that out. A thousand miles below were people, life, and home. It didn't matter what they'd done to him, or why they had done it; he'd lived through it somehow, and now he was almost there.

He shivered in the wash of emotions. His gaunt, almost skeletal body jerked under the flood of adrenalin, and his scarred, claw-like hands gripped the edge of the control board savagely. The starved hollows in his cheeks deepened, and the wisps of white hair on his head were beaded with drops of cold perspiration.

Behind him, the uneven roar of the rocket had been making the little ship quiver with subsonic vibrations. These halted suddenly, began again, and then were gone. The last of his bitterly acquired fuel was exhausted.

Weightlessness caught his tortured body, sending anguished cramps through him and threatening to end his hard-held hold on consciousness. He mastered himself after a moment of retching, and reached for the tiny crank that would spin the gyroscopes. He

turned it madly to the limit of his strength. Imperceptibly, the view of Earth in the plate that showed the ship's rear began to twist.

MOON-BLIND
By LESTER DEL REY

Either Soames or all of Earth was crazy. He knew he'd landed on the Moon in 1948. They knew no ship had left Earth and that he had died in World War II. And all the proof was on their side.

Illustrated by ORBAN

It took time to turn the ship that way, and he had little time left. The atmosphere was rushing up. He'd been luckier than he had expected; the rocket had killed most of his speed. But now he had to strike that two-hundred mile layer of air head foremost. The crank seemed to fight against him, but the ship was swinging. Here in space, Newton's third law worked perfectly. For every action, an equal and opposite reaction. A few thousand turns of the little wheel geared to the crank would turn the ship half a revolution in the other direction.

Four years before, when he had turned over to brake down to the Moon, it had been easy. He'd been strong, then, full of energy.

43

He'd been the conquering hero. Months of conditioning and training had gone by, and he had walked up the ramp to the ship entrance with perfect health and complete confidence. He'd grinned at the generals and the reporters gathered to see the first manned flight to the Moon, and he'd known he would come back.

Well, he was coming back through no help from them. The ship had been a gem, and the landing on the Moon had been almost routine. He'd sent back his radar message, located the single unmanned supply ship they'd sent ahead, and settled down to getting ready for the other ones still to arrive.

They never came, and there was no message back from Earth!

When he landed, July 5, 1948, he had had enough food to last him nearly four months, counting the supplies in the unmanned ship. He hadn't worried too much, at first. Air was renewed by the pumpkin vines and tomatoes that filled one chamber of the ship, and the water he used was recovered automatically. Something had held up his supply ships, but they'd be along shortly with the water that served as fuel for the big atomic-powered rocket; as for the message, probably something was wrong with his receiver.

In August, he began worrying, after he'd caught bits of some conversation on his microwave set and found it worked perfectly. There was still no message directed at him. He tried to reason it out, and decided that they must have somehow decided he was dead. He began cutting down on his eating, and planting more tomatoes and pumpkins frantically. There would be another ship up, to try it again, but it was going to take longer, probably. He'd have to survive until it landed, and then prove he wasn't dead by reaching it. He couldn't understand why they didn't hear his calls, since the radar seemed to transmit okay. But he could find out all about it when the next ship landed.

By the beginning of 1949, he was sick of pumpkins and tomatoes, and beginning to wonder. That was when he started looking up at Earth and cursing it. It wasn't until almost 1950, though, that he gave up all hope, along with attempts to understand.

It nearly broke him. But Bill Soames had been picked carefully, and he wasn't the type to give up. It took him over two years to build a solar oven out of the supply ship parts and begin baking water out of the gypsum he finally located. Then only a trickle seemed to come from his crude pipes. He hoarded it painfully, beginning to fill his fuel tanks.

He had to stop to find minerals to enrich the hydroponic tanks. He wasted days and weeks lying sick and near death from exposure, exhaustion, and near starvation. He developed deficiency troubles, and he refused to give in to them. He never thought of failure. They'd abandoned him, and he cursed Earth with every weakened breath. But he was going back.

Finally, he stripped the ship of every drop of water he could spare, leaving himself almost none. He had already moved most of the plants into a crude hothouse outside. Now he drained their tanks, and decided that with that, added to what he had got from the gypsum, he had fuel enough.

In the spells of sickness, he had lost track of time. But he was fairly sure it was near the end of April, 1952, when he finally blasted off and headed back for Earth.

The ship was pointing ahead towards the cloud-filled atmosphere now. Soames dropped his hand from the crank, shaking with exhaustion, and waited for the first sign of air outside. He was falling fast, but that couldn't be helped.

He let the weakness grip him for a moment longer, while cold sweat stood out on his forehead, and time seemed to hang still in his frozen mind. Then he reached for the controls that would guide the ship down on its stubby wings.

The controls resisted faintly when he touched them. The refrigerator inside the ship was whining, and he knew the hull must be hot already. This was familiar ground—he'd piloted experimental rocket planes enough to have the feel of supersonic flight. It was a matter of keeping the ship up in the super thin air until it began to lose speed, then letting it glide down to a landing.

He should hit somewhere inside the Atlantic Coast, from his rough calculations. He might do damage there—but the chances were against it. Anyhow, they hadn't thought of him for four long years—they'd have to take their chances now.

The ship was getting hot inside. He fought against the controls, trying to hold it just inside the atmosphere until its speed came down enough. The clouds below were lost from his sight. He stole a quick glance at the thin section of hull he could see. It wasn't glowing yet.

He fought mechanically, with his mind buried somewhere down in its deepest sections, trying not to think. The ship groaned, and the stubby wings seemed about to fall off. Somewhere to the rear, something gave with the sound of an express rifle. The ship grew hotter. The thin, worn coveralls were wet with his sweat, and the wristwatch seemed to burn his skin.

Then the speed was dropping and he was going into his glide.

He came down through the clouds, finally, just as he left the darkness behind. His eyes darted to the little port that would show the surface below. He should be nearing the coast.

Soames' gasp was a hoarse choke. The line that separated sea and land was directly below him! He'd overshot. He drew back on the control, trying to steepen the glide, but it was already too late. The ship went plunging down through the air, heading out to sea. He cursed to himself, but there was nothing to be done, in the time left. He began a slow turn, but he knew it would fail.

He was miles from land when the first sound of the water slapping against the ship reached his ears. She was coming down smoothly enough. Spray leaped up, and the ship lurched as the braking force of the sea hit it while it still was making better than 200 miles per hour. But he managed to avoid being thrown forward. Then she was skipping a bit, with the sound of rifle-like popping coming from the rear again. A moment later, the ship was coasting smoothly over the fairly calm sea.

He was down—home—back to Earth—and alive!

And brother, would the brass hats have some explaining to do now!

Wetness touched his bare feet. He jerked his eyes down, to see an inch of water on the "floor" of the ship—and it was rising as he looked. The ship had sprung a leak during the battle through the air and the pounding of the landing. Now it would sink almost at once.

Bill threw the straps of the seat off and was on his feet, jumping for the airlock as he saw it. With a leak, this thing would sink like a piece of lead. He grabbed down his good-luck charm as he went. The sheaf of hundred dollar bills—eight in all—had been left from the going away present his mother had sent him, and he'd forgotten them until half way out from Earth. Somehow, they had always been a symbol that he'd get back—but now, if he lived, they'd be of more immediate use. He reached for the packet of exposed film, but the water was coming up too fast; it touched the control-board and the films slid along the wet surface and vanished. There was no time to grope for them.

Soames struggled through the water as the little lock finally opened. He pulled himself out. The land was lost from view, and the sea was all around him.

But there was no time to wait. He jumped into the water and began paddling frantically. It was icy cold, and it shocked his body, driving the breath from his lungs. In his emaciated condition, keeping afloat was going to be hard work. Eight miles…

It never really occurred to him that he couldn't make it. He was heading toward the land when the suction of the ship's sinking caught him, and he didn't look back. He settled down to the best compromise between endurance and speed he could make and drove on. He was back on Earth, and they couldn't defeat him now.

Fifteen minutes later, the boat appeared. It was a Coast Guard cutter, he saw. It circled, and a line was tossed to him. On the rail, he could see the figures of men. All the loneliness of the long years on the Moon hit at him, then. He pulled on the line, dragging forward; it wasn't the thought of rescue, but the sound of human voices that drove him now.

"I'm Bill Soames," he began shouting, over and over.

They pulled him up, crying something to him—something about luck that had let them see his plane going down on their radar screen. But he hardly heard the words.

"I'm Soames," he repeated. "Major William Soames. Damn it, can't you understand? That was a rocket ship—the *Lunatic*. I've come back from the Moon. Four years—four damned long years—but I've come back."

"Shock," one of the men said. "Okay, Bill, take it easy. You'll be all right."

He shrugged off their hands. "I *am* all right. Damn it, don't you even remember me? I took off for the Moon in 1948—July 1, 1948! Now I'm back!"

He saw consternation on their faces and pity mixed with it. He shook his head. After all the publicity there had been, it hardly seemed that a man on Earth could help knowing about the trip. Yet maybe these men hadn't heard. Maybe they didn't care about rockets and the Moon.

"Didn't get a rocket out of the atmosphere until February, 1949," the Coast Guardsman said slowly. "That was when they shot the Wac Corporal up, using the V-2 to carry her. Got up about 250 miles, as I remember it. Brother, this is 1952—not 1975. You've been seeing too much fantasy on the television. Come on, we'll fix up a bunk."

A fine welcome for a hero, Bill thought. He'd expected his name to be enough to stop them cold. Now something was stopping him...tired...everything getting black...So tired, so dead... He felt himself falling, but was too far gone into unconsciousness to care.

They held him two weeks in the hospital. The semi-starvation and the exhaustion had added to the shock of the cold swim. But he hadn't been delirious, as they claimed. He'd recovered the first night. Maybe he had raved a little—surely among all those doctors and nurses, one should have known about the take-off of the Moon ship, or should have known his name. They'd pretended to, after a while; but he knew they had been lying. They really believed all that guff about Man still being unready for Space!

He finished his lunch and reached for the dessert. Then he shuddered violently, and shoved it away. Pumpkin pie! His stomach seemed to turn over at the sight of it, and he pushed it as far from him as he could. Tomatoes and pumpkins were no longer fit to eat, as far as he was concerned.

He reached for the book on the table again. *Rockets, Missiles, and Space Travel*, by Willy Ley. He'd read the original version of it in

1947. This edition bore the date of 1951. It had a good deal of new material and all the charm and sound thinking he expected of Ley. But it didn't fit with his memory of a big, black-haired man who had boomed out farewells to him while he climbed the ramp for the take-off. Ley wasn't just an expert—he was an enthusiast, and nobody wanted space travel more than he did.

Yet the book contained no mention of Bill's flight. It didn't list the method of turning water to monatomic hydrogen and ozone for rocket fuel, discovered in 1946; there was nothing on the first compact atomic motor to provide power, built late in 1947. Both had been highly secret at the time, but they had been announced publicly before his flight.

He'd expected to find proof of his facts in the book. Instead, he found only confusion for his mind. They couldn't have covered up that thoroughly. Yet the date of February 24, 1949 was listed for man's first step beyond the atmosphere—the same 250 mile flight the Coast Guardsman had mentioned.

Soames sighed, and dropped the book as the nurse came for his tray, the eternal mechanical smile on her lips. "Dr. Willoughby will see you soon," she told him.

He'd tried to talk to her, but he knew it was useless. These people really didn't know about his trip. It should have been on the front pages of every newspaper in the world, and there shouldn't be a literate person alive who didn't know of it. Instead, they had treated his facts as the ravings of a man suffering from shock.

What could account for something big enough to suppress such news—not only to suppress it, but to kill what had already gone before?

Even his former commanders had failed him. He'd been refused the right to send a telegram, but the Coast Guardsman who had visited him had promised to mail his letters to the men of Operation Space. General Bartley should have come tearing in, threatening to rip the place apart unless he was released at once. But the letters had vanished, if they had ever been mailed, without an answer.

Dr. Willoughby came in quietly. "Well, young man, how do you feel today? Still think you're chasing girls on the moon, heh?"

Soames wanted to push the smiling face back into the man's adenoids, but he managed to grin. In hospitals, you had to grin. He'd learned already that patients had to humor doctors and nurses and agree to anything they suggested.

"No more of that," he answered. "I still can't remember, but I'm sane enough. When do I get out of here?"

The doctor seemed to consider it weightily. "Well, now, I guess we can let you go. You did some fearful things to that body of yours—just what I can't tell; but you're well enough now. A little amnesia, of course, but that will wear off. Such cases happen from shock. You sure you want to leave?"

"I certainly am. I can get a job…"

The doctor wasn't listening. He nodded without waiting to hear the answer. "The nurse will bring you clothes, and then lead you to my office. I'll have some papers there. And there's a Colonel Hadley to see you."

He was gone before Soames' shout could get from his throat. So the Army had his letters! The hospital must have been holding him until Hadley could get there. They'd been stalling, but not for the reason he had expected. Now his troubles would soon be over.

He signed for the clothes they had bought at his order and the property they held for him. The clothes were picked without taste, as if some store had packaged them at random. He looked more human when he finished shaving. His face was still gaunt and tense, and his hair was thin and white, as it had grown in after a long bout of illness. But he felt almost himself again as he followed the girl to the doctor's office.

Willoughby introduced him and withdrew discreetly. Colonel Hadley was a plump, youngish man, with the rocky face and false pleasantness that could carry a man to his position quickly, but would never let him advance much beyond it. He obviously had no imagination, and couldn't trust it in others.

He got down to business at once. "These your letters? Ummm. Well, I've been talking to Dr. Willoughby. Understand you were pretty sick. So we won't discuss this nonsense about the moon. In fact, under the circumstances, perhaps we can forget…"

"Did you ever hear of Major William Soames?" Bill asked. "Before this, I mean?"

"Certainly. That's what made Bartley send me up here, instead of routine procedure. Naturally. Soames was on Bartley's flight over Berlin when the Nazis got him. Brave man. Saved Bartley's life. Got a posthumous Congressional Medal, you know. A hero."

"He—he *died?*"

"Right. May 23, 1943. Sad business. Had a brother—Lieutenant Roger Soames—on the same flight. Both got it."

Bill Soames let his legs lower him carefully into a chair, studying the Colonel's face. It wasn't the face of a man who could lie.

It was the face of a man reporting hard fact that he knew to be true. Yet it was the sheerest nonsense. Bill had started on that flight—but his plane had developed motor trouble half an hour out from England and he'd put back. He'd always felt he was somehow to blame for Roger's death. He tried to say something, but no words would come.

"Very sad," Hadley added.

"Never knew Major Soames, but I got on well with his brother. Saw the whole business myself. Felt sick for a whole day afterwards—first Roger, then the Major." He cleared his throat. "You can guess what we thought when we heard you were impersonating him. Naturally, we had to investigate. Crank letters come often enough, but not like that. Deuce of it was that Bartley swore it was like the Major's handwriting. And you know, you do look a little like the pictures I saw.... Know what happens to anyone who impersonates an Army officer, young man? Bad. But—well, Dr. Willoughby tells me it was just shock. What about that?"

"I'm—I'm Bill Soames," Soames answered, while his head went around in crazy circles. He tried to pretend it was a gag to himself, but it wasn't. He fell back on the lying that had finally convinced the staff of his sanity. "I—I guess I must have been kind of a hero worshipper; when I got the shock, I thought I was the other William Soames—and went all the way on the hero stuff. If I caused you any trouble..."

"You did. You certainly did. Two days up here, checking your fingerprints, doing everything. Prints don't match, of course. Took me a whole day in Washington just getting Soames' prints, too, you know. Funny, you'd think they'd be careful with the records of a hero; almost lost! Heh! Well, anyhow, I guess we can close the case. No sign of fraud. Hope you get your full memory back."

He stood up to go, and Bill got to his feet. He took the other's perfunctory handshake and watched him leave. He saw Willoughby come in, beaming. There must have been some exchange of words, though he couldn't remember them. Then the papers were signed, and he was going out of the hospital. The sun was shining brightly as he came down the steps, mechanically counting out the four hundred odd dollars he had left.

It *had* to be hypnotism. Hadley had thought he was telling the truth. But they had hypnotic drugs now. They might use them if they wanted to pretend a man who'd flown to the Moon had been dead years before. If General Bartley had meant to send Soames a warning that the subject was top secret, and to go slow...if he'd been unable to come himself...

It still didn't make sense. It hadn't made sense when they had abandoned him on the Moon, and it made less now. What national danger could possibly be averted by lying about this—particularly when they were still talking about the fact that the first nation to get a base on the Moon would rule Earth?

There was only one answer. He had to see Bartley in person. He was due in Washington, it seemed—overdue by some four years.

Seeing Bartley proved to be more trouble than he'd thought. The Pentagon wasn't open to casual visitors—not the part he wanted. He couldn't use his own name, either. But even Generals are human beings. They eat, and they have to have places to sleep. Soames gave up direct efforts, and waited patiently.

He was lucky. He spotted Bartley getting into a car alone on the third day, just as he was driving up to park his own rented car. He could tell the way the gears ground that the man was bound for the old familiar place. Bartley was short and plump, a little Santa Claus of a man with fierce black hair and a totally unconvincing bristle of a mustache. When he was angry, he looked more jovial than ever—which was probably why he had his favorite bar well out in Bethesda, away from the usual run of other officers.

Soames kept a casual eye on the car, but he was sure of himself when Bartley headed out Wisconsin Avenue. He drove into the little parking lot, just as Bartley disappeared into the pleasant bar across the way. Then he took his time. The General would need a beer by himself before he could be approached. When Bill finally went in, he found the place almost unchanged. He ordered his own beer and moved back to the jukebox. Bartley was sitting beside it. He set his beer on the table, and began feeding nickels into the machine. None of the new tunes meant anything to him, but luck was still with him. There was one of the old platters there— "A Long, Long Trail." He let it start and saw Bartley glance up.

Soames had worn a hat to cover his hair, but he had carefully turned his face to the light. Now he saw Bartley's eyes slip to his own, and hesitate. He smiled faintly, drew an answering doubtful smile, and slipped into the booth. The other man offered no objections.

"Beer here is worth coming a long ways for," Bill said casually. "Worth a quarter million miles."

The General smiled doubtfully, then frowned as if the joke escaped him. It was a good act, Bill had to admit. "Good beer," he finally admitted. "Like the stuff the Germans had for their officers—almost."

"Honigsbrau," Bill agreed. "A couple cases of it. They'd just started to crack it and drink when we strafed 'em. It was warm by the time we reached the shack, but it was worth all the trouble we had."

The General nodded. "Good. Dark and heavy stuff. I can still taste it. Used to…"

His mouth fell open, making him look more than ever like a comic cherub. "Good God! Man, you couldn't be! You…Bill Soames!"

Bill nodded, and the fears washed away. "In the flesh, Tom. I had a helluva time getting back—I'm still mad about being left there. But I knew you'd be glad to see me!"

"Glad! You sunovagun! We knew you were dead. You couldn't have lived in that smash-up. Bill!" He was pumping Bill's hands, his own arm jerking spasmodically. "Man, wait'll they hear about this!"

"They don't seem to want to hear about it," Bill told him.

"They will, boy, they will! We didn't go through the war together for nothing!"

"Or Operation Space? Remember how we used to dream about that, when I found you were human enough to read those stories. Rockets—space... We didn't think then..."

Bartley sighed. "Yeah. And when the V-2's fell into our hands, I did a lot more dreaming, Bill. It was tough, not getting assigned to White Sands. I really wanted to work on the rockets. But I guess they knew what they were doing when they turned me down."

"They turned you down?" Hell, Tom Bartley had been the one to get him in, after his first application was turned down. Bartley had been the first officer picked for the job.

"They did. I guess I forgot about your being somewhere in Germany— Say, when did you get back? And how? Come on, give."

Bill sat back, staring at him. It was his turn to sit with his mouth open. He glanced up to see if anyone else could have come near to cut off the honesty he'd found here before. They were alone. The bartender was at the other end, and all the booths were deserted.

"Okay," he said. "I guess you had some reason for the game, but not between us, Tom. Leaving me up on the Moon without answering my signals was a dirty trick. It took me four years to get back, and then I cracked your precious ship into the ocean, where the salt water can eat its magnesium to bits. But it's time to stop the pussy-footing. You know damned well I never cracked up on the Moon. I've left my signature up there. Now I'm back. And I want some explanations."

Bartley's face had gone white, and now was turning fiery red. His hand around the beer glass tautened until the glass snapped.

Blood seeped out on his fingers, but he didn't look at it. Finally he took a deep breath.

"For a minute you fooled me," he began in a deadly quiet voice. "For a minute. I was fool enough to think Bill Soames had managed to live somehow, when I knew he'd burned up in the plane. But I should have remembered those damned letters. You fooled Hadley—he thought you were sick, not crazy. But you can't fool me. You damned rotten..."

The fist that landed in Bill's face hardly traveled six inches, but it was backed by sheaves of muscles that only looked like fat. Bill's head snapped back against the rear of the booth, while hot pain lanced through him. He slid down, barely holding onto his aching consciousness. He heard Bartley get up and dash to the phone. He heard the crisp orders to come for him.

For a second, he wanted to lie there and let them get him. There was nothing left. The others could be fooled or try to fool him—but Tom Bartley wouldn't do that. That blow had been based on real feelings. Bartley had believed he'd never worked at White Sands. And generals weren't hypnotized, even for security.

Then the stubbornness that had carried him through four years of desertion on the Moon and brought him back alive came to the surface. He shook the blackness away from his head, sending up lancing pains, and got to his feet. The beer bottle was under his hand. He lifted it, and threw it, four feet behind Bartley. As the man turned toward it, his legs drove him forward. He was out of the bar, and across the street. He threw a bill at the parking attendant, and gunned his rented car to life. Then he began twisting crazily through side streets. Washington wouldn't be healthy for him after this.

He had no time to think, but his mind had already been made up. There was one place and only one where he could go. And he'd better get started there fast.

The key that had been with his wallet—the stuff he'd forgotten to leave behind when he took off—still fitted the lock. He opened the door of the quiet apartment when no one answered his knock. The furniture was mostly the same, and there were pictures of himself and Roger on the piano. He called, but there was no answer. Then he moved back toward the windows that opened on Central Park South.

It was hard to believe, after the war, the tests, and the Moon, that he'd grown up here, in the quiet luxury of the money his father had left them. But he found his old room still as it had been the last day before he left. He closed the door on it quickly; it brought back too much that he'd forgotten.

He found a chair near the door and settled down to wait. The rest of the world might deceive him. Even Tom Bartley might lie—he'd left Bill on the Moon, and he probably had enough guilt feelings from that to account for anything. But Bill knew that his mother wouldn't lie to the craziest stranger. Surely he'd find the truth here. She had never understood his craving for adventure beyond Earth, and she wouldn't know too much about advances in the world. But she'd accept him. All their lies about his having died over Berlin wouldn't mean anything to her, after they'd spent so many weekends here when the war was over. She'd remember the ring on his finger that had been her idea, to help him cut his way out of a Nazi prison if he were captured; she'd thought that diamonds were somehow safe and that they could cut steel bars as well as glass. She'd remember the thousand dollars that had been meant to give him a grand party with the men, since he insisted on being fool enough to try to reach the Moon. She'd been tearful then, but she'd seen something of his drive, and had seemed proud of him, at the end.

He sat there, soaking up peace and quiet from the room around him. The sunlight disappeared from the windows at the far end, and there was a bit of gloom that finally ended when the streetlights went on. They left the room thick with shadows, and rich with the fancies he'd woven around them when he was only a kid, playing with Roger. He made no effort to turn on the light, but waited quietly.

Then he heard the elevator stop, and her feet on the floor of the hall. He was still sitting as the key turned in the lock, and a beam of light struck him. She closed the door quietly, looking older and frailer than he remembered, but still upright and carrying herself with the ordered pride of good breeding.

She snapped on the lights and turned to face him. For a moment, surprise struck her. Then she mastered herself. "Good evening, young man. How did you get in here?" Her voice was firm, but calm enough, as if this were a minor upset in some fond routine.

He stood up, moving toward the light. She watched him, then smiled doubtfully. "If you're a burglar, you're quite welcome to what money I have here. Only don't make any commotion, please. I can't stand vulgarity." She was trying to make a joke of it, he knew. Then her voice caught. "But you...you look like..."

"Hi, Mom," he said, nodding.

She stood there, suddenly old and shrunken, though her back was straighter than ever. Her perfectly applied makeup was ghastly on her white face. She backed against the door slowly, while her hand went to her throat.

"You look like Bill—like Bill—like Bill. Just like Bill." It was a soft moan, unconscious. "Bill was a nice boy. He died in the war—the same time Roger died. It wasn't fair. He died—they told me he died horribly. And they sent me his papers, what was left— and half a letter he'd begun—and they gave him a medal. He was such a nice boy. I saved them all...I..."

She began to fall, still stiffly. Bill caught her in his arms, and eased her onto a couch. He'd never seen her faint before. He knew she hadn't fainted when she'd heard that Roger had been killed. He stood helpless. Finally he lowered her head and raised her feet, waiting for her to come to. His eyes moved to the drawer where she'd stared, the drawer under the two smaller pictures from their childhood.

He found them all there—the death notice, with its accusing date, half of a letter he actually had written—but completely—his papers, and some knickknacks that seemed to have been in a fire!

He pawed through them quickly, and then went back to the couch. He knew what he had to do, and began rummaging into his few belongings. He was rubbing her forehead when she came to. She looked at him, but he was holding his face as taut as he could, to build up the lines that the hard years had put on it. She shook her head slowly.

"You're—not..."

"No, ma'am. I guess I forgot, calling you 'Mom' the way Bill always did. He was my buddy, you know. Used to laugh at how we looked alike. A great guy. We were in prison over there together. That's why I came back, to bring you this—all he had left when he died. But he didn't die in the plane, ma'am. They shot him trying to escape, and it was quick and painless. That's why I came here, why I had his key..."

He'd rehearsed it in his mind, but hadn't known whether it would work. Now he saw life come back into her. She drew herself up, and straightened her hair. Her voice was calm again.

"Silly of me, of course. I—I'm glad you came. I never did believe Bill died in the plane. He was so much at home in any kind of machinery. Thank you for bringing my picture back to me. And now, can't I get you a drink, before I apologize for being so weak?"

He shook his head. "I'll have to rush, ma'am. I waited too long. Bill wanted you to have the picture—it was what he valued most. But—well, I have got to rush."

She let him go. She was not the sort to hold any nervous man against his will. She saw him to the door, and her fingers rested briefly on his arm. The smile she gave him would have been reward enough, if his story had been true.

Then he went down the stairs and out into the night on this world which had erased him and which refused to admit he had ever left it.

There had been another picture in his wallet, but he'd been a fool to look at it. He'd looked at it often enough that first year up there, wondering whether she'd wait for him, but somehow the memory of Sherry had grown weak with time. He'd been a bigger fool to spend the night making phone calls to locate her.

He knew it now as he sat on the too-lavish couch. He'd heard a faint gasp when she first saw him, but she'd never thought he was Bill Soames, and he hadn't tried to tell her he was. He'd used the same line on her as he'd finally used on his mother, with a change in the picture. It sat on the table near her now, its water-stained younger image of her face staring up.

She slid a trifle sideways, exposing one knee from under her negligee, and reached across him for her drink. She'd always had a nice bosom, and she'd always known it. She sipped the drink and put it back. "Poor Bill," she said throatily. "He was such a kid—but I guess I was too, then. I suppose he really expected me to wait for him?"

"I don't know—maybe not," Bill answered her. "Things were pretty tough in the prison."

"I meant to wait for him. But it was so long. I guess it wasn't very nice, marrying Bob Stanton just six months after Bill went overseas, but you know how it is. And then we heard Bill had died, but I was just having Junior…"

"Junior?" Bill jerked at that, his eyes flickering over the slightly too-decorated room. She couldn't have had a child in 1943—she *had* waited for him; she'd promised to wait again when he left for the rocket in 1947. And imagination wouldn't supply a child…

She laughed and pointed to a picture of a boy of about eight. "He's away at school now, of course. You know how important it is to give them the *best* education." She sighed, and reached for the drink. "But it's terribly hard on a boy's mother, having him away. The place gets so lonely, now that Bob's away in Washington so much of the time. Sometimes I think I'll go mad…"

She wasn't even subtle about it. For a moment, it worked. Bill had spent too long away from women. Then the ease of her passion was too much for him; it told him too strongly what a fool he'd been ever to believe her accounts of the missing dates that had always come between them. He pushed her away, pulled her negligee shut firmly, and added insult to the injury by making no attempt to turn his eyes away.

She was just switching from surprise to querulous hurt as his feet carried him across the living room to the foyer. Her voice was rising to a shriek of outraged anger as he closed the door behind him. This time the night air felt good. There were worse things than being marooned on the Moon. He might have come back and married her!

Then he frowned. It wasn't night, anymore, after all. The streetlights were still on, but day was breaking in the east.

He grimaced. Well, he'd gotten things out of the night. He'd found that his mother knew he was dead, and had been dead years before he took off for the Moon; he'd found the papers that had the authentic appearance of age to prove it. He'd found that the girl who'd been single and willing to wait for him in 1947 had not only been married, but had had a child in 1943 or 1944. That would take some explaining! He couldn't swear to some things about her, but he knew damned well there had been no marriage or child in the past from which he came.

It hit him, then—the stories he'd read once had been filled with the idea that time is a matter of multiple choice, and that the future is a fan-shaped thing, with many branches. If he'd gone to the Moon from one such probability world and somehow rotten switched over to another on the return—a world where he had never left...

He shrugged. It was fine for speculation, but there was no way to account for such a switch. Anyhow, that stuff was based on the need for a good story-gimmick, and not on facts. There was a lot more sense in a universe where there was an absolute relation between cause and effect. This was the same world he'd left—however much deceit was involved, and whatever the tricks they used to deny him. It might be a crazy world, but not one of those improbable ones.

He considered that. A crazy world—or one person who was crazy. Then he grinned savagely.

He didn't feel crazy. It was no solution, anyhow. If he were crazy, he wouldn't know it. The same stubbornness that had let him survive for four years on the Moon made him reject the idea at once. There *had* been times when the whole world was wrong and only one man was right; as far as he was concerned, this was another such case.

He came up to a newsstand and stood staring at the magazines. There were more dealings in the fantastic than he remembered, but they looked familiar. Spaceships and weird landscapes vied with half-nude girls and bug-eyed monsters. He started to buy one, and then gave up the idea; after being up there, he didn't want someone else's guess. As for alien life-forms...

He thought about it for a second, but little more. Maybe some alien civilization that wanted to keep man Earthbound might suppress knowledge and even change memories; but it didn't fit the case. It would have been easier for such a race to eliminate him, or to prevent the ship ever having taken off. There was no answer there.

He bought a newspaper and went into a coffee shop for breakfast. He still enjoyed eating real food. The sight of two eggs, over light, surrounded by crisp bacon, together with toast and coffee was better than any scene off Earth. He took his plate to a little table and began glancing through the paper as he ate. Most of the news meant nothing to him—the war beginning in Asia now so soon after the last war was something he preferred to ignore. Most of the rest of the paper was filled with things that he couldn't understand or didn't care to read. Even the comics were dull, without the continuity of regular reading.

Then he stopped, and looked back at a picture. Professor Arnold Rosenblum had delivered a lecture on the need for a space station outside Earth's atmosphere. When interviewed later at the Weldon Arms Hotel, he had stated...

Rosenblum had been the man who had invented the method of using water as the propellant! He'd been part of Operation Space from the beginning. If Bill could see him...

He knew the result. Rosenblum wouldn't remember. Yet the man was a scientist, and science isn't something that deals with belief. It sticks to facts. Bill turned it over, considering. The man might not believe a word he would have to say—yet he couldn't argue against provable facts. And to a real scientist, there were facts that could be proved!

The phone booth was in the back, and there was no trouble in getting his message put through to the scientist. Apparently, men of science still didn't have to be suspicious of callers, as did movie stars. The voice at the other end was sleepy, but not hostile. "Yes?"

"Dr. Rosenblum? I'm James Cross, a former student—class of '44. I was wondering whether I could see you—about the space stations? I—" He halted his story about being a reporter,

considering what he knew of the man. Then he hesitated deliberately. "I—I don't have any reason to bother you, but I missed your
lecture, and I couldn't get much out of the newspaper articles. For
breakfast, perhaps?"

"Cross?" Rosenblum seemed to turn it over and decide names
didn't matter. "Well, why not? I don't wonder you couldn't understand the newspaper account. Ten minutes—wait, where are you?"

"Ten minutes will be fine," Bill told him. "And thanks."

"Pleasure. Always glad to find someone still curious. Usually
they forget after college." The phone clicked down, covering the
last of a yawn. Bill went outside quickly to flag a cab.

It took fifteen minutes, but he managed to beat the professor to
the lobby. Rosenblum was tall and thin, with a face like that of
Lincoln, and eyes that managed to be both sharp and friendly, even
with traces of sleep in them. He made no comment at not
recognizing Bill.

Soames had given up expecting recognition. He ordered
breakfast again, and grinned at Rosenblum's order—the scientist
obviously believed in enjoying life. Then he plunged into it.

"I've been thinking that problem of fuels over, Dr. Rosenblum.
You mentioned fluorine and beryllium as a theoretical ideal. What
about ozone and monatomic hydrogen? Wouldn't they have a
higher exhaust velocity? Maybe enough to avoid the need for a
step rocket?"

"Very fine," Rosenblum admitted with a grin, around a thick
slice of ham. "Excellent—if you'll tell me how to get them and
store them."

"Don't. Make them out of water. Like this." Bill pulled out a
pad and began scribbling on it, mixing it with comments as he gave
all that he could remember of what Rosenblum had originally
discovered. He was watching for signs of suspicion, but there were
none. The professor showed interest, but no indication that this
was some highly secret discovery of his own.

He studied it. "You'd need power for this, of course, Mr.
Cross. But I suppose the work being done on submarine atomic
motors might provide that, for a large ship. Still…"

Bill relaxed at the interest on the other's face. Facts—science
had to deal with facts. And no casual interviewer could know

enough about both fuels and atomics to reveal such information—Rosenblum would have to believe him. "I've been thinking about it. If we use a heavy-water moderated pile, but design it..."

He plunged into that. It was hard work, trying to remember it all, but he was sure he'd covered most of the points. Rosenblum sat back, his breakfast forgotten, nodding. Bill looked up with a final nod of his own at the scrawls on the paper. "Well?"

"Interesting. Unfortunately, it won't work. I tried to do exactly that with water for a fuel back in 1946—and it failed. The theory looks good—but it takes too much power. I had some students working on it, too, but we had to abandon the idea. As for your atomic motor..." He shook his head sadly. "Well, that's out of my field, but some of the material they've just released covers such an idea. I understand it isn't controllable."

"But—"

Rosenblum shook his head and began attacking his breakfast again. "Oh, I think you've done a lot of clear thinking, and I'm not calling you a fool, young man. I only wish I had a few more students like you. But you have to remember that there are hundreds of men working on these things today, and they've had these ideas, too. It's a beautiful piece of logic—but unfortunately, logic isn't everything; it won't work."

"It did work!" Bill told him grimly. "It worked when you tried it in 1946! Security be damned! I know it. I was the guy who rode the rocket using it to the Moon and back! I tell you, I *know!*"

A change crept over Rosenblum's face. He studied Bill for a moment, then shook his head, making clucking sounds.

"Another one, eh? Last week it was my colleague, Dr. Dickson, who had invented a variation of this, late in 1949. Now *I* invented it in 1947. And of course, the man who told him about it had been to the Moon personally, too. You don't fit the description, or I might think you were the same man. Mr. Cross, in spite of what the papers say, college professors are neither credulous idiots nor crazy."

He picked up his check, and put down change for the tip. "I have no intention of reporting you to the establishment. But I think you'd be wise to leave...at once! Good day."

Rosenblum walked toward the cashier, leaving Bill to stare down at the working diagrams that had taken him to the Moon, but had been proven not to work. Sure, science dealt in facts! It had been a beautiful theory.

The library had a complete file of the *New York Times* back through 1947. Bill had half expected to find missing issues, but they were all there. He riffled, back to June, thumbing through. The advance feelers put out by the Army were there—meaningless by themselves, of course, but leading up to what was to come. He came to July, and tensed.

There were no missing headlines—but there was nothing on the flight of a rocket to the Moon. He combed July thoroughly. There was no mention of him. He went back to July 2nd, when the news should have been broken. On the front page, one of the men who had covered the take-off had a by-line story; it dealt with ordinary news, though, and would have required that the man be in New York the day before. Bill turned to the science columns—and again, a name that had been among those covering the take-off hit his eye. But the story dealt with something totally unrelated to the flight, and again would have had to be written by a man nowhere near the take-off spot!

It took him four hours to complete his search, and netted him only one item. That stopped him when he came to it. It was in the same month; this time it was a more sensational paper, and the account was buried under a miscellaneous collection of scandals, *Ham Claims Contact with Man in Moon!* It seemed that a radio amateur had picked up a signal from someone who claimed to be marooned on the Moon, asking for supply ships. It must have been *his* signal!

He took it to be photostatted, amazed at his violent reaction to even this bit of evidence. His hands were trembling as he held it up and pointed out the piece. But the man who came to help him only glanced at it with amusement.

"Fortean, eh? Well, I get a kick out of such things, too. But you'll find a lot of things like this printed in the summer. That's why reporters call it the silly season, I guess." He read through it, grinning again. "Mm-hm. They ran almost the same story in

1950—I remember it, because my father was visiting us... You know, I had a man here a couple weeks ago who told me he sent the message. Never cracked a grin... Hey, mister, don't you want your stat?"

Bill went down the street slowly. He'd have to get a room, of course. And a job. His money wouldn't last forever—even if he hocked the diamond ring and his watch. Time for lunch. Hell, he wasn't hungry. He glanced at a television store, noticing that the screens looked immense, though the prices were lower than he'd thought they would ever be. But men could make progress in amusement, even if their leading scientists insisted they'd failed at work that might have sent man to the planets, given time.

He bought a paper and skimmed it. He found the first of the "silly season" accounts on Page 7, though it wasn't summer yet. It dealt with the flying saucers, of course, since they were still the current fad. He turned on. Maybe it was a lean day, and news was scarce. Three pages further he found a brief mention of a 97-year-old woman who could recite the Bible in Hebrew, though she'd never spoken a word of it in her life. Telepathy, she claimed; thought communication with a scholar who had lived two thousand years before.

He threw the paper in the disposal can, and stared up at the sign moving across the Times Building...

They'd covered up perfectly. There wasn't any real evidence left. A ship had disappeared on the Moon, but nobody had missed it. A man who waited for help was tagged as dead years before, and even his own mother could remember how he had died. Science had proved that he couldn't make the trip with the equipment he had. The papers were complete—and spurious.

It was the stuff of madness. Yet he knew inside himself he wasn't mad. Somehow, reality had been altered for everyone here. A thousand men who had seen the ship take-off now probably all knew that they had been doing something else. Papers had been changed.

Men had invented the steamboat long before Fulton. Their attempts had been buried, though some of them had worked. Leif

Ericson had crossed the Atlantic and discovered America before Columbus—and the account had been lost, until the evidence was found. Had the facts been altered then? Had Ericson come home to find that everyone knew he had been in Iceland all along? And then, when the evidence was finally found, centuries later after America had been discovered again, had things been doctored up the opposite way, so that people thought the evidence had been there all along?

What about the hot-air engine? It was known before the gasoline motor, and it had been just as good. Yet it had lain unused for decades, until after gasoline was powering every car on the road; then it had been rediscovered, and someone had scratched his head and wondered how it had been overlooked. Prontosil was developed during World War I, but the sulfa part wasn't used to kill germs until twenty years later. Penicillin had appeared and proved its germ killing power before 1930, but no one got around to using it until World War II.

Why was everything so significant overlooked? And would some man, a hundred years from now, stand on the Moon and stare down at his crude solar still, to recognize he'd been there first? Would they mysteriously find the accounts in old papers then, and wonder why they hadn't known about it before?

Or would this ultimate step of mankind be buried for good, while the race went on warring its way to destruction? A base on the Moon could spell enforced peace, if they got it in time.

Bill walked on, without purpose. He was finished. There was no use fighting now. Maybe he really wasn't Bill Soames. Maybe he'd been James Cross all along—maybe a nephew of old Robert Cross, who'd inherited a small fortune when the old man died. Gone on a hunting trip by airplane, gotten lost, half starved before he could find the plane, then landed in the ocean. Three children, one a girl with amazing dark red hair and the deepest blue eyes that could smile at a man. A vision of a pleasant apartment swam into his mind. He'd better call home...

He cut it off savagely. He was Major William Soames, back to a crazy Earth after four years on the Moon. Neither his own mind nor any outside force was going to change his knowledge of that.

For a second, he was tempted to call the phone number that had been in his mind. Maybe there was such a number under the name of James Cross, and such a family. Maybe they had a convenient slot for him to fit into, just as they'd destroyed his own slot. But he couldn't fool with it. Giving in might be just what they wanted—whoever or whatever *they* were.

He shook his head. It was too late to change his mind. The doubtful number had disappeared, along with the phantasms that went with it. He was no longer uncertain about himself, at least. Yet he knew that he had to find some kind of proof, if he didn't want the fantasy thoughts to come back.

Where could he go for specific information? How could he locate the news from all the papers, dealing with a specific subject, instead of having to plow through edition after edition, requiring a life-time of effort?

Then he had it. There were clipping bureaus that did that for one. They could cull out everything except articles dealing with rockets, spaceflight, and so on. He had no idea of the cost, but he could find out. He studied the signs along the street, and began pulling off the ring. He'd never get what it was worth—but even at a discount, five carats should be worth a considerable sum. Then he could investigate the clipping bureaus.

Again, luck changed capriciously. The ring had brought more than he'd expected—at least half of what it was worth—and he found the bureaus listed in the classified section of the phone book. Most of them obviously specialized in names, rather than subjects. Some agreed that they could get him such clippings. And one stated rather doubtfully that they had some. But the seventeenth one seemed pleasantly surprised when he broached the idea.

"How about photostats? They do you as well?"

Bill could see no reason to object to that. The voice at the end of the line became even more pleasant. "Fine. We've been making up a file on that subject. Another day and you'd have been too late. But we can run off a copy for you tonight, and have it ready at nine tomorrow. It'll save you a lot of expense, too. We've had to get extra copies of some of the papers from back years, and that runs into money, not counting the overtime work. This way, that's all paid for, and we can be pretty reasonable."

"Nine o'clock tomorrow," Bill agreed. "I suppose you'll want some money in advance?"

The voice brightened again. They made arrangements for a messenger to pick up the money in the lobby of a nearby hotel. Bill registered at the desk while waiting, using the same fictitious name he had given the agency. He was tired in a way that he'd never been during all the grueling effort to get back to Earth. It would be easy to relax and pretend the world was right—it was hard to keep fighting it. But something in his head refused to surrender. Somehow, he was going to collect the recognition they owed him, if it took him his whole remaining life time to get it!

He should have felt better after a night's sleep, but bitterness was apparently getting to be a habit again. Nine o'clock found him outside the clipping bureau. He saw tired, lackluster women entering and punching their cards into the time clock; they began gathering up newspapers and filing towards desks, where the routine job of marking, cutting, and pasting the items began. They'd probably throwaway a thousand hints of new ideas and inventions that would be buried for years or decades, and never know what they had missed—if the news was even there. They'd go on collecting the names of men who liked to see those names in print. And at night they'd go home too tired and dreary to look up at the sky. Would it really make any difference if they knew that somewhere up there parts of a supply rocket had been turned into a solar still, so that a starved, crazy fool could come back here to bring them news nobody would believe?

"Mr. Foster?" a voice behind him said for the third time, and he suddenly remembered that he'd chosen that as his name the day before. "Ah, good morning. Everything's ready—and quite a file, too. I was looking it over last night. Strange material here—enough for a book, at least. People hear messages from the Moon, people see big ships land, people announce they've built a rocket to go to Mars. A Coast Guard yeoman even reported picking a man out of the sea who claimed he'd just come from the Moon.

Something about living up there four years without air or water. People! Are you a writer?"

"Sort of." Bill evaded his question. He picked up the file with a shudder at realizing he had made the news, even if it hadn't been quite the way he'd intended.

The clerk was busy making a flourish of computing the sales tax, then counting the money. Bill picked up the bulky envelope and started to leave, just as a big, blond man entered. The clerk nodded toward him. "The man who ordered this originally," he started, as if to introduce them.

But Bill didn't wait. He'd seen a quiet little bar on the corner, and he headed for it. It was nearly empty, and he found a booth off by himself, where he could go through the photostats.

Most of it was what he had expected, and it had been padded out with flying saucer stories, of course. He began weeding out the junk, keeping everything that seemed to have the faintest use. There was an account on July 1 of a kid who'd run away—it made no sense until a July 8 follow-up pasted to it showed that the kid had been found, safe enough, but swearing he'd gone to see the big rocket go up. Bill checked the date again. It was 1948, and the location had been about right. The kid could have run off to see him leave, if word had leaked. But it was no proof by itself.

"Hi," a soft voice said. The big blond man was sliding down across from him. "Hear you got a bargain. Not that I care nothing exclusive. Interested in space flight?"

Bill frowned, and then decided he could use a little chance to talk socially. "You might say so," he admitted. "Mostly about the Moon. I got interested in Professor Rosenblum's lecture. It gets to be a bit expensive as a hobby, though."

"Pays off, if you know how. That's my angle. I make process shots for the movies, now that they've gone in for this stuff. Do it cheaper and better than they can. I figured some of this might give me some ideas." The man's voice was friendly, but he seemed vaguely disappointed, as if he had expected something else from Bill.

For his own part, Bill was wondering about leaving. It had seemed to offer some possibility for interest when he'd realized that the other was sinking money into finding all he could about such things. But Bill wasn't interested in process shots. The films that had been lost on his ship were the real thing—and they showed it. No trick of photography could give the same effect.

He started to gather up the mess of photostats, but the other had signaled for more beer. "I'm Brad Wollen."

"Bill Soames," he answered automatically, and then cursed himself as the other's eyebrows lifted. "A cousin of the fellow who got the Medal of Honor, if that's what you were thinking."

Wollen nodded. "Funny. And I'm the cousin of the Army test pilot who cracked up in that new supersonic job back in '49. Quite a coincidence, isn't it? Hey…wait a minute…didn't I see something about a guy who claimed he was your cousin in one of these…"

He began searching through the clippings busily. Bill swore hotly to himself. He'd thought his name had escaped publication—they usually left out names, in such cases. He shoved back his beer, and began framing an excuse to leave.

Then he stopped. Lying on the table was an eight-by-ten glossy picture. And it was no process shot. The lighting couldn't be duplicated. That was a shot of the Moon—the real Moon!

His hands fumbled with it as he tried to pick it up. No tricks could do that! And the rocket ship in the background was too detailed for any of the stuff they were doing now. It was different from his—but it might have been another model of the same ship, just as this picture was like the crater he'd known, though not quite the same.

"It's real!" he said slowly. "The way the light bounces, the way those rocks look eroded, yet aren't rounded off! Damn it, you can't fake that."

He realized he was being a fool as he said it, but the words piled out before he could stop them. It wasn't the stupidity that brought him to a halt, though. It was the sudden blanched shock on the other man's face. Wollen had heaved himself half out of his seat and was staring at him as if he'd just come out of hell, complete with brimstone.

"Mister, how do *you* know how those rocks look?" The man's voice was a hoarse whisper.

Bill sighed wearily. "Because I was the fool that took off in the first ship—in 1948, for the record. The blind fool who couldn't die, but managed to live up there four years until I could come back here to be shown what a real fool is. Now go ahead and laugh. Tell me you never heard of a rocket then and that Bill Soames died over Berlin. Tell me I'm a liar now!"

I never heard of a '48 rocket and I did hear you died." Wollen was sinking back slowly. "But it fits—oh, how well it fits. Then—you did crash in the sea!"

He didn't wait for Bill's tensed, unbelieving nod. "I was luckier. I came down in a swamp not sixty miles from here. Make way for the hero, home from the Moon! Did they abandon you without supplies, too? Yeah. It isn't fun, baking out water if you did it the way I did. And it isn't fun when you find you're dead—were dead before you took off, and your wife swears your kids belong to the man she married the same day she married you, and... But I had the films. When the guys I showed them to told me they were nice process work, I caught on fast. I came closer to starving here than up there, at first. Now—well, I'm doing all right, that way. They like my process work! Almost looks real, they tell me. The blind fools! They won't even look at the ship—they call it clever of me to make such a big mock-up for my shots!"

His voice quieted suddenly. "I've been back three months. Sometimes I begin to think I never took off from Earth at all. I get funny ideas. But all the same, I took off in 1950, and I was up there seventeen months on food enough for less than six."

They sat staring at each other while Bill cursed himself. It had been thrown at him—the man who had approached Rosenblum's colleague, Dr. Dickson, must have been Wollen. Rosenblum had discovered the fuel method in 1946; Dickson had found it in 1949...

His eyes dropped to the clippings, but Wollen was gathering them up. "It's a nice ship, still," he said. "It needs raising upright, and a little work. But you'll like it."

It *was* a nice ship—a better model in some ways than Bill's had been. But they'd discussed that, and agreed it was natural. While the fuel trick had been buried, technology in other lines had advanced a little. If there was another, later ship, it would probably be better, though still not good enough.

And there was going to be another. The clippings had proved that. All the signs that Bill and Wollen could remember from their pasts were out again, obvious to those who could read the meaning. Somewhere, someone else had discovered how to use water in an atomic power plant for fuel, and they were building a ship. In another year, it would be winging up towards the Moon. And the whole story would start over again; the fuel supply rockets would not arrive, and somehow the headlines and memories on Earth would change.

Bill had a picture of thousands and millions of people scuttling about, destroying that "ridiculous" bit of evidence, or "correcting" some mistake, to hold man down from his great leap. It had been easy to keep him fooled once. The Greeks had invented a toy steam engine twenty-five hundred years ago, and the idea had somehow been glossed over until Watt came along. It was harder now—it must take more work each time.

Whatever was causing it was losing. But that whatever might still win. Man was getting close to destruction now. He had bombs that could annihilate great masses. He had a thousand new toys of war. And he was blundering along, closer and closer to using them all.

Bill helped Wollen unload the new batch of supplies off the little truck into the shed beside the rocket. Around them, the swamp was a perfect camouflage, and the hollow into which the rocket had settled in its landing glide concealed it almost completely.

The blond man wiped his hands, and stopped for a breather, picking up the conversation where he'd dropped it. "You can't give them—or it—a name, Bill. Maybe it's caused by aliens, in spite of what we believe. Maybe it's caused by a group right here on Earth who can control men's thoughts on any one limited subject at a time. Maybe it's some supernatural drive. I've even thought about the old idea of the mass-mind, capable of taking over individual humanity; that would be a pretty basic, conservative force, and it wouldn't want newfangled ideas. The thing has been operating for a good many thousand years, fighting a constant delaying action. But this is its last stand. Once we spread out, we can't be controlled—one planet will discover what the next one doesn't. It has to win now. And that means we have to win."

"We'll win," Bill answered him, and began unloading the truck again. "We've got to win, so we will."

Unconsciously, they both looked up to the sky, where the Moon would be. There was time enough for them to get the big ship righted and ready to take off. The repairs needed were minor, and the fuel for the rocket was all around them, while the atomic motors were good for at least one more trip. They'd make the Moon, and still have some leeway to maneuver about, or to jump from one crater to another.

Men had struggled with electricity and tamed it before they knew what it was. They'd been fighting gravity for millennia, whenever they did work, and still knew nothing about it, really. They knew nothing about their own minds and the minds of the larger groups being studied in mob psychology, beyond a hint and a suggestion. Men somehow always had to beat down the opposing forces and only learn what they were after the battle was won.

It didn't matter what had been doing it. Maybe they'd never know. Or maybe they'd learn as soon as it was finally overcome. All they had to do was fix it so they couldn't lose.

In another year, the third rocket would go up. This time two men would be watching for it from the Moon—men in a worn spaceship, who'd spent months baking out supplies of water from gypsum for fuel. Bill and Wollen would be ready. They'd ferry the fuel to wherever the next ship landed, and the new ship could head back for Earth less than a day after it touched the Moon.

That wouldn't leave time enough for the records to be changed and old memories replaced with false ones.

Bill grinned to himself. So he'd be a hero, after all, with his supposed death probably explained as a cover-up for his initial flight. They'd find some way to explain it all, of course.

He shouldered another load of hydroponic tanks to replace those Wollen had left on the Moon, and his face sobered. It would take more than heroism. It would take men too stubborn to have good sense.

"Pumpkins!" he said with a new depth of feeling. "Tomatoes!"

He carried the tanks into the ship and began bolting them down, ready for an early planting.

THE END

The Barrier

By MURRAY LEINSTER

Men proved once that the speed of sound was a barrier which no airplane could crack. It took new ideas, tough men, and a lot of time to beat it. Then men got out of the atmosphere where a worse barrier was waiting. They knew that ships had to go faster than light to reach the stars. It's a lot tougher to beat the speed of light than to crack the sonic barrier. It would take a hero to do that—or the world's number one prize fool!

I get a laugh out of the way they tell the story of how Joe Harper broke the Barrier. All the visicasts carry it on the anniversary of the *Star Pup's* return. There's a big, full-hour program about it, and school kids have to watch it for school credit, and all that day the comedians make cracks about it, and they fly flags at half-mast and have ceremonies yapping about it. Joe Harper broke the Barrier, they say, and he's a planetary hero—the first one—and Bill Todd makes a speech and says what a good guy Joe Harper was, and how everybody wishes he'd lived, and they hold Joe Harper up for all the kids to model themselves by. They say with proud and wistful grief that they can't build a memorial over his grave, but that every Earth colony in the skies is his memorial. They say a lot of things like that.

I knew Joe Harper; I knew him when. I knew him better than anybody else who ever lived. I know more about him than anybody who makes speeches or writes the visicasts for the anniversary of the Breaking of the Barrier. I know!

The Barrier was space, of course. It was the distance between Earth and the nearest star. It was the difference between the distance to the Moon—we could make that then—and Alpha Centaurus. It was less than two light-seconds to the Moon. It was four and a half light-years to Alpha Centaurus.

I'm not going to spoil the story. When I kick off, this goes to the Joseph Harper Memorial Fund—which educates boys who can't swing it themselves. They can use it or not, just as they please.

THE BARRIER

BY MURRAY LEINSTER

Illustrated by ORBAN

If they give a damn about actual facts, they'll publish it, though. This is the truth about this precious hero of theirs, Joe Harper.

It was the Bessenden Comet that started it. If you're more than a kid you'll remember. It was a comet that they picked up on the Moon Observatory telescopes first. They'd already spotted two planets of Alpha Centaurus, then. They picked up Bessenden's Comet a half-light year out. It took plenty long to arrive. By the time it was a naked-eye object they had its orbit figured, and they were shivering with joy. It came in and swung around the sun, and they checked some more, and then they went crazy with excitement.

There were three good reasons. One was that Bessenden's Comet didn't visit our sun only. It had a closed orbit, of course, and our Sun was at one end of it, but Alpha Centauri was at the other. It made a round trip between them every twenty-three zillion zillion years.

That was one excuse for going nuts. Another was the spectrum of its tail. There was some stuff in it that didn't fit into the periodic table. It had atoms with double nuclei. Like double suns. Two nuclei spinning around each other, and the planetary electrons running around outside. The physicists went out of their minds, figuring out what it would mean. They called the stuff bessendium, after the guy who'd picked out the comet on a photographic plate in the first place. He never did anything else of any importance in all his life. The third reason for excitement was the news that Earth was due to pass through the comet's track in just three months.

That meant there might be meteoric falls of the same stuff the comet was made of. Meteors go barging around in the orbits of comets. The Leonids and the August meteors anyhow. Maybe some scrap from this comet would fall.

The physicists started showing their figures to the big-money boys. By the time we were ready to pass through the comet's trail there was an offer of a thousand dollars a gram for any meteoric material from the comet. And you could write a book about that night with everybody watching for millions to fall from the sky!

A half-ounce piece fell in the middle of Rio de Janeiro. A fire-ball exploded over Lake Erie, and three pieces fell on shore. There was a fall in Kamchatka—sixty pieces, total weight twenty-three pounds. Up near the Moon observatory they got another piece. With all the Earth watching here and on the moon besides, there were less than thirty pounds of meteoric material picked up—and there was less than an ounce and a half of pure bessendium in it. That was where Joe Harper came in.

He'd been working on rockets. He was the one who worked out compound-explosion rocket motors, and got forty thousand feet exhaust-velocity for the first time. The big-money boys were putting up for something big, and they wanted him to design the engines. They were going to build a spaceship with their ounce and a half of bessendium. Because bessendium turned out to be an atomic catalyst. You could get controlled atomic energy out of anything from lead to mushroom soup if you had as much as an ounce and a quarter of bessendium. You couldn't use less. There was a critical mass for catalysis, like there's a critical mass for a bomb. They could make one ship. Just one. They could never make another ship unless they got some more bessendium. And they called in Joe to build the drive.

You've heard the stuff about him. Poor boy, self-educated, brilliant mind, genius for seeing into the heart of things, high ideals, chivalrous—everything a planetary hero ought to be. Sure! That's what the visicasts say. Let's skip that hogwash. The compound-explosion rocket motor was only a twist on the principle of the long-barreled cannon. He got it from the Big Bertha that bombarded Paris from seventy miles, back in 1917-1918, fifty years before he was born. Of course he had to work out a tricky electronic-circuit cooling-system to keep his engine from melting.

It turned waste heat to electricity, and they use that to generate current on Earth, right now.

They were going to use the *Star Pup* to go to Mars. A quick petrological exploration—for traces of bessendium—and they would push off for Saturn's rings. If that failed they'd start checking over the asteroids, one by one, for bessendium. Earth had the stuff to make one atomic-drive ship. Just one. No more. They had to use it to try to find more stuff for more ships. And Joe Harper designed the *Star Pup's* engines.

He did a good job on those engines. You can give him that. They were good engines. But he put something over on the rest of the designing crew. Those engines could have pulled the *Star Pup* straight out from the sun. They could accelerate the ship at forty-seven gravities. If you figure what forty-seven gravities would do to anybody inside the ship, you'll see how often it would be used!

The funny thing was that nobody realized it while the ship was building. Not even Bill Todd—but he was an astronomer. Nobody got it but Lila Hunt, who was the biological designer; she worked on the air-freshener and ozone apparatus and the interior environment to keep the crew from cracking up from space-nerves. A nice-looking girl, Lila. A little bit on the tall side, but she had good eyes and plenty of brain cells working, and she was a human being besides. Even she didn't really tumble until they'd finished putting on the *Star Pup's* outer plating and were working on the outer helix.

Joe Harper was puttering around on top of the hull, watching the workmen mold welding the silver conductor-bars from the cooling circuit. The *Star Pup* was funny looking. Her rockets were outside her skin. There was a helix of heavy silver bar around the whole hull. It was supposed to be communication stuff. Lila watched Joe raising hell with workmen fixing up a weld. They had blueprints and a wiring-diagram, and they argued with him. He took the diagram and changed it and signed the change. He snapped.

"That puts you in the clear! Go ahead and fix it my way!"

Then Lila said:

"Joe."

He climbed down from the hull and went to her. He liked her a lot, Joe did. She was a couple of inches taller than he was, but he thought about her a lot when he should have been doing something more sensible. He never made any passes at her, though. He was conceited, but not that conceited! He knew she wouldn't look at him. So he acted curt and hard-boiled to her, but he always thought over everything she'd said, afterward, just liking to remember the way she looked and how her voice sounded.

This time, when he climbed down off the *Star Pup*, she smiled at him and said, "Joe, those engines are too big. I've been reading up. You had an article in the last *Electronics Engineering*. I studied it."

"Why?" asked Joe. Pretty stupid. A girl doesn't read a technical article outside her field unless it's by a man she wants to understand.

"Oh, I like to read what my friends publish," said Lila. "But those engines are big! You'd never dare turn them on full, according to the figures in your article. You're putting something over. Come have lunch with me and tell me about it, will you?"

He pretended to hesitate, but he went to the commissary of the moonship yard where all the rockets that had ever gone to the moon had been built—but the *Star Pup* was the first one ever built to go farther. A moon rocket could get to Mars, but it would have to coast eight months, and carry eight months of food for the crew that went along—and then it couldn't get back. So nobody'd gone. No use in it. Joe and Lila found a table and sat down.

"So I'm putting something over!" said Joe. "What?"

"I wouldn't know," admitted Lila. She smiled at him very nicely. "But if you turned on your engines full power you'd kill everybody in the ship unless you turned on the coolers full power. Then you wouldn't get much drive, but you'd draw off a couple of hundred thousand kilowatts of power. Maybe more."

"So what?" said Joe, challenging.

"So what are you going to do with two hundred thousand kilowatts of power, out in space?" asked Lila.

"It's three hundred thousand," said Joe. He ordered a meal, for her and himself, and said, "I want to try something."

"To try melting the ship?" asked Lila. She said softly, "Tell me, Joe. The engines are in. It's too late to tear them out. I won't tell. What do you want to try?"

"You saw the helix outside the hull," said Joe. "It's half-inch silver bars, to send radio signals and pick them up, they say. Quite a loop. What'd happen if you sent three hundred thousand kilowatts through that helix—four hundred thousand horse-power?"

"Wouldn't they blow?" asked Lila. She watched his face.

"Not if they were cold enough," Joe told her. "Not at four degrees Kelvin. That's the temperature out there. Silver's a superconductor there—zero resistance. They wouldn't blow. They'd carry the current. What would happen?"

Lila thought it over. She shook her head. It was queer, this stuff. He talked technicalities and noticed the way she smiled and thought about that. She talked technicalities and smiled at him in a strictly untechnical way.

"All I can see is that there'd be the strongest magnetic field anybody even thought about," she said. "What good would that be to a spaceship enclosed in it?"

"Take a thing that makes heat," said Joe, noticing that her hair had funny little golden lights in it. "A resistance wire, say. Put in enough power and it stops making heat. It gives light. Put in more power and if it didn't blow it'd stop making light. It'd give off ultra-violet and X-rays. Put in still more, and if anything could take it, it'd give cosmics. Right?"

She nodded.

"Take a coil that'll make a magnetic field," said Joe. "Put in enough power, so it's not magnetism any more. What'll it be?"

"What would it be?" she asked, surprised into paying attention to what he was saying, instead of just to him.

"I want to find out," he told her, grinning. Then he said, "You're a good-looking girl, Lila."

"Ah!" she said, making it sound like half a joke. "Come up to my house tonight and tell me that again!"

"You'd pump me," he said wisely. "About what I think that field would be. I don't fall for that."

"I might want you to tell me I'm good-looking," she protested.

"Not with Bill Todd hanging around."

She said very firmly indeed, her eyes anxious, "He hasn't any mortgage on me! I'd like you to come, Joe. I—you never have talked to me about anything but work."

"And I won't," said Joe. "Not until I get rich. Remember my cooling-circuit for my rockets?' "

She nodded. That was a bad deal that Joe Harper got. It made him the fool he turned out to be. But of course, if he hadn't been something of a halfwit to start with, it wouldn't.

"I never did appeal to girls," said Joe deliberately. "I was pretty well resigned to it. Then I met a girl who seemed to fall for me, hard. She liked to talk about my work…even I was figuring out that cooling-circuit, then, and I bragged about it to her. I drew the circuit for her to admire. She admired it a lot. She admired it so much that she carefully took my sketches and a tape-recording of what I'd said about it to the corporation that patented it and is making very nice dividends from it. They're building all the new power plants on Earth with my circuit. But I didn't get anything out of it. I guess the girl did, though."

Lila knew it had been taken from him, of course. She'd never known how. It was one of those things that couldn't be proved.

"Do you think I'd do that?" she asked, hurt.

"I wouldn't take the chance," he told her. "That's all."

"That's hardly a nice thing to say to me," she protested.

"I know," he agreed. "It isn't nice. But I said it."

She bit her lips.

"If that's why you act as you do, Joe," said Lila quietly, "—because some girl did you a dirty trick—I'll promise not to say one word about work or the *Star Pup*. I would like you to like me, Joe. I've tried to make you."

She looked like she meant it, and he was tempted. This was in the commissary restaurant. She was the prettiest girl in the room. He liked her better than he'd ever liked anybody else. But he'd been hit hard. He'd made a bitter resolve never to be fooled again by a girl. He would have given Lila his left arm and leg, if it would have done her any good. But he couldn't trust anybody. He couldn't tell the difference between Lila and the kind of girl who could be hired to make a fool of him.

"I'll tell you," he said. He grinned, but he meant it. "If my trick is what I think it is, I'll get a lot richer than that cooling-circuit ever would have made me. I've got you in my mind. When I'm rich, I'll come and ask you to marry me. I mean it," he added. "That's what I want."

Then Lila went pale. She said very quietly, "I think you mean that, Joe. You're just crazy enough to mean it. But I'm crazy too, in my own way. I've been telling myself I was in love with you. I've been making passes at you in a ladylike way. Now that you've said this—I'd marry you tomorrow if you asked me. Right now. But if you dodged me until you got rich—not trusting me—and then came... I wouldn't marry you if you were the last man in the world!"

Then she got up and went out of the commissary, fast. Joe looked after her. He felt rotten. He had an idea that she hoped he'd come over to her house that night. But he was not the brilliant, impulsive, splendidly normal character the visicasts say he was. He didn't go. Next day he saw her at the moonship yard. He nodded how-do. She turned away. He was sorry, but he was that kind of a fool. He didn't know what to do.

Then he had that run-in with Bill Todd. The *Star Pup* was pretty nearly finished, and Bill was feeling good. He was the official head of the organization that had bought up all the bessendium from the meteoric falls, he was in over-all charge of designing and building the *Star Pup*, and he'd be her skipper. An astronomer, Bill Todd. Big and handsome, and he could turn on the charm and make a swell speech before a woman's club or a banker's luncheon. He liked Lila.

All of a sudden he came to Joe Harper and said angrily, "Look here, Joe! What's this about Lila?"

Joe was working, then. He was making an instrument to go on the *Star Pup*, and it was tricky adjusting it, because all he had to go on was theory. He was irritable because he couldn't have any of the stuff it was supposed to measure to calibrate it by.

"What about Lila?" he asked.

83

"She told me she's not sure she'll sign on the *Star Pup* for the cruise. Even the try-out cruise! I asked her what was the matter and she said you wouldn't want her along. If you think you can decide who makes up the crew of the *Star Pup*...I raised the money for that ship! I'm to be her skipper! If I want Lila in the crew, she's in the crew!"

"All right," said Joe. "She's in the crew, then."

He was having trouble with his work. He was fretting. And Bill Todd was a nuisance.

Bill said more angrily still, "You're a good engine man, Joe, but don't get any ideas! You're not the boss of this business! If you've got something on your mind, you can say it right now!"

Joe turned from his workbench and snapped, "The scheme is crazy! It's crazy to hunt for bessendium on Mars. Erosion has pulled it down flat and covered over all its rocks anyhow. It's crazy to hunt for bessendium in Saturn's rings. It makes nice dramatic picture, but the specific gravity's low. There won't be any heavy elements in bessendium. If there's any in this solar system it'll be on Mercury, but I don't think there is. The comet came from Centaurus. I don't believe there's an atom of bessendium closer than that. It would take some freak conditions to make a double-nucleus atom! We'd have found it on Earth if there were any around. Earth's got the best assortment of elements any planet has. It could be on Mercury—but not anywhere else. I think it'll have to be found in the Centaurus system."

Bill Todd said, "Ambitious, you are! It'd take six years, counting acceleration and deceleration, to get to Centaurus at point eight light speed. That's the best the *Star Pup* could do with all the time it needed for acceleration. And a crew would starve on the way. Six years each way? You're the one who's crazy!"

"Want to bet?" asked Joe.

"I do not want to bet," said Bill Todd with dignity. "I want you to attend to your part of this business and leave the rest—including the selection of the crew—to me!"

"Else I'm likely to be left out, eh?" asked Joe.

"Figure it yourself!" said Bill.

Joe went back to his instrument. Bill Todd was a pretty good astronomer. He could raise money and give a charming lecture, and he was good at changing the photographic plates in a telescope. He stood there, watching Joe belligerently.

"And I want Lila on the *Star Pup!*" he said firmly. "That's settled!"

He stalked away, leaving Joe to figure it out. And Joe figured. He could see through Bill Todd easily enough. Bill was the sort to gloat over being skipper of the first ship to land on Mars, and the first to touch the rings of Saturn—nobody'd want to land on Saturn—and he was the fair-haired boy who would revel in being the hero of the first romance out in space. He'd love the visiscreen appearances he'd be asked to make as a great scientist and a great lover, holding the hand of the girl he'd won with Saturn filling half the universe as he told her of his love... Sure! Even Joe could figure that one out.

He saw Lila next day. He went up to her and said, "You told Bill you want me left behind? Why?"

"I didn't say that," said Lila quietly. "I said I might not go along myself. I don't think it's a good idea to have a crew of a ship not able to trust each other."

Joe said coldly, "All right. Suppose I put three hundred thousand kilowatts through that helix. It'll be as much more than magnetism as light or X-rays is more than heat. It'll be a stress in space, of course. It'll be a new kind of stress in space. I think it'll make a field in which the speed of light will go up out of sight, and a field that can travel at that speed. I think it'll give the *Star Pup* a faster than light drive. Is that what you want to know? You wanted me to trust you. I've told you. Satisfied?"

She shook her head.

"That's not what I want you to say," she said in a low tone.

"I've got to be part of the crew," said Joe practically, "to find out if that works. I might be wrong. It might blow us to hell-and-gone. I'd rather you stayed behind."

"Why?" asked Lila bitterly. "Nobody cares if I go on a dangerous expedition!"

"I do," said Joe. He meant it.

"If you'll ask me," said Lila, "I'll go with you and be with you when you try it. I'll even help you do it without the others knowing—because they wouldn't let you. That's not right, but I'll do it. You haven't the right to risk their lives without their consent, but I'll help you do that—if you say what I want you to say."

Joe shrugged.

"They'd never agree," he told her. "Besides, there's the bessendium. It's all there is. Bill wouldn't risk either his neck or the bessendium except for glory. He'd never risk both."

"I will," said Lila. "But you've got to ask me to, Joe, haven't you ever wanted anybody to be part of you? To share everything with you? Even danger?"

"No," said Joe. "Not danger. If I get a lot of money I'll want to share that with you."

"You're crazy!" cried Lila fiercely. "I won't let you do it! I'll tell Bill Todd what you intend! I'll stop you!"

She ran away. He didn't run after her. He just stared where she'd vanished. Plain stupid.

He took off in the *Star Pup*, alone, two days before the ship was officially finished. It was practically done, of course. The air-plant was in, and the heaters, and the fuel was loaded—but anything would do for fuel. The bessendium was in its place, built in. Joe Harper went to the ship and got a workman to help him get a couple of heavy cases inside. Said it was instruments for testing the rockets. Then he got all the workmen away. He was going to test the rockets.

He tried them. One by one, at minimum power, he set every one at work. But even so, they made a noise that was something to crack a man's eardrums. The noise was terrific. It went beyond the moonship yard. It filled the offices. It was a growling, snarling thunder. Lila heard it. She turned her head, going white. Bill Todd was talking to her at the time.

"Who's turned on the rockets?" she demanded, white as chalk.

"Joe," said Bill, easily. "He told me he was going to make a check. Just routine. You didn't tell him he'd have to stay behind, did you?"

Lila didn't answer. She was out the door. She ran. She ran down the steps and into the yard, and she ran crazily toward the *Star Pup*, sobbing as she ran and blubbering, "Joe! Joe! Wait for me!"

Somebody tried to stop her when she was a couple of hundred yards of the ship. She dodged them, and ran down a lane of unscorched ground where the rocket flames didn't touch. She saw the ports were closed. The entrance port closed as she got to the ship's side. It seemed like Joe had closed it in her face, but actually he'd done it from the control room. She pounded on it with her fists, crying, "Joe! Joe! Let me in!" The booming of ten thousand thunders was in her ears.

Then the ship up-ended and went away from there with as many of the forty-seven gravities that its engines could give as Joe dared put into them. There was a flash, and it was darting up. It went up into the sky. It was out of sight in seconds. And there wasn't anything where it had been. Not anything.

So Joe went to Centaurus. They got word to the Moon Observatory, and they got a telescope trained on the *Star Pup* and saw it head out. Joe put it through all its paces on atomic rocket drive. Very conscientious, he was. Then he lined up for Alpha Centaurus—and suddenly the ship wasn't there. He'd waited, watching the outside temperature, until the silver helix was down to four degrees Kelvin, and it didn't have any resistance at all. Then he turned on the engines and the cooler full power. Three hundred thousand kilowatts went into the helix. There was hardly any power left as rocket thrust, but there was enough. The magnetic field became something else. It became an area of stress in which the speed of light went way up—and therefore an area in which the *Star Pup* could travel hundreds of times faster than in normal space. The stress went ahead of the *Star Pup*. She went out of sight. There wasn't even a streak of ions left behind that anybody could see. There was a streak, but the ions were too far apart. Miles and miles apart.

The *Star Pup* had cracked the Barrier.

He was gone something over three weeks, living on the food he'd gotten into the ship in those two cases he'd said were instruments. Then, one day, the *Star Pup* winked into being again. She came on toward Earth. The radio receivers at the Moon Observatory picked up this message.

"Star Pup *reporting back from Alpha Centaurus planet two,*" was the message. *"Have nearly ton bessendium ore for cargo. Contact Lila Hunt care of moonship yard Star Pup project. Message for her: quote, I know what I should have said. I say it, I love you. We'll get married please. Unquote."*

The Moon Observatory relayed the message to Earth, while the *Star Pup* came on. They went crazy down there, of course. But Bill Todd phrased the message back to Joe. He did a beautiful job of it.

It told Joe that Lila had been in the blast area when he took off. It had been quick. That was the blessed part of it. It didn't last the thousandth of a second.

Joe went out of his mind, out there in the *Star Pup*, heading for Earth. There was a time when he started to head for the Sun and dive in it. But that wasn't fair. So he landed on Earth.

But Joe got one break. The only break he ever got out of the whole business. He set the Star Pup down. The minute she was on the ground the planes hovering around broke all barriers and came swooping over to see the *Star Pup* close. Joe got out of the ship and began to run. He wanted to hide. He didn't want to be a hero. And he got his break.

A four-passenger job collided with a light plane and they started to fall; they gathered up two other planes on the way down. They landed at the very edge of the crowd that was rushing out on the field to mob Joe for being a hero. They blew up when they hit. There were eighty-some people killed, right away, and some hundreds burnt or injured in the crush. They never found Joe's body. They never found Joe.

When they picked me out of the mess and hauled me to the hospital with all the other injured, I was burnt pretty badly. The first thing they asked me was, "What's your name?"

I told them, "John Smith." I didn't want to be a hero. I wanted to hide. I wanted not to remember anything. I was pretty bitter because I didn't die. It was three months before they turned me out of the hospital, and then nobody would have recognized me anyhow. So that's that.

Joe Harper wasn't any hero. He was a damn fool. I should know. I used to be him.

THE END

The Fence

By CLIFFORD D. SIMAK

There are two sides to any fence, even an invisible one. But can you be sure which is really the inside?

He came down the stairway into the hushed sanctuary of the lounge and stood for a moment to allow his eyes to become accustomed to the perpetual twilight of the place.

A robot waiter went past, tall glasses balanced on the tray.

"Good afternoon, Mr. Craig," he said.

"How are you, Herman?" asked Craig.

"Will you wish something, sir?"

"No, thank you," said Craig. "I'm going out directly."

Herman left. Craig crossed the room and he walked almost on tiptoe. He realized now, for the first time, that he almost always walked on tiptoe here. The only noise that ever was allowed was a cough and even then it must be a cough that was most discreet. To have spoken to anyone within the confines of the lounge would have been high treason.

The ticker stood in one corner of the room and, in keeping with the place, it was an almost silent ticker. The tape came out and went into a basket, but the basket was well watched and often emptied and the tape never, never spilled out on the carpet.

He picked up the strand of tape and ran it through his fingers, bending low to read the characters, backing through the alphabet until he came to C and then he went more slowly.

Cox, 108½; Cotton, 97; Colfield, 92; Cratchfield, 111¼; Craig, 75...

Craig, 75!

It had been 78 yesterday and 81 the day before and 83 the day before that. A month ago it had been 96½ and a year ago 120.

He stood with the tape in his hand and looked out over the room. The place seemed, at first glance, to be deserted. But as he looked, he saw them. There was a baldhead peeking over the back

89

of one chair and over the back of another rose a telltale trail of smoke from an invisible cigar. There was one who sat facing Craig, but he seemed so much a part of the chair that at first he seemed invisible. He sat quietly, with his gleaming black shoes and white shirtfront and the folded paper held stiffly before him.

THE FENCE

BY CLIFFORD D. SIMAK

Illustrated by GARI

Craig turned his head slowly and saw, with a sinking feeling, that there was someone in his chair, just three removed from the right wing of the fireplace. A month ago it would not have happened; a year ago it would have been unthinkable. His personal satisfaction had been high, then.

But they knew that he was slipping. They had seen the tape and talked about it. And they felt contempt for him despite their mealy mouths.

"Poor Craig," they had said to one another. "Such a decent chap. And so young, too."

They would have been consoling.

"He'll come out of it," they'd said. "It's just temporary."

And they had been quite smug about it, no doubt, sure that it was the sort of thing that would never happen to anyone of them.

The counselor was kind and helpful and Craig could see at a glance that he was a man well satisfied and that he liked his work.

"Seventy-five," he said. "That is not good, is it, Mr. Craig?"

"No, it's not," said Craig.

"You are engaged in something?" asked the counselor and he simpered just a little, a professional, polished simper that said he knew that Craig was, of course, but he had to ask.

"History," said Craig.

"Oh," said the counselor. "A most engaging subject. I have known a number of gentlemen who were quite wrapped up in history."

"I specialize," said Craig. "One acre."

"Acre?" asked the counselor, not a little puzzled. "I'm not quite sure..."

"The history of one acre," Craig told him. "Trace it back, you know, with a temporal viewer. Hour to hour, day to day. Record in detail, and with appropriate comment and deduction, everything that transpired upon the acre."

"Most novel," said the counselor. "I've never heard of it before."

"You do some screwy things," said Craig.

"Screwy?"

"Well, you strive for effect. You try to be spectacular, but spectacular in a scholarly way, if you understand."

"Yes, I am sure I do," the counselor said, "and yet it seems to me that the study of one acre of the Earth's surface is quite legitimate. There have been others who have limited their studies. There have been histories of families and of cities and of certain rather obscure causes and of the development and evolution of such commonplace things as teapots and coffee cups and antimacassars and such like."

"Yes," said Craig, "that is exactly what I thought."

"Tell me, Mr. Craig," asked the counselor, "have you run across anything spectacular on your…ah, acre?"

"I have traced the growth of trees," said Craig. "Backwards, you know. From decaying giants to saplings, from saplings to seed. It is quite a trick, this backward tracing. It is a bit confusing, but soon you get used to it. I swear you finally get so that you think in reverse. And then, of course, I have kept a record of birds' nests and the birds themselves. There's one old lame robin that was quite a character. And flowers, naturally. And the action of the elements on boulders and soil. And weather, I have a fine record of the weather over several thousand years."

"Most interesting," said the counselor.

"There was a murder, too," said Craig, "but it happened just outside the boundary line, so I can't actually include it in the study. The murderer, however, did run across the acre after he committed the deed."

"A murder, Mr. Craig?"

"Exactly," said Craig. "One man killed another, you understand."

"How ghastly," said the counselor.

"I suppose it would be," admitted Craig. "But it was done, you know. The records are filled with murders."

"Anything else?"

"Not yet," said Craig, "although I have some hope. I found some old foundations."

"Buildings?"

"Yes, of buildings. Go back far enough and I'm bound to find the buildings before they went to ruin. That might be interesting. There might be people in them. One of the foundations looked like a residence. Had what appeared to be the footing for a fireplace."

"You might hurry it up a bit," suggested the counselor. "Get there a little faster. People are most interesting."

Craig shook his head. "To make the study valid, I must record in detail. I can't slight the detail to get what's interesting."

The counselor managed to look sorrowful.

"With such an interesting project," he said, "I can't understand why your rating should go down."

"I realized," said Craig, "that no one would care. I would spend years at the study and I would publish my findings and I would give copies to my friends and acquaintances and they would thank me and put the book up on the shelf and never take it down again. I would deposit copies in libraries and you know yourself that no one ever goes to libraries. The only one who would ever read the thing would be myself."

"Surely, Mr. Craig," comforted the counselor, "there are other men who have found themselves in a like position. And they have managed to remain relatively happy and contented."

"That is what I've told myself," said Craig, "but it doesn't work for me."

"We could go into many of the closer aspects of the case," said the counselor, "but I think we should leave that until some future time if it proves necessary. We'll just hit the high points now. Tell me, Mr. Craig, are you fairly well convinced that you cannot continue to be happy with your acre?"

"Yes," said Craig. "I am."

"Not conceding for a moment," said the counselor, with dogged determination, "that your statement to that effect closes our avenue of investigation in that direction, tell me this: Have you considered an alternative?"

"An alternative?"

"Why, certainly. Some other line of work that might prove happier. I have counseled a number of gentlemen who changed their line of work and it has proved for the best."

"No," said Craig. "I haven't the least idea what I might go into."

"There are a number of openings," said the counselor. "Almost anything you wish. There's snail watching, for example."

"No," said Craig.

"Or stamp collecting," said the counselor. "Or knitting. A lot of gentlemen knit and find it very soothing."

"I don't want to knit," said Craig.

"You could make money."

"What for?" asked Craig.

"Well, now," the counselor said, "that is something I've often wondered, too. There's no need of it, really. All you have to do to get money is go to a bank and ask for some of it. But there are men who actually set out to make money and; if you ask me, they use some rather shady methods. But be that as it may, they seem to get a great deal of satisfaction doing it."

"What do they do with it once they get it?" asked Craig.

"I wouldn't know," the counselor told him. "One man buried it and then forgot where he buried it and he remained happy the rest of his life running around with a lantern and a shovel looking for it."

"Why the lantern?"

"Oh, I forgot to tell you that. He never hunted it in daylight. He hunted in the night."

"Did he ever find it?"

"Come to think of it," the counselor said, "I don't believe he did."

"I don't think," said Craig, "that I'd care for making money."

"You might join a club."

"I belong to a club," said Craig. "A very fine old club. One of the very finest. Some of the best names and its history runs back to…"

"That's not the kind of club I mean," the counselor said. "I mean a group of persons who work for something or who have special interests in common and band themselves together for the better enjoyment of those mutual interests."

"I doubt," said Craig, "that a club would be the answer."

"You might get married," the counselor suggested.

"What! You mean to one woman?"

"That is what I mean."

"And raise a bunch of kids?"

"Many men have done it," said the counselor. "They have been quite satisfied."

"It seems," said Craig, "on the face of it, just a bit obscene."

"There are many other possibilities," the counselor told him. "I can just run through a partial list of them and see if there is anything you might care to think about."

Craig shook his head. "Some other time," he said. "I'll come back again. I want to mull it over."

"You're absolutely sure that you're sour on history?" asked the counselor. "I'd rather steer you back to that than interest you in an alternative."

"I'm sour on it," said Craig. "I shudder when I think of it."

"You could take a vacation," suggested the counselor. "You could freeze your personal satisfaction rating until you returned. Maybe then you could boost it up again."

"I think," said Craig, "that to start with I'll take a little walk."

"A walk," the counselor told him, "is very often helpful."

"What do I owe you?" Craig asked.

"A hundred," the counselor said. "But it's immaterial to me if you pay or not."

"I know," said Craig. "You work for the love of it."

The man sat on the shore of the little pond and leaned back against a tree. He smoked while he kept an eye on the fish pole stuck into the ground beside him. Close at hand was an unpretentious jug made of earthenware.

He looked up and saw Craig. "Come on, friend," he said. "Sit down and rest yourself."

Craig came and sat. He pulled out a handkerchief and mopped his brow.

"The sun's a little warm," he said.

"Cool here," said the man. "I fish or loaf around when the sun is high. When the sun goes down I go and hoe my garden."

"Flowers," said Craig. "Now there's an idea. I've often thought it would be fun to raise a garden full of flowers."

"Not flowers," the man said. "Vegetables. I eat them."

"You mean you work to get the things you eat?"

"Uh-huh," said the man. "I spade the ground and rake it to prepare the seed bed. Then I plant the seeds and watch them sprout and grow. I tend the garden and I harvest it. I get enough to eat."

"It must be a lot of work."

"I take it easy," said the man. "I don't let it worry me."

"You could get a robot," Craig told him.

"Yeah, I guess I could. But I don't hold with such contraptions. It would make me nervous."

The cork went under and he made a grab for the pole, but he was too late. The hook came up empty.

"Missed that one," he said placidly. "Miss a lot of them. Don't pay enough attention."

He swung in the hook and baited it with a worm from the can that stood beside him.

"Might have been a turtle," he said. "Turtles are hell on bait."

He swung the tackle out again, stuck the pole back into the ground, and settled back against the tree.

"I grow a little extra corn," he said, "and run a batch of moon when my stock is running low. The house ain't much to look at, but it's comfortable. I got a dog and two cats and I fuss my neighbors."

"Fuss your neighbors?"

"Sure," the man said. "They all think that I am nuts."

He picked up the jug, uncorked it, and handed it to Craig. Craig took a drink, prepared for the worst. It wasn't bad at all.

"Took a little extra care with that batch," the man said. "It really pays to do that if you have the time."

"Tell me," said Craig, "are you satisfied?"

"Sure," the man said.

"You must have a nice P. S.," said Craig.

"P. X.?"

"No. P. S. Personal satisfaction rating."

The man shook his head. "I ain't got one of them," he said.

Craig was aghast. "But you have to have!"

"You talk just like that other fellow," said the man. "He was around a while ago. Told me about this P. S. business, but I thought he said P. X. Told me I had to have one. Took it awful hard when I said I wouldn't do it."

"Everyone has a P. S.," said Craig.

"Everyone but me," said the man. "That's what the other fellow said, too. He was some upset about it. Practically read me out of the human race."

He looked sharply at Craig. "Son," he said, "you got troubles on your mind."

Craig nodded.

"Lots of folks have troubles," said the man, "only they don't know it. And you can't start to lick your troubles until you see and recognize them. Things are all upset. No one's living right. There is something wrong."

"My P. S. is way off," said Craig. "I've lost all interest. I know there's something wrong. I can sense it, but I can't put my finger on it."

"They get things given to them," said the man. "They could live the life of Riley and not do a tap of work. They could get food and shelter and clothing and all the luxuries that they want by just asking for them. You want money, so you go to a bank and the bank gives you all you need. You go to a shop and buy a thing and the shopkeeper don't give a tinker's damn if you pay or not. Because, you see, it didn't cost him nothing. He got it given to him. He doesn't have to work for a living. He ain't keeping shop, really. He's just playing at it, like kids would play at keeping store. And there's other people who play at all sorts of other things. They do it to keep from dying of boredom. They wouldn't have to do it. And this P. S. business you talk about is just another play-mechanism, a way of keeping score, a sort of social pressure to keep you on your toes when there is no real reason on all of God's green Earth that you should be on your toes. It's meant to keep you happy by giving you something to work for. A high P. S. means high social standing and a satisfied ego. It's clever and ingenious, but it's just playing, too."

Craig stared at the man. "A play world," he said. "You've hit it on the head. That's what it really is."

The man chuckled. "You never thought of it before," he said. "That's the trouble. No one ever thinks. Everyone is so busy try-ing to convince himself that he's happy and important that he never stops to think. Let me tell you this, son, no man ever is important if he tries to make himself important. It's when he forgets that he's important that he really is important.

"Me," he said. "I have lots of time to think."

"I never thought of it," said Craig, "in just that way before."

"We have no economic worth," the man said. "There's not any of us making our own way. There's not a single one of us worth the energy it would take to kill us.

"Except me," he said. "I raise my own eating and I catch some fish and I snare some rabbits and I make a batch of drinking likker whenever I run out."

"I always thought of our way of life," said Craig, "as the final phase in economic development. That's what they teach the kids. Man has finally achieved economic independence. There is no government and there is no economic fabric. You get all you need as a matter of a hereditary right, a common right. You are free to do anything you want to do and you try to live a worthwhile life."

"Son," said the man, "you had breakfast this morning and you had lunch this noon before you took your walk. You'll eat dinner tonight and you'll have a drink or two. Tomorrow you'll get a new shirt or a pair of shoes and there will be some equipment that you'll need to carry on your work."

"That's right," said Craig.

"What I want to know," said the man, "is where did all that stuff come from? The shirt or the pair of shoes might have been made by someone who likes to make shirts and shoes. The food was cooked either by robots or by someone who likes to cook, and the drawing set or the typewriter or the power tools that you use might have been made by someone who likes to mess around making stuff like that. But before the typewriter was a typewriter, it was metal in the ground, the food was grown, the clothes came from one of several raw materials. Tell me…who grew the raw materials, who dug and smelted the ore?"

"I don't know," said Craig. "I never thought of that."

"We're *kept*," said the man. "Someone is keeping us. Me, I won't be kept."

He pulled in the tackle and twirled the pole to wrap the line around it.

"Sun is getting down a bit," he said. "I got to go and hoe."

"It was good talking to you," said Craig, getting up.

"Nice path over that way," said the man, pointing. "Good walking. Lots of flowers and it's shaded, so it'll be nice and cool.

If you go far enough, you'll reach an art gallery." He looked at Craig. "You're interested in art?"

"Yes," said Craig. "But I didn't know there was a gallery anywhere around."

"Well, there is," said the man. "Good paintings. Some wood statuary that is better than average. A few pieces of good jade. Go there myself when I have the time."

"Well, thanks," said Craig.

"Funny looking building," the man said. "Group of buildings, really. Architect who designed them was crazier than a coot, but don't let it prejudice you. The stuff is really good."

"There's plenty of time," said Craig. "I'll drop in and have a look. Thanks for telling me."

The man got up and dusted off his trousers seat.

"If you're late in getting back," he said, "drop in and spend the night. My shack is just across the way. Plenty of grub and there is room for two to sleep."

"Thank you," said Craig. "I may do it."

He had no intention of accepting the offer.

The man held out his hand. "My name is Sherman," he said. "Glad you came along."

They shook hands.

Sherman went to hoe his garden and Craig walked down the path.

The buildings seemed to be quite close and yet it was hard to make out their lines. It was because of some crazy architectural principle, Craig decided. Sherman had said the architect was crazier than a coot. One time when he looked at them, they looked one way; when he looked again they were different somehow. They were never twice the same.

They were pink until he decided that they weren't pink at all, but were really blue; there were other times when they seemed neither pink nor blue, but a sort of green, although it wasn't really green.

They were beautiful, of course, but it was a disturbing beauty—a brand new sort of beauty. Something, Craig decided, that Sherman's misplaced genius had thought up, although it did seem funny that a place like this could exist without his ever hearing about it. Still, such a thing was understandable when he remembered that everyone was so self-consciously wrapped up in his work that he never paid attention to what anyone else was doing.

There was one way, of course, to find out what it was all about and that was to go and see.

The buildings, he estimated, were no more than a good five minutes' walk across a landscaped meadow that was a thing of beauty in itself.

He started out and walked for fifteen minutes and he did not get there. It seemed, however, that he was viewing the buildings from a slightly different angle, although that was hard to tell, because they refused to stay in place but seemed to be continually shifting and distorting their lines.

It was, of course, no more than an optical illusion.

He started out again.

After another fifteen minutes he was still no closer, although he could have sworn that he had kept his course headed straight toward the buildings.

It was then that he began to feel the panic.

He stood quite still and considered the situation as sanely as he could and decided there was nothing for it but to try again and this time pay strict attention to what he was doing.

He started out, moving slowly, almost counting his steps as he walked, concentrating fiercely upon keeping each step headed in the right direction.

It was then he discovered he was slipping. It appeared that he was going straight ahead but, as a matter of fact, he was slipping sidewise as he walked. It was just as if there were something smooth and slippery in front of him that translated his forward movement into a sidewise movement without his knowing it. Like a fence, a fence that he couldn't see or sense.

He stopped and the panic that had been gnawing at him broke into cold and terrible fear.

Something flickered in front of him. For a moment it seemed that he saw an eye, one single staring eye, looking straight at him. He stood rigid and the sense of being looked at grew and now it seemed that there were strange shadows on the grass beyond the fence that was invisible. As if someone, or something, that he couldn't see, was standing there and looking at him, watching with amusement his efforts to walk through the fence.

He lifted a hand and thrust it out in front of him and there was no fence, but his hand and arm slipped sidewise and did not go forward more than a foot or so.

He felt the kindness, then, the kindness and the pity and the vast superiority.

And he turned and fled.

He hammered on the door and Sherman opened it.

Craig stumbled in and fell into a chair. He looked up at the man he had talked with that afternoon.

"You knew," he said. "You knew and you sent me to find out."

Sherman nodded. "You wouldn't have believed me if I told you."

"What are they?" asked Craig, his words tumbling wildly. "What are they doing there?"

"I don't know what they are," said Sherman.

He walked to the stove and took a lid off a kettle and looked at what was cooking. Whatever it was, it had a hungry smell. Then he walked to the table and took the chimney off an antique oil lamp, struck a match and lit it.

"I go it simple," he said. "No electricity. No nothing. I hope that you don't mind. Rabbit stew for supper."

He looked at Craig across the smoking lamp and in the flickering light it seemed that his head floated in the air, for the glow of the lamp blotted out his body.

"But what are *they?*" demanded Craig. "What kind of fence is that? What are they fenced in for?"

"Son," said Sherman, "they aren't the ones who are fenced in."

"They aren't..."

"It's us," said Sherman. "Can't you see it?"

Craig looked puzzled.

Sherman continued, "*We* are the ones who are fenced in."

"You said this afternoon," said Craig, "that we were kept. You mean they're keeping us?"

Sherman nodded. "That's the way I have it figured. They're keeping us, watching over us, taking care of us. There's nothing that we want that we can't have for the simple asking. They're taking real good care of us."

101

"But why?"

"I don't know," said Sherman. "A zoo, maybe. A reservation, maybe. A place to preserve the last of a species. They don't mean us any harm."

"I know they don't," said Craig. "I felt them. That's what frightened me."

He sat in the silence of the shack and smelled the cooking rabbit and watched the flicker of the lamp.

"What can we do about it?" he asked.

"That's the thing," said Sherman, "that we have to figure out. Maybe we don't want to do anything at all."

Sherman went to the stove and stirred the rabbit stew.

"You are not the first," he said, "and you will not be the last. There were others before you and there will be others like you who'll come along this way, walking off their troubles."

He put the lid back on the kettle.

"We're watching them," he said, "the best we can. Trying to find out. They can't keep us fooled and caged forever."

Craig sat in his chair, remembering the kindness and the pity and the vast superiority.

THE END

The Undying Ones

By FREDRIC BROWN

*Alone among the uncaring stars, Donross stalked a mighty, invincible prey—
the thing that men called Death!*

ON A tiny planet of a far, faint star in a globular cluster at the
very edge of the galaxy, fifty thousand parsecs away—five times as
far as man has yet penetrated into space—there is a statue of an
Earthman. It is a tremendous thing, ten inches high, exquisite in
workmanship.

Bugs crawl on it, but they have a right to; they made it, and they
honor it. It is unquestionably the figure of an Earthman, but it
bears no real resemblance to its particular subject, for they never
saw him. They know his name, though: Donross.

The statue is of very hard metal. On an airless world it will last
forever—or until Earthmen find that world and blast it out of
existence. Unless, of course, by that time Earthmen have changed
an awful lot.

IT WAS a routine patrol in Sector 1534, out past the Dog Star,
ten parsecs from Sol. The patrol ship was the usual two-man scout
used outside the system. Captain May and Lieutenant Ross were
playing chess when the alarm rang.

Captain May said, "Reset it, Don, while I think this out." He
didn't look up from the board; he knew it couldn't have been
anything but a passing meteor. There weren't any Terrestrial ships
in this sector, except their own little scouter. And that meant that
there weren't any ships. Man had penetrated space for a thousand
parsecs and hadn't yet encountered an alien form of life intelligent
enough to talk, let alone build spaceships.

Ross didn't get up either, but he turned around in his chair to
face the instrument board and the telescreen. He glanced up
casually and gasped that there was a ship on the screen. He got his

THE
The screen was filled with a flare of energy. . . .

UNDYING ONES

By FREDRIC BROWN

breath back enough to say, "Cap!" and then the chessboard was on the floor and May was looking over his shoulder.

He could hear the sound of May's breathing, and then May's voice said, *"Fire,* Don!"

"But that's a Rochester Class cruiser! One of ours. I don't know what it's doing here, but we can't—"

"Look again."

Don Ross couldn't look again because he'd been looking all along, but he suddenly saw what May had meant. It was almost a Rochester, but not quite. There was something *alien* about it. Something? It *was* alien; it was an alien imitation of a Rochester.

104

And his hands were reaching for the firing buttons almost before the full impact of that had hit him.

Fingers on buttons, he looked at the dials on the Picar estimator and the Monold. They stood at zero.

He swore. "He's jamming us, Cap. We can't figure out how far he is, or his size and mass!"

Captain May nodded slowly, his face pale.

Inside Don Ross's head a thought said: *"Compose yourself, men. We are not enemies."*

Ross turned and stared at May. May said, "Yes, I got it. Telepathy."

Ross swore again. If they were *telepathic*—

"Fire, Don. Visual."

Ross pressed the buttons. The screen was filled with a flare of energy, but when the energy subsided, there was no wreckage of a spaceship...

ADMIRAL Sunderland turned his back to the star chart on the wall and regarded them sourly from under his thick eyebrows.

He said, "I'm not interested in rehashing your formal report, May. You've both been under the psychograph; we've extracted from your minds every minute detail of that encounter. Our logicians have analyzed it. You are here for discipline. Captain May, you know the penalty for disobedience."

May said stiffly, "Yes, sir."

"It is?"

"Death, sir."

"And what order did you disobey?"

"General Order Thirteen-Ninety, Section Eight. Quad-A priority. Any Terrestrial ship, military or otherwise, encountering an alien ship is ordered to destroy that ship immediately, if possible. If unable to do so, ship must immediately blast off toward outer space, in a direction not exactly opposite that of Earth, and continue until fuel is exhausted."

"And the reason for that, Captain? I ask merely to see if you know; it is not, of course, important or even relevant whether or not you understand the reason for any ruling."

"Yes, sir. So there is no possibility of the alien ship following the sighting ship back to Sol and learning the location of Earth."

"Yet you disobeyed that ruling, captain. You were not certain that you had destroyed the alien. What have you to say for yourself?"

"We did not think it necessary, sir. The alien ship did not seem hostile. Besides, sir, they must already know our base; they addressed us as 'men'."

"Nonsense! The telepathic message was broadcast from an alien mind, but was received by yours. Your minds automatically translated the message into your own terminology. He did not necessarily know your point of origin or that you were humans."

Lieutenant Ross had no business speaking, but he asked, "Then, sir, it is not believed that they were friendly?"

The admiral snorted. "Where did you take your training, Lieutenant? You seem to have missed the most basic premise of our defense plans, the reason we've been patrolling space for the past four hundred years on the lookout for alien life. *Any alien is an enemy.* Even though he was friendly today, how could we know he would be friendly next year or a century from now? And a potential enemy is an enemy. The more quickly he is completely destroyed the more secure Earth will be.

"Look at the military history of the world! It proves that if it proves nothing else. Look at Rome! To be safe, she couldn't afford powerful neighbors. Alexander the Great! Napoleon!"

"Sir," said Captain May. "May I ask—am I under sentence of death?"

"Yes."

"Then I may as well speak. Where is Rome now? Alexander's empire or Napoleon's? Nazi Germany? Or Tyrannosaurus Rex?"

"Who?"

"Man's predecessor, the toughest of the dinosaurs. His name means 'King of the Tyrant Lizards.' He thought that every other creature was his enemy, too. And where is he now?"

"Is that all you have to say, Captain?"

"Yes, sir."

"Then I will overlook it. Fallacious, sentimental reasoning. You are *not* under sentence of death, Captain. I merely said so to see what you would say—how far you would go. You are not being shown mercy because of any humanitarian nonsense. A truly ameliorating circumstance has been found…"

"May I ask what, sir?"

"The alien *was* destroyed. Our technicians and logicians have worked that out. Your Picar and Monoid were working properly. The only reason they did not register was that the alien ship was too small. They will detect a meteor weighing as little as five pounds. The alien ship was smaller than that."

"Smaller than—"

"Certainly. You were thinking of alien life in terms your own size. There is no reason why it should be. It could be even submicroscopic. The alien ship must have contacted you deliberately, at a distance of only a few yards. And your fire, at that range, destroyed it utterly. That is why you saw no charred hulk as evidence that it was destroyed."

He smiled. "My congratulations, Lieutenant Ross, on your gunnery. In the future, of course, visual firing will be unnecessary. The detectors and estimators on ships of all classes are being modified immediately to detect and indicate objects as small as a fraction of an ounce."

Ross said, "Thank you, sir. But don't you think that the fact that the ship we saw, regardless of size, was an imitation of one of our own Rochester Class ships is proof that the aliens already know much more of us than we do of them, including, probably, the location of our home planet? And that—even if they are hostile— the minute size of their craft is what prevents them from blasting us from the system?"

"Possibly. Either both of those things are true, or neither. Obviously, aside from their telepathic ability, they are quite inferior to us—or they would not imitate our design in spaceships. And they must have read the minds of some of our engineers in order to duplicate that design. However, granting that, they may still not know the location of Sol. Space coordinates would be extremely difficult to translate, and the name Sol would mean nothing to them. Even its approximate description would fit thousands of other stars. At any rate, it is up to us to find and exterminate them before they find us. Every ship in space is now alerted to watch for them—and being equipped with special instruments to detect small objects. A state of war exists. Or perhaps it is redundant to say that a state of war always exists with aliens.

"That is all, gentlemen. You may go."

Outside in the corridors two armed guards waited. One of them stepped to each side of Captain May.

May said quickly, "Don't say anything, Don. I expected this. Don't forget I disobeyed an important order, and don't forget the admiral said only that I wasn't under sentence of death. Keep yourself out of it."

Hands clenched, teeth clamped tightly, Don Ross watched the guards take his best friend. He knew May was right; there was nothing he could do except get himself into even worse trouble than May was in—and make things worse for May.

But he walked almost blindly out of the Admiralty Building. He went out and got drunk, promptly, but that didn't help.

He had the customary two weeks' leave before reporting back for space duty, and he knew he'd better straighten himself out mentally in that time. He reported to a psychiatrist and let himself be talked out of most of his bitterness and feeling of rebellion.

He went back to his schoolbooks and soaked himself in the necessity for strict and unquestioning obedience to military authority and the necessity of unceasing vigilance for alien races and complete extermination whenever one was found.

He won out; he convinced himself. He even convinced himself how unthinkable it had been for him to think Captain May could have been completely pardoned for having disobeyed a definite order, for whatever reason. He even felt horrified for having himself acquiesced in that disobedience. Technically, of course, he was blameless; May had been in charge of the ship and the decision to return to Earth instead of blasting out into space—and death— had come from May. As a subordinate, Ross had not shared the blame. But now, as a person, he felt conscience-stricken that he had not tried to argue May out of his disobedience.

What would the Space Corps be without obedience?

How could he make up for what he now felt to be his dereliction, his delinquency? He watched the telenewscasts avidly during that period and learned that, in various sectors of space, four more alien ships had been destroyed. With the improved detection instruments, all of them had been destroyed on sight; there had been communication only on that first contact, the one he had been in on.

On the tenth day of his leave, he terminated it of his own free will. He returned to the Admiralty Building and asked for an audience with Admiral Sunderland. He was laughed at, of course, but he'd expected to be. He managed to get a brief verbal message carried through to the admiral. Simply: "I know a plan that may possibly enable us to find the planet of the aliens, at no risk to ourselves."

That got him in, all right.

HE STOOD at rigid attention before the admiral's desk. He said, "Sir, the aliens have been trying to contact us. They have been unable to because we destroy them before contact is established—or, in the case of the first contact, after a single telepathic thought had been put across. If we make that contact and permit them to communicate, there is a chance that they will give away, accidentally or otherwise, the location of their home planet."

Admiral Sutherland said drily, "And, whether they did or not, they might find out *ours*, by following the ship back."

"Sir, my plan covers that. I suggest that I be sent out into the same sector where initial contact was made—this time in a one-man ship, *unarmed.* That the fact that I am doing so be publicized as widely as possible, so that every man in space knows it—and knows that I am in an unarmed ship for the purpose of contacting the aliens. It is my opinion that they will learn of this. They must manage to get thoughts at long distances, but to *send* thoughts—to Earth minds, anyway—only at very short ones."

"How do you deduce that, Lieutenant? Never mind; it coincides with what our logicians have figured out. They say that the fact that they have stolen our science—as in their copying of our ships on a smaller scale—before we were aware of their existence proves their ability to read our thoughts at—well, a moderate distance."

"Yes, sir. At any rate, I am hoping that if news of my mission is known to the entire fleet, it will reach the aliens. And knowing my ship is unarmed, they will contact me. I will see what they have to say to me—to us—and possibly that message will include a clue as to the location of their home planet."

Admiral Sunderland said, "And in that case, that planet would last all of twenty-four hours. But what about the converse, Lieutenant? What about the possibility of their following you back?"

"That, sir, is where we have nothing to lose. I shall return to Earth *only if I find out that they already know its location.*

"With their telepathic abilities, I believe they already do—and that they have not attacked us only because they are not hostile or are too weak. But, whatever the case, if they know the location of Earth they will not deny it in talking to me. Why should they? It will seem to them a bargaining point in their favor, and they'll think we're bargaining. They might claim to know, even if they do not— but I shall refuse to take their word for it unless they give me proof."

Admiral Sunderland stared at him. He said, "Son, you *have* got something. It'll probably cost you your life, but—if it doesn't, and if you come back with news of where those aliens come from, you're going to be the hero of the race. You'll probably end up with *my* job. In fact, I'm tempted to steal your idea and make that trip myself."

"Sir, you are too valuable. I'm expendable. Besides, sir, I've *got* to. It isn't that I want any honors, I've got something on my conscience I want to make up for. I should have tried to stop Captain May from disobeying orders. I shouldn't be here now, alive. We should have blasted out into space, since we weren't sure we'd destroyed the alien."

The admiral cleared his throat. "You're not responsible for that, son. Only the captain of a ship is responsible, in a case like that. But—I see what you mean. You feel that you disobeyed orders, in spirit, because you agreed at the time with what Captain May did. All right, that's past, and your suggestion makes up for it, even if you yourself did not man the contact ship."

"But may I, sir?"

"You may, Lieutenant. Rather, you may, Captain."

"Thank you, sir."

"A ship will be ready for you in three days. We could have it ready sooner, but it will take that long for word of our 'negotiations' to get throughout the fleet. But you understand— you are not, under any circumstances, to deviate on your own initiative from the limitations you have outlined."

"Yes, sir. Unless the aliens already know the location of Earth and prove it completely, I shall not return. I shall blast off into space. I shall not deviate from that in the slightest way. I give you my word, sir."

"Very well, Captain Ross."

THE ONE-MAN spacer hovered near the center of Sector 1534, out past the Dog Star, ten parsecs from Sol. No other ship patrolled that sector...

Captain Don Ross sat quietly and waited. He watched the visiplate and listened for a voice to speak inside his head.

It came when he had waited less than three hours. *"Greetings, Donross,"* the voice said, and simultaneously there were five tiny spaceships outside his visiplate. Not one, but five. The detectors and estimators registered now; he could tell that the five ships weighed a fraction less than three pounds each.

He said, "Shall I talk aloud or merely think?"

"It does not matter. You may speak if you wish to concentrate on a particular thought, but first be silent a moment."

After half a minute, Ross thought he heard the echo of a sigh in his mind. Then: *"I am sorry. I fear this talk will do neither of us any good. You see, Donross, we do not know the location of your home planet. We could have learned, perhaps, but we were not interested. We were not hostile and from the minds of Earthmen we knew we dared not be friendly. So you will never be able, if you obey orders, to return to report."*

Don Ross closed his eyes a moment. This, then, was the end; there wasn't any use talking further. He had given his word to Admiral Sunderland that he would follow orders to the letter.

"That is right," said the voice. *"We are both doomed, Donross, and it does not matter what we tell you. We cannot get through the cordon of your ships; we have lost half our race trying."*

111

"Half? You mean—"

"Yes. There were only a thousand of us. We built ten ships, each to carry a hundred. Five ships have been destroyed by Earthmen; there are only five left. These five. You see before you the entire race of us. Would it interest you, even though you are soon to die, to know about us?"

He nodded, forgetting that they could not see him, but the assent in his mind must have been read.

"We are an old race, much older than you. Our home is—was—on a tiny planet of the dark companion of Sirius, far out; it is only a hundred miles in diameter. Your ships have not found it yet, but it is only a matter of time until they do. We were intelligent beings for many millennia, but we never developed space travel. There was no need and we had no desire.

"Twenty of your years ago an Earth ship passed near our planet and we caught the thoughts of the men upon it. And we knew that our only safety, our only chance of survival, lay in immediate flight to the farthest limits of the galaxy. We knew from those thoughts, that friendly contact was impossible; that we would be found sooner or later, even though we stayed on our own planet, and that we would be ruthlessly exterminated upon discovery."

"You did not think of—fighting back?"

"No. We could not have, had we wished—and we could not even wish. It is impossible for us to kill. If the death of one Earthman, even of one lesser creature, would insure survival of our race, we could not—would not—bring about that death.

"That you cannot understand. Wait—I see that you can. You are not like other Earthmen, Donross. But back to our story. When we learned we must flee or be exterminated, we took details of space travel from the minds of members of that ship and adapted them to the small scale of the ships we built.

"We built ten ships, enough to carry our entire race. But we find that we cannot escape through your patrols. Five of our ships have tried and have been destroyed. Half of our race."

Don Ross said, grimly, "And I did a fifth of that. I destroyed one of your ships."

"You merely obeyed orders. Do not blame yourself. Obedience is almost as deeply rooted in you as hatred of killing is in us. That first contact, with the ship you were on, was deliberate; we had to be sure that—as we had thought— you would destroy us on sight.

"But since then, one at a time, our other ships have been trying to get through your patrols and the first four to try have been destroyed. We brought

112

all five of the remaining ones here, when we learned you were coming out to contact us.

"Even if you disobeyed orders and returned to Earth, wherever it is, to report what we have just told you, no orders would be issued to let us through. There are too few Earthmen like you—as yet. Possibly in future ages, by the time Earthmen reach the farthest side of the galaxy, which we are going to try to reach, there will be more like you and we will survive the second contact and be friends. Now the chances of even one of our five ships getting through your cordon seem remote.

"But now we may as well separate and try. Just possibly one ship out of our present five may get through. Goodbye, Donross—what is that strange emotion in your mind, and that convulsion of muscles? It is something foreign to us. I do not understand it.

"Wait, I do—partially. Laughter is one word, humor another. But— Yes, it is your reaction to perceiving something incongruous. But your thought is too complex, too mixed. What is incongruous to you?"

Don Ross finally managed to stop laughing.

"Listen, my alien friend who cannot kill," he said. "I'm getting you out of this. I'm going to see that you get through our cordon and to the safety you want, on the galaxy's edge. But what's funny—incongruous—is the way I'm going to do it.

"You can't otherwise get through, because you'll be detected. But I'm about to take off for outer space, am I not, to die there? You, all of you, can come along, and *live* there. Hitchhike. *Your tiny ships won't show in the patrol's detectors if they're touching this one.* Not only that, but the gravity of this ship will pull you along and you won't have to start using your fuel until you're forty more parsecs out, and through the cordon."

There was a long pause before the voice in Don Ross's mind said, *"Thank you."* Faintly. Softly.

He waited until five ships had vanished from his visiplate and he had heard five sounds against the hull of his spacer. Then Don Ross laughed once more. And obeyed orders to the letter, blasting off for outer space and death.

THE END

Too Many Worlds

By IRVING E. COX JR.

Would you like to wake up in a nightmare world where none of the old laws work? Then take this trip into a strange hell...

HE WAS HALFWAY to the city, barreling along the express arterial before he recovered from the numbing hypnotic of the nightmare. He remembered nothing of the dream, except the feeling that invisible cords were being drawn tight on his mind, slowly smothering him. He had awakened exhausted. Mechanically he went through the morning routine of dressing, kissing Irene, and leaving for work.

As his mind began to function again, he became aware that his speedometer had climbed past eighty. He decreased the speed. Then, with a cold shock shivering along his spine, he looked again at the chromium dial and its surrounding field of red leather. He was driving a sleek, Nile-green Cadillac convertible. And he had never seen the car before.

He turned off the arterial and pulled to a stop on a deserted side street near the Bay. Wisps of cold morning mist hung in trailing threads over the road, dancing gray shadows against the dismal sky. With trembling fingers he twisted the registration slip, fastened to the steering column, so that he could read it. The owner of the Cadillac, he discovered, was Albert Hammond, of 3754 Via Wanda Way.

But that was his own name! And he drove a Buick, two years old.

Hammond snapped open the glove compartment. There was his old brier, Irene's scarf, the familiar Auto Club map book, and a letter, which he recognized at once. Irene had given it to him three days ago and asked him to mail it on his way to work. As he sometimes did, he had stuffed it into the glove compartment and forgotten it.

But that had been in the Buick! He was sure of that. Or nearly so. He checked the registration slip again, and saw that he had bought the Cadillac six months before. Sweat broke out on his forehead. Somehow he had forgotten his own actions for the past half-year.

He felt ashamed—and frightened. He wondered if he should see Dr. Betts. But, if he did, what would he say? That he thought he was cracking up? That his mind was failing him at thirty-five, when he had reached the floodtide of mental and physical vigor? There was nothing in his life to drive him to madness. He was in good health, successful in business, immensely happy with Irene and their two children.

No, it was impossible to allow even a doctor to know what had happened. Hammond had to handle this himself.

He went on to work. The General offices for his freight line were on the top floor of a warehouse terminal, on Market Street not far from the Ferry Building. The first overnight rigs from Los Angeles and Portland were pulling into the yard, scarlet boxes lettered in flaming orange THE RED ARROW LINES. Hammond took the elevator up to his office.

THE BILLING-ACCOUNTING department, spread over forty desks in the main office, was in a chaos of activity. Hammond was used to a friendly, relaxed office atmosphere. He had always prided himself on his good relations with his employees. No more than a score had quit the Red Arrow Line in the past decade. Most of them called him by his first name.

Now, only one or two nodded, and their greeting was hesitant and fearful. The violent onslaught on work redoubled as he entered the office. It was a burlesque of efficiency, set to a driving tempo. It was not a business office, but its caricature, the sort of farce dreamed up for a musical comedy or a slapstick parable out of Hollywood. The switchboard girl actually cringed when Hammond approached, as if she expected him to lash her with a whip. And Joe Kelly, the chief biller, leaped fully three feet when Hammond addressed him.

Hammond fled into his private office. He jerked a pint of whisky out of his desk drawer and poured himself a stiff drink.

**Illustrated by
William Slade**

Willie wooed Irene with his success—to find her not worth the winning

This office comedy must be something else he had created during the past six months. If so, the Red Arrow Line would have been driven close to insolvency. Hammond then called his chief

TOO MANY WORLDS

BY

IRVING E. COX, JR.

accountant on the intercom and asked to see the profit statements for the last two periods.

After he had read the report, he snatched up the whisky and drained what was left from the bottle, for the profits had been enormous. The accountant hovered over his shoulder anxiously, pulling at a loose button on his frayed coat. For all the world, he reminded Hammond of Mr. Cratchit in *the Christmas Carol.*

"Sit down, Tim; sit down!" Hammond had intended to speak softly, as he always did, but he was amazed at the vicious bite in his voice. He had a feeling that he was someone else, not himself—an actor playing a role in a ridiculous farce.

"Mr. Hammond, sir—you see, sir—this report—"

"Out with it, Tim!" The bark was angrily ferocious.

"The truth is, sir, I know we're not showing quite the profit that we should this period. It's the new ship line you bought last week."

Mentally Hammond reeled. What ship line? So far as he knew, he was only in the trucking business, and, as such things went, a very small operator.

"Trans-Pacific is basically sound, of course," the accountant assured him. "We've taken over twelve more good freighters, and thirty new tankers; but their receivables have to be overhauled. I'm sure we'll show our usual profit next month."

"And just what is our usual profit, Tim?" Hammond had intended to make the question cautiously exploratory. Instead, his tone was heavy with slashing sarcasm.

"We aim at forty percent on the gross revenue, Mr. Hammond, sir, and I'm fully aware that we're not—"

Hammond dismissed the accountant weakly and slumped down in his chair, his face and hands wet with sudden sweat. Forty percent on the gross! No business made such a profit. This whole situation was a travesty of reality, grossly overdone.

For the first time Hammond wondered if this was the nightmare, rather than the nameless terror that had closed on his mind during the night. Conscientiously he tried to pull himself awake from the dream. He used every trick he could think of, but with no results.

As the initial shock subsided, Hammond began to adjust to the situation. Or, rather, the adjustment came in spite of himself, as if he were speaking a part in a rather badly written play. The correct words, tone, and gesture came involuntarily—no matter what he intended. The rest of the players seemed to accept him quite seriously in the new characterization. Even when he tried to be himself—to act, at least, as he assumed he had six months ago—he was misinterpreted.

THE BOARD of Directors met this afternoon. The Red Arrow Line had never had such a board, to Hammond's knowledge, and the men who gathered in his office were strangers.

Yet they knew him intimately. Furthermore, he seemed to know precisely how to preside; he was amazed at the lucid presentation he made of the unfinished business of the previous meeting—which, so far as he knew, he had not attended.

The Board Meeting, however, proved very instructive. Hammond learned that he was the president of the largest trucking line on the Pacific Coast. He had general offices in Portland, Seattle, San Diego, and Los Angeles, in addition to this terminal in San Francisco. He owned a fleet of freighters and cargo vessels, a commercial airline, and miscellaneous parcels of city real estate.

By all accounts, he was a captain of industry with a very unsavory personality. As a landlord of slum property, he took delight in evicting the destitute. He boasted of the blatant devices he used in order to evade his proper taxes, apparently so sure of his immunity that he could make the discussion a part of the Board minutes. And, finally he seemed to take pride in the systematic cruelties he practiced toward his employees.

None of it was good business, as Hammond understood the term. Nor was it his personality, as he understood himself. Yet nothing he did or said made any difference. The words he spoke were not his own; they were entirely divorced from the thought he intended. He was helplessly playing a role, and so was everyone else.

It was not insanity; Hammond was sure of that, because the internal logic of the situation was too highly integrated, the detail of reality too tangible. Something had happened, but not to him alone. The whole world around him had changed; to what extent, he was afraid to guess.

In the uncertainty, there was one thing he could cling to, his love for Irene. They had been married for ten years, and they were still as much in love as when they had their first high school date. If Irene had not changed, the rest could become bearable.

He drove home slowly that afternoon, pushed by his anxiety to see Irene and reassure himself, and yet afraid to find out. Around him the city of San Francisco glittered in the golden sunlight, beautiful and unchanged—until he began to notice the bizarre differences.

The Ferry Building was enormous. The Top of the Mark was like a gigantic glass cube weighing down on the insignificant building beneath it. The presidio was a vast acreage of grass plots and old cannon. Knob Hill soared up like a craggy Everest, studded with sprawling, gleaming mansions. And tremendous, blazing neon signs, brighter even than the setting sun, proclaimed the location of the Barbary Coast and Chinatown. The rest of the city was indistinct in a gray haze.

San Francisco, as Hammond knew it, had given way to San Francisco as a tourist might have remembered it, or as an archeologist of the future might have reconstructed it from the evidence of penny postcards.

MUCH THE same thing had happened to his home. Yet he knew that it was his. Yesterday's modestly comfortable white-walled bungalow had been transformed into a formal granite fortress, modeled on the Palace of Versailles. A tall, thin, aloof butler met him at the door.

"The master had a good day, I trust?"

"So-so, James. Is the madam ready?" It was by no means what Hammond had meant to say, but he was hardly surprised. He was growing used to playing his part. He began to feel that he was splitting into two people. One, himself, was being slowly driven out of the physical body named Albert Hammond by an aggressive stranger who seemed entirely at home in this weird world.

"She is waiting in the Red Room, sir."

Hammond found Irene standing by an elegant Louis XVI lounge, motionless in a blaze of sunlight. When Hammond opened the door of the Red Room, it was like the rising of a curtain on a new scene. He had the impression that she had been immobile and lifeless for an eternity, waiting for the moment of his coming, which would bring her reality.

Hammond plunged into bitter despair, for only faintly did this woman resemble the Irene he knew. Dressed in a clinging, ornate evening gown, she was very young, sensuously beautiful, and graceful. When she spoke her voice rang out with the tinkling music of a high school girl, not the comfortable assurance of a mature woman.

"I was so afraid you might be late, Albert," she cooed. "We're going to the Berkeleys', you know."

"It's hard to get away early on Board Meeting day."

"Fortunately, you don't have to change, dear; none of the men are going formal." He hadn't heard her use those exact words, in that tone, since the night of their high school Junior Prom. For a split second that forgotten quarrel was very vivid in his mind. She had changed her mind only when she found that none of the other boys were going to wear Tuxedoes, but until the afternoon of the Prom she had threatened to go with someone else. What was his name? Willie. Willie Tuttle!

As he remembered the name, a pain stabbed into Hammond's mind, and vanished. It was like the dream that had crushed into his soul during the night, numbing, hypnotic, and terrifying...

Hammond knew neither the Berkeleys nor their guests, but the usurper who ruled his body seemed to be on excellent terms with them all. The party was quite in the romantic tradition of the gushiest of women's magazines. Hammond caught tantalizing scraps of talk that could have served as captions for full-page, full-color illustrations.

"I know my baby comes first, always, but does that mean that I must give up the only man I love?"

"Oh, Charles, must we part again, so soon—so terribly, terribly soon?"

"And then he swept me into his arms, and our lips met, warm and tender, pulsing with the purity of our newfound love."

Hammond was slowly nauseated by the appearance of the guests. The women were all alike, resembling Irene—polished, highly glazed adolescents, masquerading as women. And the men were pretty companion pieces, big, virile, young, heavily tanned, and forever smiling tenderly.

BUT, IN SPITE of himself, Hammond joined heartily with the others, mouthing inanities he would have held back if he could.

On the way home he found the courage to ask Irene about their two children. The question had been seething in his mind since he had returned from work, but he had been afraid to ask it. Now, though he guessed the truth and already writhed in its agony, he could not put if off.

"Tom and Jean?" Irene repeated, without understanding. "Who in the world are they, Albert?"

"Our children, Irene!"

"Are we supposed to have any?"

"Don't you know?"

"Why, Albert, you're joking! Of course not." She nestled close against his arm, like a starry-eyed girl on her first date, gently caressing his sleeve. "You're so big and strong, Albert, and it's so wonderful having you beside me. Wasn't the Berkeley party just scrumptious?"

The next day Hammond saw a psychiatrist. He was a good man, highly recommended by Dr. Betts. While Hammond talked, he listened patiently. Afterwards he laced his fingers and leaned back in his leather chair, pursing his lips.

"A fascinating delusion, Mr. Hammond," he conceded. "I've never encountered another case quite like it."

"Then these things aren't real?"

"On the contrary, they are all very real. It's this other thing—this normal world, as you call it—that makes your story interesting. In most psychiatric situations, the patient escapes from the everyday world by building a hallucination for himself. You have done the reverse. You see the world around you exactly as it is, but you're convinced that it is an illusion."

"But I do have two children, doctor—two of the finest kids you've ever seen! And now Irene tells me—"

"The children, too, are part of your delusion."

"This—this reality is a distortion of everything I've ever known!"

"Mr. Hammond, there is an external reality of material things which we all know and share. But a person's only contact with external reality is through the interpretations of his own senses. You see and feel and hear the things around you, just as I do, but your own mind gives meaning to the sensations. If the meaning you get is reasonably like everyone else's, we say you are normal and sane. That's the only basis for judgment that we have. For all I knew we might all be quite wrong. But my point is this: in actual fact, what each of us does is create our own private universes. This delusion of yours is that sort of thing. It is your world as you would make it ideally, not as it is."

The psychiatrist got up, extending his hand. "I'm going to prescribe a lot of rest and relaxation for you, Mr. Hammond. For a while, don't live your business problems so intensely. Get out and enjoy yourself more. Come and see me in a week or so and we'll see how you're feeling then."

The psychiatrist was Hammond's last resort, and he had answered nothing. Hammond left the office frustrated by the words and utterly bewildered.

THE FIRST day set the pattern for Hammond for nearly a week. His business life consisted of making monotonously caddish coups, which always turned out to be enormously profitable. And every night Hammond and Irene went out, or entertained themselves. It was an exhaustive routine, but Hammond felt no fatigue. His sleep was sound and dreamless.

Dreamless, except that once he awoke in the early morning hours, screaming aloud the name of Willie Tuttle. He couldn't remember why he felt so terrified, why his body was cold with sweat. But the name clung tenaciously to his mind.

Willie Tuttle! Hammond remembered him vaguely as a mousy, insignificant, dreamy boy who had gone to high school with him and Irene. He hadn't seen Willie in fifteen years. Yet the name rang so persistently in his thoughts, Hammond wanted to find him again. Somehow he was sure that Willie could explain the transformation that had taken place in the world.

In the morning Hammond telephoned the high school and began the slow process of tracing Willie through the series of mediocre jobs he had held since graduation. It was two days before he found that Willie was currently employed by the Red Arrow Line as a biller in the Los Angeles office. Hammond determined to summon him to San Francisco the next day.

But that night he had his second nightmare.

Insensible to every stimulus except the choking fog he was fighting slowly out of his mind, Hammond dragged himself through another morning routine. It was routine in the sense that he knew by instinct what he must do, but he was also aware that his environment was totally different once again.

He bolted a breakfast of cereal and toast at a battered kitchen table, with Irene and their two brawling children. There was no time for family niceties. As usual, they were all just a little late. Irene, work-worn and tired, wearing a faded dressing gown that was splattered with stove grease, tried ineffectually to keep peace at the table. Hammond—again as usual—stormed and threatened punishment but the bickering of the children went right on.

Irene kissed him and handed him his scarred lunch pail. He banged out of the house and climbed into his car. The motor whined and whined and finally started. Hammond clattered out of the drive, narrowly missing the scrawny palm that grew in the parkway—as he always did.

When he was able to think rationally, he found that he was on the Glendale-Los Angeles Freeway, and he was driving a Ford, twelve years old. Acrid banks of smog blotted out the city of Los Angeles, yet Hammond knew precisely where he was going. He was a junior rate clerk in the Los Angeles terminal of the Red Arrow Line. It was a job he had held for a decade, without promotion and afraid to quit because he had a family to support.

The situation was understandably sound and logical. The only thing wrong was that it was also quite mad. Yet, if he were insane, would the appearance of this new environment have seemed so very tangible? He could feel the worn seat covers beneath his thighs; he could see the blistered, faded paint on the exterior of the sedan. The bent left fender—he remembered smashing it on a foggy night, five years ago. The stain on the back seat—he remembered how Jean had spilled her bottle there when she was still a baby.

IF THIS were an illusion, it came equipped with a detailed and integrated peripheral reality. A week ago he had felt that he was being split into two persons; now it was three. He had distinct memories of three entirely separate pasts; three distinct personalities, three separate worlds were crowded into the physical being of Albert Hammond. If only one of them were real, as other people defined reality, which of the three was it?

The shock of the second transformation was minimized by the memory of the first. Hammond proceeded cautiously to feel his way into this new world, but the caution was unnecessary. He could draw upon an accumulation of past experiences as the underpaid, overworked rate clerk for the Red Arrow Line. He did his day's work without a hitch.

He went home to the familiar nagging of an overcrowded house and a family trapped by the bitterness of economic mediocrity. None of the equipment in the tiny jerrybuilt cottage functioned properly. Doors sagged and squeaked. The refrigerator clattered so that it shook the paper-thin walls. The ancient radio spluttered and faded and sometimes did not work at all. The plumbing either dripped or was plugged up, and the floor lamps waved back and forth when anyone strode across the living room.

The children had no place to play except the living room, and they quarreled continuously over their few cheap toys. Irene was always worn out by her daily conflict with the house, and the strain of stretching a slim budget to meet the needs of a family of four.

Hammond no longer had the feeling that he was playing a part. He had full control of what he said, and he could have asked Irene for any explanation he wanted. But it was impossible to talk to her. In this world their love had died years ago beneath the steady hammering of work.

This was a special night, apparently, for as soon as the dinner dishes were cleared away, Irene said she was going in to dress.

"I made over the blue that Mrs. Slovena gave me," she said. "I think it'll do. You'll wear your Sunday suit, won't you, Al?"

"Are we—are we going out?"

Something fixed in his memory told him that the question was superfluous, but he couldn't place the details.

"Don't tell me you've forgotten!" Irene's voice was shrill with anger, yet she was close to tears. "It's the Red Arrow anniversary dinner, and we're invited."

"Oh, yes." Comfortingly he tried to put his arm around her, but she shrugged him away.

"Willie Tuttle only invited us for old time's sake, because we all went to high school together."

"Willie Tuttle?"

125

"Just the president of the company, that's all. And he asked us on his own personal stationery! Oh, Albert, maybe you'll have a chance to put in a word about your job!"

The anniversary dinner was held in the Beverly-Wilshire. It was definitely a big-time affair. The mayor, the governor, a delegation of Congressmen, Hollywood stars, and lesser politicians were crowded at the table of honor, like celestial dignitaries at the feet of President Tuttle. Willie himself ate in a blaze of spotlights, seated on a level slightly higher than his guests; Hammond and Irene were shabby poor relations in so much glitter. They were grateful to have a tiny table hidden away in the rear of the room.

THE SPEECHES were long and monotonously identical. Governor, mayor, and assembled Congressmen all lavished ecstatic praise on Willie Tuttle for his services to mankind, to business, and to the great and glorious State of California. Through it all Willie basked in the spotlight, modestly sipping gallons of champagne and smiling upon the multitude after each rousing round of applause.

When the speeches were over the cloth-of-gold curtain at one end of the room was pulled back, revealing the Los Angeles Philharmonic Orchestra, which had come to play for the dancing. Followed by his halo of spotlights, Willie Tuttle walked the length of the hall toward Hammond and Irene.

His progress was slow because guests kept crowding around him crying for his autograph. With a gracious flourish, Willie always obliged. As he came closer, Hammond saw that Willie was amazingly handsome, combining qualities of Charles Atlas, Allan Ladd, and Tyrone Power with the atmospheric culture of Ronald Colman.

Hammond arose and went to meet him. Willie was related to the weird series of transformations that had overturned Hammond's life and, despite the throng, Hammond intended to force an explanation from him. The two men met in front of Hammond's table. Willie was smiling broadly, exuding an air of success. But when Hammond tried to speak, to ask the questions crowding his mind, he mumbled and stuttered helplessly. Once again he knew he was playing a part.

"How do you like it with things reversed, Al? Which of us do you think Irene would choose now?"

The thought was Willie's, but somehow he had spoken to Hammond without saying the words aloud. In that instant Hammond understood many things, as if Willie had suddenly told him the drab story of his life—of his yearning, his frustration, his bungling incompetence; of his bitter envy of Hammond's success; and of his driving desire for Irene.

The realization came in a flash and was gone. Subservient and servile, Hammond stepped back, bowing a little as Willie moved toward the table and Irene. Irene stood up, her tired face radiant, her lips trembling.

Willie stopped, staring at her. His smile faded. His face drained of color. As it did, a flood of energy flowed into Hammond's soul, as if he had been released from an invisible bondage. He clenched his fists and sprang at Willie. Indecisive and frightened, Willie backed away; but his hesitation was momentary. He paused and cried out in anguish.

"No—no! This won't work! It has to be done differently!"

As if the projected scene of a motion picture had been suddenly stilled, the activity and sound in the banquet hall became frozen and immobile. Dancers stood like statues; waiters were dead, in the act of removing dishes from tables; the curtain, waving in the wind, hung like a thing made of grass; and the air throbbed with the single note the orchestra had been playing when the paralysis came upon them.

Hammond was lifeless, like the others; a part of his mind went blank, but his two other worlds remained intact. Hammond saw the room as a picture, hidden in the depth of a body of water. Only Willie Tuttle had life. Willie looked for a moment at the lifeless statues around him, and then he approached Irene.

HE FINGERED her straggling hair; he ran his hand over the wrinkled gray skin of her face; he lifted her hand and touched the reddened calluses. When Willie looked up, he was crying. Furiously he lashed out at Irene, to sweep her aside, but his swinging arms passed through her body like knives cleaving quiet water.

Willie stepped back, surveying the motionless throng. As he reached a decision a sly smile crept over his face. With a flick of his wrist he removed one of the men standing near Hammond's table and replaced him with a dignified, white-haired gentleman.

He turned and faced Hammond, grinning.

In a burst of light and sound, motion came back to the room, but the time element had been altered. Hammond was back at the point where he went to face Willie and force an explanation from him.

A thick, pulsing hatred arose within Hammond, like the quaking of an unleashed volcano. He began to shout into Willie's smirking face, crying that Willie did not own the Red Arrow Line, that it belonged to him, to Albert Hammond. He would have smashed his knuckles into Willie's gleaming teeth, but men rose on all sides to hold him back.

They carried him, screaming, into an empty lounge. As Hammond's rage subsided, he saw that the dignified, white-haired gentleman was with him.

"Feeling better, Mr. Hammond?"

"I guess I did go off my rocker a little, didn't I?"

"It sometimes happens if we work too hard. Mr. Tuttle asked me to tell you he won't press any charges, but if there's a repetition of this outburst he'll take steps to have you committed."

"The strange thing is, I—somehow I know I'm right! I do own the company, but I live in San Francisco and my wife—"

"Mr. Hammond, we all daydream. It's normal for a man to envy his boss and to imagine how things would be if he were in his place. Our dreams are our own private worlds. We can build them as we like, fill them with puppets of our own making. But it's madness if you allow yourself to confuse your own dream-world with reality."

"A psychiatrist told me that same thing almost a week ago, in San Francisco—but I owned the company, then."

"I'm advising you to get a lot of rest, Mr. Hammond. If this happens again, you won't get off so easily. I'll give you a tablet to take before you go to bed tonight."

Hammond drove back to Glendale in a seething storm of disgrace. Irene's quarrelsome voice picked fitfully at the bones of his brief and one-sided battle with Willie. She heaped high her scorn and denunciation, never pausing for breath, never asking him for his explanation.

Hammond took the sleeping tablet and went to bed. Irene was still talking. Twice she shook him awake to tell him again how much he had embarrassed her and to demand,

"Whatever can we do, now? Of course Willie won't keep you on at the office after this!"

Eventually Irene ran through even her score of bitterness and the tiny, dismal bedroom fell silent. Hammond dozed and the tension in his muscles began to relax. To sleep was to forget. To sleep was to—

TO DREAM! He jerked himself back to consciousness, fighting the creeping paralysis of the drug. When he slept he was helpless, trapped by the nightmares that overturned his world. He sat up, staring at the pattern of light the corner streetlamp threw on the bedroom ceiling.

Very slowly he began to understand what had happened. A madman created a dream world and escaped into it, and for him that world was real; it would be real, too, from the point of view of the dream itself.

Hammond, then, had become caught in dream worlds made by someone else.

Willie Tuttle! These were his puppet universes, the gaudy delusions of a futile, ineffectual, timid nonentity, envying Hammond his success and his possession of Irene. The first trans-formation had framed Hammond's San Francisco existence in the romantic nonsense Willie botched together out of his restricted experiences and his imagination. And the second had reduced Hammond to a poverty and a drabness comparable to Willie's. Willie had meant, then, to move across the stage, a glittering lion of success, captivate Irene, and snatch her away. But Willie's dream went wrong, because Irene necessarily had to share Hammond's economic environment. Willie found her an undesirable, work-worn wench, the only possible product of the world Willie had given her.

Willie's only solution was to create another dream in a hurry. He used the white-haired gentleman to engineer a situation that would force Hammond to take a sleeping pill. Willie hadn't had recourse to that particular trick before, but he was apparently frightened and rattled now. He couldn't be sure that Hammond had not guessed the truth, and the only time Willie could bring about the transformation was while Hammond slept.

Hammond dragged himself out of bed, sluggishly fighting off the drug. If Willie could make the dreams, he could unmake them, too. Hammond had some slight control of the situation now. He knew Willie was staying at the Biltmore. If he could get his hands on Willie, Hammond could force him to restore his own world of reality. Perhaps that was as much an illusion as this, but at least Hammond was at home there and held dominion over his own destiny.

Hammond drove back to Los Angeles. The encroaching weariness rose up against him like an invisible force. He fought it with all his strength, but it was a losing battle.

He left his car in an all-night lot on Hill Street and reeled through Pershing Square toward the Biltmore. He staggered drunkenly, as if his feet were trapped in a sea of mud. His breath came in gasps. His heart lurched.

He dropped on a green bench to rest and he did not get up. His head fell on his chest. The screaming nightmare closed over his mind.

But a spark of himself stayed doggedly alive, whispering over and over again, "This is not real; this is not real." Desperately Hammond seized upon it, while the storm of the dream raged across his soul; the steady whisper gave him courage. Slowly he began to build upon it. If the torment were not real, he could dismiss it simply by refusing to accept it.

TO DREAM! He jerked himself and then a shout of triumph. Abruptly his fatigue passed. Hammond stood up and looked at the square. All motion was frozen into the one-dimensional reality of a photograph. The leaves on the trees stood still. The water of the fountain hung in midair, clear crystal tears without weight.

This was Willie's world. By the strength of his conviction, of his belief in himself, Hammond could destroy it. To believe, however, was a desperate struggle against his own established concepts of reality. For a long time he stood where he was, as motionless as the rest of the picture; but the conviction mounted slowly in his mind, and slowly he found that he could walk.

Hesitantly he began to pull the world apart. The edges of the picture blurred into a gray shadow, folding inward like sheets of water. Suddenly he saw Willie running toward him across the square.

"No—no!" Willie screamed. In spite of his effort, he ran sluggishly, fighting the force that dragged against him. When he came close to Hammond, he was livid from exertion. "Leave it be, Hammond, if you want to save either of us!"

"If you can make this dream, Willie, I can destroy it."

"Yes. Yes now that you know how. But, when you do, you'll create a vacuum. There'll be nothing to take its place."

"I don't like your dream, Willie. I want to get back to my own."

Willie pulled himself up and spoke with courage, although his face paled. "You have to depend on me to do that, Hammond, and I'll never do it. I'd rather have the other thing."

"The other thing?"

"Look!" Willie gestured vaguely. Already the buildings in the background had peeled away; the trees were fading, colorless; the brick walks were graying into indistinctness. An emptiness, like a thick fog, was closing around the two men.

"I can create for myself, then," Hammond said.

"You haven't the ability!"

"If I can wipe out your world, why can't I make my own?"

"Because you know you're part of my dream; since you really believe that, you can destroy it. But you're too practical, Hammond, too much the materialist to believe that much in your own. You can erase what I've made; that's as far as you can go. You're too normal to accomplish the other thing; you believe too much in the external reality of things."

Furiously Hammond advanced on Willie. Willie backed away, still talking, still pleading. Underneath a hedge Hammond stumbled upon an electric clipper left there by a park gardener. He picked it up and swung the blade. Willie cringed and screamed. Hammond swung again, and the clipper hit Willie's head. In a final frenzy of angry words, Willie vanished. His world went with him. Hammond stood alone in a vast, gray-white emptiness. He stood on nothing. He felt nothing. He moved freely, but he moved in no direction.

Willie's dream was gone. Hammond began to create his own. He tried to visualize Irene, their white-walled bungalow, the two-year old Buick, and the children that he loved. Very faintly the house began to take shape in the mist, but it disappeared when a new thought occurred to him.

IF HE COULD make the world as he wanted it, why not create perfection? He began with the things he thought he needed: wealth, prestige, power, good health; and he discarded them all. He had grown up in a universe in turmoil, among sheeting demagogues and in the thunder of war. The one thing above others that he had learned to desire was security.

Begin with that, then. Make his universe absolutely secure in all things.

He built up the image in his mind, but the gray mist did not lift. He knew that he could create as he pleased; he believed that as he had believed that he could shatter Willie's dream. Yet still the mist held fast.

After a time he was exhausted. He thought that he slept for a while, but he could not be sure. When he awoke, the mist was still there. He knew that hours had passed, but he felt no hunger, no discomfort, nothing except the cold touch of the gray mist.

No discomfort! Then this was the thing that he had created—a universe of absolute security. He was forever safe—and forever alone.

Security by itself meant nothing, then. It was one-half of a balanced scale. Security became meaningless unless it was opposed to insecurity.

As he reached that conclusion, the gray fog began to stir. He knew he had found the way back. For a moment he was tempted to pursue the security of absolute power, and a tentative world took form, but it was a madness of screaming adulation for an aloof godhead that was himself. He fled from it back into the blankness of the mist.

He did not want perfection, then, but the semblance of it that he once had had.

The white house took shape. He saw the sun warming the lawn. The colors brightened. He saw children playing in the drive. The detail of the picture took form. He heard the sound of birds in the trees, the splutter of a distant motor on the highway, the whine of a lawn mower.

From out of the void he moved into the house. He saw the white, emaciated form lying on the bed, motionless under the sheets. Slowly that form became himself. Irene was bending over him as he opened his eyes. He became aware of the bandages that bound his shoulder, of the pain throbbing in his throat.

"You're going to be all right, Al," Irene said. Her hand was cool and soft on his forehead.

"What happened?" His voice was, husky, his throat sand dry.

"Yesterday, when we were working in the garden, a man sprang at you from a break in the hedge. He tried to kill you, dear."

"I—I don't remember, Irene."

"No wonder; the doctor gave you a sedative! In an hour or so you'll be feeling more yourself again."

"Someone tried to kill me? Why, Irene?"

"Goodness knows. He was drunk, I think. You beat him off with the hedge clipper, but he cut your throat very badly with a broken bottle."

"Who was it, Irene? Do I know him?"

"That's the strangest part of it, Al. It was Willie Tuttle. Remember him? He went to high school with us. I almost gave him a date once, for the Junior Prom."

THE END

City of Lost Souls

By RALPH MILNE FARLEY and AL P. NELSON

Three thousand Martian Legionnaires faced more than they could handle when they attacked the holy city of Daloss to rescue captured comrades.

"WARREN!" cried Hammersmith, as he thrust his shaggy head between my tent-flaps. "The desert chieftain, Mu-Lai and his blasted Mauros have wiped out our garrison at Wacco. Two hundred Legionnaires and a hundred Martians!"

Hammersmith, a rangy red-haired Australian, with cold blue eyes, was the only Earthman to hold a commission in the Martian Foreign Legion; for all the other officers, and even some of the non-coms, were copper-skinned Martian aristocrats.

He eased his rangy frame into my tent and sat down at the foot of my canvas cot. Little Cedric, the Englishman, followed him in.

"It happened last night!" Cedric breathlessly added. "One of the survivors has just reached camp—he's over at headquarters right now reporting to Colonel Ak-Ak. He says the Mauros fell on the little city at midnight and slaughtered nearly every man, woman, and child. Babies—little babies—torn from their mothers' breasts and slit open with swords. Oh, my God!" His boyish face was blank with horror.

Hammersmith's leathery jaw was set and grim. His blue eyes flashed in the light of my tent lantern.

"That's not the worst of it. The dead are dead, but think of what's going to happen to our buddies who were taken prisoner. Ten of them! Dragged off to Daloss to be tortured and then burned alive on the golden altar as a sacrifice to the Dark Star, Erlik. One of them in particular!" His voice broke.

Daloss. In spite of my horror at the fate of my comrades, I could not restrain a thrill at the magical spell of that name. Daloss, hidden deep in the fertile valleys between the ranges of the mighty Fobian Mountains was the age-old mystic city of the Mauros, a stronghold that bristled with guns and superstitions.

Here the worship of the Dark Star was most devout. Here plans were daily reviewed for the mighty holy war, which some day would find all followers of Erlik rising to wipe infidels from the face of the planet.

Scourge of Mars for generations, Daloss was known as the most holy city of the worshippers of Erlik. If a nonbeliever should venture to reach its borders, the curses of the dark religion, yea, the curses of Erlik himself would most certainly fall upon him. Disease and misfortune, like a raging storm, would seize the infidel crraat, * or would fill his soul with an evil dark spirit to torture him the rest of his days upon the planet, should he escape death from the Mauros themselves.

This city it was that the Martians dreaded to approach too rapidly, despite the despotic orders from the Capital city to seize the Mauro gold mines at any cost.

No believer in any other religion had ever come back from the holy city. Infidel captives were anointed with rare Martian perfumes, then burned alive on the great altar of gold in the Maadar, largest and most sacred of all of Erlik's temples. Then their ashes were scattered upon the fields, where the heavy hooves of lumbering ox-like Martian beasts of burden ground them into the soil, so that no trace of the unbelieving crraats might remain to taint the city of the Dark Star.

Truly a City of Lost Souls—Christian souls, Martian souls, doomed by incantation of Erlik's high priests to roam in misery over the red planet, pursued by evil dark spirits.

And yet there was a romantic side to this city of mystery. The tales that reached us from Daloss were not all horror. There were things to draw us there, as well as to repel us. For not only was there the fabulous wealth of its gold mines—but there were its women!

Little Cedric, the English boy, was telling us this. But somehow it went against my prejudices.

"Filthy wenches!" I snorted.

"Not all," said Cedric quietly.

Something in his tone caused me to look at him searchingly.

---

* "Crraat," a particularly repulsive desert rodent-like reptile—Ed.

"Well?" I asked.

"There was one," the boy said dreamily. "Blue eyes, golden curls, skin pink and white like a sea shell. Her father was a very wealthy Mauro, and sent her to finishing school on Earth, in England. She was from Daloss. I'd like to see her again."

"A Mauro—as beautiful as that?" I exclaimed.

"A Mauro, not a gunmetal-blue Martian," said Cedric, with disdain, "nor a copper-red member of the Martian aristocracy. A Mauro, most of whom are white like ourselves. One of the reasons I came to Mars and joined up with the Legion, was the hope of seeing that little beauty again."

Then he went on to tell us of what he had heard of the midnight ritual of the City of Lost Souls.

IT was said that, on moonlit Martian nights, these beautiful Mauro women, shedding their flowing white shawls and silken tunics, roamed the streets of Daloss, to perform weird, naked,

CITY OF LOST SOULS

by Ralph Milne Farley and Al P. Nelson

"I can kill the infidel now!" Warren heard her sob. "He deserves to die!"

worshipful dances in honor of Erlik the Unspeakable, while hidden
stringed instruments throbbed with wild barbaric music. Every
male inhabitant cast his eyes upon the floor of his hut while these

dances held sway, for worthy only is Erlik himself to gaze upon so much naked loveliness.

A growl from Hammersmith snapped our minds back from these dreams, to the horrid fate awaiting our ten captured comrades.

"Who were they?" I asked. "Any whom we know?"

"Well, there's Gustav Schmidt," little Cedric began.

I shook my head. The name was not familiar.

"And Victor Lafontaine."

"Not Vic?" I cried. I knew him well, a lovable roly-poly Frenchman.

"And Hammersmith's own brother!"

So that was the reason for the catch in Hammersmith's voice a few moments ago.

"The others," the young Englishman ended harshly, "were not of our outfit."

"Well," I demanded, "what are we going to do about it?"

"The Legion is wild with rage!" Hammersmith declared. "You and Cedric are the two senior Sergeants—other than the Martians. I want you two to come with me to headquarters to talk to Colonel Ak-Ak."

"You're on!" I cried, jumping up and jamming my desert hat onto my head.

Together the three of us made our way to the whitewashed stone house, which served as headquarters and dwelling for the red Martian aristocrat, who was our commandant.

Colonel Ak-Ak, a gross swarthy Martian with long drooping moustaches, received us with an air of graciousness, and listened quietly to the suggestions of Captain Hammersmith.

"Sir," our Captain concluded—in Esperanto, of course, the official interplanetary tongue, "the men are eager to avenge this damned massacre and to rescue their comrades from bloodthirsty Mu-Lai and his savage Mauros. Is not this what you have been waiting and hoping for? An incentive to drive us to capture the gold mines which the Capital City is anxious for us to seize?"

The Colonel seemed pleased at the suggestion, promised to take it up with the Staff early in the morning, thanked us profusely, and poured out some excellent wine—quite different from the rancid syrup, swimming with desert insects, which formed a part of our daily ration.

Then we returned to our encampment and spread the word of the rescue plans. The whole camp buzzed with excitement. Weird tales of the City of Lost Souls, and its beautiful women, were told far into that desert moonlit night.

Now at last we Legionnaires could look forward to a real war! No more mere slow skirmishing across the sun baked red sands. No more cautious advances. Quick action, desperate action, decisive action would be necessary, if we would save our ten comrades.

NEXT morning we awoke—those of us who had slept at all— eager to set out for Daloss. But no call to the colors came. All through that sweltering day, we fretted and chafed beneath the boiling sun, watched the red haze of the mighty Fobian range, and waited.

We questioned the junior Martian officers and non-coms concerning plans for the advance. But they merely shrugged their shoulders.

"What are a mere ten men? And especially mere Earthmen, mercenaries?" they said, snapping their fingers. "Nothing, in a war like this. And the massacre? 'Tis but the fortunes of war, nothing more; a mere desert wind, which blows some good, some ill."

The Legion seethed. For with every minute that slipped by, rescue was becoming more and more difficult. So finally Captain Hammersmith and Little Cedric and I went back again to the Martian Colonel, Ak-Ak.

We intended to make demands—perhaps even to threaten a mutiny. But we never got that far. For, as we entered the Colonel's office, after cooling our heels in the outer room for an hour, we were set upon by a squad of men from one of the native Martian regiments.

"Seize—bind them!" shouted the swarthy red-skinned Colonel.

It would take more than eight Martian regulars to seize the three of us. Cedric and I dropped back several paces, and raised our fists to defend ourselves. But Hammersmith, our leader, seemed to slump with servility, as he meekly held out his wrists for the shackles.

Doubtless anxious to get him out of the way, before tackling Cedric and me, one of the native soldiers leaped forward, with the open handcuffs in both hands, ready to clap them on Hammersmith's wrists.

This was what Hammersmith had been waiting for. Lunging suddenly, he reached beneath the extended manacles, seized the soldier around the waist with both hands, lifted him aloft, and hurled him full in the faces of the others.

Then, our fists flying, all three of us waded in.

Through one corner of my eye, I saw Colonel Ak-Ak whip out his atomic pistol. I crouched low, and mixed up closer with the Martian soldiers, so that Ak-Ak wouldn't dare try to blast me. I heard several toots of the Colonel's whistle, and then more men came running.

It was a glorious fight while it lasted, but at length we were downed, and our wrists and ankles firmly tied. Big, gross Colonel Ak-Ak twirled his long black drooping moustaches, his fat copper-hued face purple with suppressed rage.

"It may interest you crraats to know," he hissed, "that there will be no advance on Daloss. On the morrow, we retire to winter quarters at Ricca, there to await reinforcements for the spring campaign. *That* for your impertinence! Your comrades can rot in hell!"

He snapped his fingers; and strode, still bristling, from the office.

"Damn!" muttered Hammersmith to me, as the three of us were led away in the wake of Colonel Ak-Ak. "Now we've put our foot in it! Losing our tempers, when we needed to keep them at all costs. Poor brother, I have failed you!"

"Shut your face," snapped one of the guards, slapping him across the mouth.

We were led to the stinking guardhouse and locked in separate cells, so that we got no chance of further conversation.

ALL the rest of that hot stifling afternoon, I worried about the fate of our ten captured comrades. But occasionally—I must admit—my thoughts wandered to the *attractions* of the City of Lost Souls, as well as to its *menace.* To the unlimited gold of its mines, and to its beautiful blonde Mauro maidens.

At last came evening, with its weird green shadows cast across the desert's hot sands, its soft cooling winds, its vast desert beauty. Black bat-like desert reptiles sped through the green darkness with eerie flapping of leather wings. Over the red desert lay a satisfying peace; but not on us three incarcerated ones, nor—so we later learned—upon the rest of the Legion of Death. Time was fleeting, and there was an outrage to be avenged, and comrades to be rescued.

In the corridors of our jail, we heard the sound of scuffling—a muffled groan—a dull thud. Then cautious footsteps approached our cells.

"Captain Hammersmith! Sergeant Warren! Sergeant Cedric! Speak up, where are you?"

"Here!" we whispered in reply.

A furtive group of enlisted men from our own outfit unlocked our cell doors, and then untied our wrists and ankles. Next they dragged in the Martian guards, bound and gagged, and left them in our places.

"What's up?" Hammersmith whispered, as we slunk through the green darkness, back toward our own outfit.

"The men have organized everything," one of our rescuers explained, "but we want someone to lead us. If you will take command, Sir, we're all set to fall upon the officers, truss them up, seize the sliths,* and then off to Daloss. What do you say, Sir?"

"It's a go!" the Captain exclaimed, his blue eyes glinting eagerly. "Who made the plans?"

"Zenoff, Duke Keating, Bloch, and Kuswa."

"Good!" he exclaimed. "Send for them."

A few minutes of discussion with the plotters convinced him that the plans had been well laid. So he gave the word for action.

A single long low barking howl, like that of a crraat, this was our

---

* "Slith," a gray horse-like reptile, ridden by the Martian cavalry. Its splay feet enable it to travel with ease over the red desert sands, and it can go for long periods without water—Ed

signal. Instantly every Martian officer and non-commissioned officer in our regiment was set-upon, gagged, and bound. Then we crept silently like dark shadows toward the picket lines. Most of the guards were our own buddies; the few Martians we quickly overpowered.

We had saddled and mounted as the red disk of one of the two Martian moons climbed above the mountains, quickly shrinking and paling as it rose.

Leather creaked, sabers clanked in their scabbards; rifles were clasped in taut hands. Breath came in quick gasps; eyes flashed; faces were grim with determination.

Down the moonlit red slope we raced, past spiky argan trees, past a honeycombed slag bluff, and out onto the open desert. Past the encampment of the native portion of the Legion we rode. Bedlam broke loose among the tents that dotted the floor of the broad valley. Atomic rifles sizzled, and hoarse commands rose on the night air.

Then the whole three thousand of us were gone—vanished into the night before the sleepy fire of the waking Martians could become destructive. Only a few men were lost to us in that encounter.

THUNDERING over the desert toward the distant Fobian Mountains, we headed for Daloss, the city of mystery. Behind us lay Martians and martial rule. Ahead lay rescue for our comrades, and adventure and perhaps death for us! What a step it was! We had outlawed ourselves. We were fugitives, subject to the wrath of a whole planet.

"Isn't it great?" screamed Little Cedric, wonder and awe shining in his young eyes, as we pounded along on our gray desert mounts.

"Great?" mocked the deep voice of Ivan Zenoff. "Wait until you see the wild Mauros before you say that. They fight like hell, and torture like the demons of their own black saint, Erlik. Say, buddy, you haven't seen or heard anything yet...?"

"Wait until you see the Mauro girls!" Cedric shot back at him.

Several miles onward, above the pungent stench of slith-sweat, drifted the thin English voice of the man whom we called the Duke.

"By Jove, they say the Mauro women are devils, too! They sneak out on the field of battle at night and sink knives into the wounded enemy, the bally things! No man comes back from this part of the world, what!"

Southward over the red dunes we swept, and up them again almost to the hurtling desert moon, yelling, singing, fair-warning the enemy. Fighting fever ran high. Singing rose louder. Our men shouted defiance at the moon, and shook their fists at the desert sky. Who cared if the Mauros heard? Who cared if anyone heard? Ahead of us lay a mission of rescue and adventure.

Hours later, small squat bushes and sparse blue-knobbed gray lichenous trees loomed before us, as the country became more hilly. We passed a black ersite shrine, solemn in its lonely glory. The hooves of our sliths clicked sharply on the bones of animals and of humans, left to scorch in the desert sun. Other battles had been fought here, grim to the very end. Life had pulsed at this spot long ago; caravans had come from the canal cities in long lines of swaying sliths, carrying plunder and Mauros, frowning Mauros with wide hats and colored capes.

"Something's going to happen!" yelled Little Cedric, his eyes glowing. "I can feel it…"

"We ought to meet them soon," I answered. "We've been riding for hours, advertising our whereabouts to all the planet. Where is the enemy?"

On thundered the three thousand, past lonely, rocky slag-bluffs, past salt-beds, weirdly white beneath the desert moon. Looming steadily nearer ahead of us, rose the mighty Fobian range. The second moon rose in the West, and hurtled across the sky, in reverse direction to its more sluggish brother.

Then suddenly from a grove of thick lichens on a rocky slope, spurts of livid flame streaked the night, as atomic rifles sizzled. Sliths shrieked and stumbled in our ranks, men fell, gasps and cries rent the air. The Legion of Death slowed down as though a huge wave had rolled against it. Again many shots sizzled forth, pouring death into our ranks. We were ambushed!

WAVING his saber, Captain Hammersmith shouted to us to follow him. Straight into that grove of fragrant blue-knobbed lichens he dashed. And we three thousand followed close behind. Sabers slashed down into the bushes; atomic pistols spurted sharply; atomic rifles sizzled sudden death. Cries rang out. More rifle shots sounded. Men and sliths tumbled into the bushes.

White-clothed Mauros appeared from everywhere, like ghosts in the moonlight. They poured from every bush, firing at close range.

A sharp cry of pain beside me, a youthful cry! It was Little Cedric. There was an agonized expression on his boyish face as he slid heavily from the saddle of his plunging slith, to be trampled and crushed by the splay feet of the sliths behind.

Poor Little Cedric! Never would he meet again his beautiful golden-haired Mauro maiden, whom he had come so far and lived through so much hell to see.

But we had no time to worry about Little Cedric or any other of our lost comrades, for we had a fight on our hands. And fight we did! Many a swarthy Mauro rose from behind a blue-knobbed lichen, and toppled, never to rise again. Many were crushed under the thundering sliths of the Legion. But there were countless others to take the places of those who fell. From the hill beyond they poured in never ending numbers, white capes flowing in the breeze.

Cries from the mouth of a gorge ahead rose above the din of battle. Shots rang out, and a moving wave of men and sliths streamed forth, looming wild and fierce against the night's eerie horizon.

"Daloss must be close at hand!" shouted Hammersmith, his face streaked with blood, and his red hair disheveled. "These are the devils who massacre women and children, and who would burn our comrades at the altar of Erlik. Charge, men! Charge!"

The enemy cavalry met us with a fierceness that stunned us, that stopped us momentarily. Some were old bearded Mauros with flowing white capes wrapped around them, fighting with a recklessness like that of youth, their short broad-bladed lances darting back and forth with flying speed. Some, equipped with atomic rifles, fired like mad as they came forward. Some were young Mauros, haughty and disdainful, their white teeth flashing in snarls of rage, their practiced arms wielding spears with quick thrusts of death. And among them were many men with skins as white as our own—strange phenomenon of a strange planet!

Cries of the wounded rose on all sides. It was close in-fighting now, every man for himself. You could hear the sharp gasp of breath as blades sank into soft flesh. Then the agonized moan as the sabers or lances were pulled out, the heart blood leaping thickly on the slayer's arm. A wracking cough—some Mauro or Earthman choking on his own life's blood.

It was fight and slash, and slash and fight. At close quarters, rifles—even atomic pistols—were ineffective. The whole air seemed filled with stabbing spears and sweeping sabers, streaked red in the moonlight.

Suddenly a hoarse, victorious shout went up, rose loudly on the soft desert, wind. The fighting mass began to shift toward the mountains. The Legion of Death was moving on!

MAD glorious joy surged in our hearts, and swelled in our throats. The enemy, battling desperately, retreated slowly at first, and then broke into a rout, the Legion following close behind.

At the entrance to the pass—a gash in the mighty Fobian range—we were met by a volley of shots. Here again were wild Martian natives hidden behind every rock and shrub. Determined hundreds, armed with atomic rifles, standing in the narrow defile, blocking our way.

Twice we swept against that line of white-caped Mauros, to be thrown fiercely back. But on the third charge we broke through into the rocky canyon. Clatter of hooves against the stony bottom, as we charged on; clank of scabbards echoing up the dark walls. Then we poured out into a broad valley, diminished in number but still compact enough for battle array.

Ahead in the moonlight rose the majestic spires and minarets of a city, beautiful in its lonely glory. Jagged mountain ranges flanked it, while beyond it stretched a high plateau, red and barren and forlorn.

"Daloss!" shouted Hammersmith, digging his spurs deep into his slith. "God grant that we are in time to save our comrades!"

To a man, the two thousand who were left in the Legion of Death gave rein to their sliths and raced toward the high red mud wall that circled the city. But the gleaming metal gate of fretwork design in the arched doorway was closed. From the walls, hidden riflemen opened a sizzling death-dealing fire, shouting to Erlik to save their holy of holies.

Then Hammersmith, our leader, commanded our trumpeter to sound retreat. At the first notes of that well-known but little-used bugle-call, a snarl of incredulous rage arose from the parched throats of the Legion of Death.

Shouts of protest filled the air.

"What th' hell! Come all this way for nothing? Are yez yeller, Hammy? Have youse fergot yer own brother?"

But our Captain rose in his stirrups, held up one hand commanding silence, and cried.

"It's only to rest a moment, and take stock of losses, and form again for the final assault. Come on! To that lichen-grove over there!"

To a little lichen-grove, on a hill overlooking the city, he led us. There we found a spring and a small brook,* where we drank, and watered our winded steeds—but scantily, only scantily—and washed off our dust and clotted gore.

Scare two thousand of us remained, out of our original three thousand. Hammersmith left seven hundred in the grove as a reserve and a rear guard, to cover our return—if we ever should return. In command of them he placed a bull-necked bullet-headed Hungarian named Kuswa.

WITH thirteen hundred refreshed and determined men, as the sky began to turn pink above the mountain tops to the eastward, he moved once more toward the city gates. On the way we found two water-soaked argan logs in the winding creek. With them we battered at the gate. Back and forth those battering rams beat upon the metal doors, shaking them with every blow.

The reorganized Mauro cavalry attacked our rear; but so fiercely did our rear-guard ward them off, that the work at the gates was

---

* Apparently the land of the Mauros is watered by seepage from some of the quite distant canals, as no canal runs anywhere near it.—Ed.

not interrupted. For some reason, the firing from atop the wall and from within the gates was not heavy.

At last the grilled gates crashed open. We pushed, we surged through, with wild cries. Down the wide central street of the city we rode at terrific pace, toward the great rounded dome of the Temple of Erlik, which loomed ahead.

Low red-walled buildings flanked the street on both sides. Mosaics, blue and white and turquoise green, were visible in the pale light of early dawn. In the doorways, veiled women gave us hasty frightened glances, then scampered inside. A nearby grove of some unknown flowering tree poured its fragrance on the breeze. From a house on a narrow side street, a baby wailed, and its cry was quickly muffled.

Could a man ever forget that ride? Soft winds blowing on tired cheeks, worn bodies, steaming sliths. And behind the latticed windows that lined the streets, frightened faces staring out at us: children's faces, women's faces. Shutters quickly slammed shut.

On toward the looming black-domed temple we rode. High stone walls, with windowed stone towers atop them, stretched far to the east and west. Beyond this wall waved the velvety tops of many blood-green ktath-trees indicating vast, cool gardens. And deep in the center stood the immense, black-plastered temple itself, with its seven rainbow-hued spires, and its vast black dome reaching into the Martian sky.

The sight stirred our blood. Within those walls, within that temple, were our comrades, perhaps even now being roasted to death on the sacrificial altar of gold! With a growl of rage we spurred our sliths on again, firing spurts of atomic flame back at the charging Mauros behind us, firing sidewise at the snipers who lay flat on the roofs of nearby houses.

A sudden sharp twinge in my right shoulder twisted me in my saddle; then, a moment later, burning pain. I felt myself slipping from my saddle, and grabbed madly for the pommel, missing it. The ground struck my head a stunning blow. Thundering, thudding splay hooves sped by me, over me. Then a silent darkness swept down upon me, and I knew no more.

LATER, through moments filled with wild dreams, came the sound of women's voices in the universal tongue of Mars. My years in the Legion had given me enough knowledge of the language so that I could understand what they were saying. A strident voice was scolding, commanding.

"You are a little fool, Esta! Do as I tell you!"

A low sweet voice replied in pleading tones.

"But mother mine, I cannot kill them. Even to think of it makes my heart chill!"

"What! You will not slay these foreign crraats, these beasts from another world, who have killed our own men, these infidels who desecrate the holy city of the Black Star?"

"N—no! No! The thought of it makes my hand shrink to my body."

"Fie, child. Is the betrothed of the handsome Ab-Nadik a coward?"

"I care not what Ab-Nadik thinks! I—oh, mother, *what* are you doing?"

"See, it is like this, my child. Open his shirt, pull back his head by the hair, and let the point of the knife tickle before you sink it deep into the Earthman crraat's throat. Ah! In Erlik's name! Hear his cursed blood gurgle!"

"Mother, mother! It is terrible!"

"Nonsense, child. Every Mauro woman must do her duty. Away with your soft-hearted foolishness— See over there! An Earthman stirs into consciousness. Slit his throat, my child, and praise Erlik."

It was all a horrible nightmare to my slowly awakening consciousness. Cautiously I opened my eyes, and stared about me.

I was lying on the paving-stones of a broad street lined with red clay houses. Far down this street in one direction was the grillwork of the city gate, now closed and guarded by swarthy men in wide hats and flowing white capes. Down the street in the other direction rose the rainbow spires and the black dome of the Temple of Erlik, with a surging thousand or so of Legionnaires massed in front of it. Around me on the pavement lay many dead and dying men, some clad in flowing white, and some in the red uniform of the Foreign Legion of Mars. And a few disemboweled sliths.

But what caught and held my eyes was the girl whose voice I had heard. Curls of burnished gold. Skin, shell-pink. Eyes of sapphire blue. And a slim but voluptuous figure, half concealed, half revealed by her flowing white shawl and diaphanous garments beneath. My heart beat wildly at such sheer beauty.

And standing with her, a hawk-faced crone—a white woman too, but gnarled and old and fiendish.

They moved away from me toward the side of the street, the mother leading; and almost I raised myself and called to them to return, so smitten was I at the sight of the blonde young Mauro girl.

Louder voices, closer, shriller. More native women slinking through the streets, like gaudy vultures, tearing at men's throats and hearts. Then the wail of the hawk-faced crone near the wall of a building.

"Great Erlik! It is my son, your brother Ben-Stu, who lies here! He is badly wounded!"

The younger woman ran toward the wall, but the mother pushed her away. She put her scrawny old arms around the body of the young wounded Mauro, and weeping, hugged him to her breast.

"I will take him home," she cried with fierce mother love. "But you, Esta, be about your work. The cursed Earthmen have almost killed your brother!"

"Yes!" the young girl exclaimed, her beautiful face now bitterly contorted. "Give me the knife, mother. I can kill them now!"

SHE strode directly toward me, a long kris in her hand, and her glinting yellow curls stirring in the wind. As she neared me, she stumbled and fell, but even as she fell she made a lunge at me, the knife sinking between the stones of the street within inches of my side.

In another moment she had righted herself. Her slender hand ripped open my shirt. I tried to roll over, but was too weak. I groaned. Her hand took hold of my hair and jerked my head back cruelly. Her pink cheeks were flushed, and there was a wild light of fanaticism in her heaven-blue eyes.

My fingers reached up and fastened about her wrist, to stay that knife which was ready to plunge into my breast. I rose on my elbow, my grip still on her arm.

"I want to live a little longer," I said slowly. "And that knife is very sharp—Esta."

Her tense and panting body was close to mine. Fiercely she struggled to get the knife free, to plunge it into my heart. Then our glances met and held. I gazed deep into the blue pools of her eyes, and smiled—smiled happily, confidently, though I was close to death. Her gaze fell. Thick long lashes masked her eyes. Her face went white—then flushed again.

I took the knife from her nerveless fingers, and flung it to clatter against the wall of a nearby house.

"You are too beautiful to be a killer!" I said as I released her. Unthinking, I had spoken in English.

And she replied in the same tongue, but with a strange lilting cadence, which gave to the language a beauty that it had never had for me before.

"No," she said levelly, although her lips trembled slightly. "I cannot kill you. Yet why did you and your comrades come, bringing death to our peaceful city, if you expect not death in return?"

"Beautiful one," I replied, "I know now that I came here for you! Tell me that you believe it!"

My words were as unexpected to me as they were to her. Her blue eyes widened for one startled moment. Then she smiled shyly, frightenedly, wonderingly. I slipped one arm around her slim waist, but she pushed me slowly away and stared at me, as if searching, seeking for something. A subtle joy vibrated through my war-tired body. This lovely girl and I—there was a bond between us, growing stronger every moment. We two were alone together, in spite of the dead all around us, and the stalking vulture-women. Words were unnecessary; words were not swift enough to convey the flood of thoughts and feelings that swept through us.

For a long time we sat in silence. Finally she spoke.

"You must be an American, for the English are not like this."

"What do you know of Englishmen or of Americans, or of any of the races of my Earth?" I asked. "And how does it come that you speak my language?"

"Ah," she laughed. "I went to school in England on your Earth for two Earth years. I am the daughter of the rich Mu-Lai."

I STIFFENED. Mu-Lai! Slaughterer of defenseless women and children. Scourge of the trackless deserts of Mars. The fiend who was about to offer up my ten comrades on the altar of gold! It was to rescue these comrades that I had waded through blood to this holy city. I had come here to fight against fiends—not for a love tryst with an angel.

Sternly I thrust the girl from me and staggered to my feet.

"Esta," I harshly declared. "I came here for rescue and revenge. When that is over I shall return to you."

"Oh, do not go," she cried in alarm. "You will be killed. You cannot hope to prevail against the forces of my father, and against the curses of Erlik, our god."

"I can try."

"I will not let you go to your death. Erlik has sent you here not to rescue your comrades but to rescue me. Against my will my father betrothed me to one Ab-Nadik, whom I do not love. You can—but no, no! What am I saying? I must keep my promise. Still I want you to live. I can hide you. Perhaps you can escape from Daloss under cover of night, when the two moons have set."

I shook my head, though the temptation to be with her was strong. I had work to do—man's work.

"I go to rescue my comrades," I cried. "But wait here for me, Esta. I'll come back."

"If you must go, you must," she sighed wearily. "I shall wait. I shall watch, and hope."

Drawing my saber, I strode toward the towering black dome of the Temple of Erlik, scattering the gaudy-caped white-clad vulture women, who hovered about the dead and dying in the street.

"You carrion!" I shouted at them in Martian. "Leave them be! Begone, or may Erlik curse you!"

They scurried for cover, like the ghouls that they were. In a side street I spied a wild-eyed slith, stirrups swinging as it sniffed irresolute. Quietly I approached the animal. It permitted me to touch its velvet hide, to pat the smooth flow of its neck.

Painfully I raised myself into the saddle, though my wounded side burned. The quivering animal quieted as I took the reins and swung it about. Together, we clattered down the street toward the temple, where sounds of fighting rose loud upon the morning air. Rising in my stirrups and turning, I stared behind me for a moment. Standing where I had left her was Esta, her hands clasped to her heart. My blood pulsed wildly. She was mine—mine! No Ab-Nadik, nor any other blue or red Martian—or even a white Martian, for that matter—would ever take her away from me.

Then I faced toward the battle ahead, and gave my slith the spurs.

The whine of atomic impulses sped past my ears, and sang on into the morning, as I rode. The wide metal gates of the temple grounds were open. The Legion had already forced their way in. Two old Mauros in dirty capes, lashed out at my slith's legs with their short broad-bladed lances, as we thundered on past them into the temple gardens.

At the entrance to the temple itself I saw large numbers of the Legion, fighting with Mauros. Many of our men were now on foot, their sliths slain.

IN front of the main doorway of the temple stood a giant one-eyed blue Martian, with a mighty broadsword in each hand. On each side of him stood others of the enemy, clad in flowing capes, javelins darting as they tried to halt the rush of our Legion. Still others, hidden behind the ktath-trees, were pouring devastating spurts of atomic fire upon our men.

But the Legion did not stop. The unconquerable urge to rescue our comrades drove us on.

Never have I seen such a splendid physical specimen as that one-eyed blue giant, standing there guarding the temple gates. Naked to the waist, he stood, with a four-foot blade circling in each ham-like hand. His knotted shoulders were at least a yard across, and above them rose a neck corded like that of a bull. The muscles of his chest and arms rippled and rolled beneath his sleek blue hide, as he swung and lunged.

As I edged through the jostling throng, I saw our Legion surge against him three times like waves against a rock, and three times fall back in thwarted spray.

Then Hammersmith alone on slith-back charged the doorway of the temple. The huge Martian giant braced his feet, and gripped his two swords to resist this onslaught. But, just before our captain came within range of a cutting slash, he jerked his reins taut, and his charger reared up, to strike at the blue giant with its front splay feet.

The Martian gave backward not an inch. Dropping one of his swords, he seized the nearest foreleg of the slith with one mighty hand, and held the beast aloft with effortless ease, as he lunged at its heart with his remaining weapon.

With a gurgling cough, the slith collapsed. For an instant the blue giant held it up, then cast it from him with a gesture of disdain, and stooped to retrieve his second sword.

As the slith fell, Hammersmith slid from its back, and rushed the giant. Swinging his saber with both hands, he brought it down on the Martian's head with a blow that would have cleft the skull of an ox.

It never even fazed the blue man. Jerking suddenly erect, as though merely annoyed by a scratch, he swung one of his own blades at Hammersmith. But the Australian was in too close to be cut, and the weapon merely felled him with a glancing blow on the side of the head.

He dropped to the temple steps, and his adversary placed one huge bare foot on his shoulders, lowered one broadsword to get the aim, and then swung it aloft.

I charged. On my saber I caught the descending blow, and turned it aside. The very fury of my foolhardy onslaught forced the giant back up the steps. He stumbled on the step behind him; and, by that time, I had recovered from my parry and swung at him with a low cross-body swipe.

Through the knotted muscles of his belly slashed my blade. But the blue man, though mortally wounded, was a powerful menace still. With a bestial roar of rage, he raised both his weapons aloft, and brought them convergingly down at my shoulders. The blood from his slit belly gushed out over my riding boots. I slipped and fell. The swords clashed together above me. Then the body of the Martian giant lurched on top of me, crushing me down to the foot of the temple steps.

SOMEONE pulled the carcass off and I staggered to my feet and stared around. Captain Hammersmith stood beside me, his desert headgear gone, his red hair disheveled, rubbing a bump on the side of his head. The remaining Mauros had been brushed aside, now that the huge one-eyed blue Martian was no more; and the Legion of Death was surging past us up the steps.

Then Mauro reinforcements mounted on slith-back thundered into the gardens behind us, yelling wildly, their javelins flashing in the morning sunlight that now bathed the planet with pink-tinted glory.

But even this attack from the rear could not stay us. In fact, it drove us on. On we charged, fighting madly, till we streamed through the main entrance into the temple itself.

Into the high-ceilinged inner room of the Temple of Erlik we swept. All its defenders had fallen. We halted, panting for breath, and stared about us at the beautiful iridescence of the holy place. Intricate geometric weavings of pale blue, rose, and green greeted us on every side. At the south end of the vast structure, high in the glossy black vault, the sun—streaming in through many small windows in the dome—played upon a riot of colors. A million golden filaments sparkled, filling the air with a luminous haze that blended now to pale rose, now to delicate mother of pearl.

High above us, from the depths of a barred gallery, a loud unruffled voice chanted with Martian fatalism:

"Erlik! Erlik, the Dark Star! Erlik, the Unseen God!"

Then there burst upon us more spouts of atomic energy from unseen places. Mauro riflemen, hidden throughout the temple, determined to glorify Erlik by killing the Earthman crraats who had dared to set foot therein.

We scattered to seek shelter behind the great round pillars in the labyrinth of intricate doorways and passages, which angled from the spacious open center of the temple. Loud sizzling detonations echoed through the sacred place. Acrid smoke rose in gray clouds to mingle with the haze of color in the black dome of the god Erlik.

At the main doorway a small detachment of the Legion of Death were holding back the Mauro slith-mounted cavalry who had attacked our rear.

The radiance of the rising sun, constantly lighting more and more of the great dome, fell full upon a huge shining altar, filling the whole temple with bright rays of glinting gold. The altar gleamed as though it were the sun itself. It was the great golden altar of Erlik, famed throughout all of Mars.

But it was not the sight of this fabulous fortune in gold that sent us charging forward over the vast tile floor, disdainful of the atomic blasts that dropped our men like wilted insects.

No, it was the sight of the ten bodies that lay naked upon that golden altar—bodies with white skin, the bodies of our comrades captured two days ago by the Mauros.

AMONG them, I recognized the fat roly-poly face of my friend Victor Lafontaine. And the slim keen features of the brother of our Captain.

Golden straps clasped their ankles, their waists, their arms, their shoulders. And all were gagged with cloth of gold. Beyond the altar we could see leaping red tongues of flame licking at the thick dry faggots of lichen-wood piled there.

The bound men lying on top of the altar tried in vain to squirm, to roll away from that blistering heat. Their bodies were wet with perspiration; their eyes mirrored intense pain; and their fingers clenched and re-clenched in agony.

Furiously Hammersmith raced in front of us, his red hair awry, his blue-gray eyes flashing.

"Look what the heathen devils have done to our comrades!" he shouted. "We must save them, even if it costs our own lives. I come, my brother! I come!"

As we rushed forward, two gold-encrusted doors, leading to a small chapel to the left opened. Fierce, bearded Mauros debouched, atomic rifles in their swarthy hands. The leader, a tall hawk-nosed white-skinned man with thin lips, held up his left hand.

"Halt, you Earthmen!" he shouted. "Or all of you will be shot down where you stand. I, Mu-Lai, command you in the name of Erlik! Touch not the sacred altar of the Dark Star, lest your bodies and souls be bled with a thousand tortures!"

Only for an instant did that command stay us; then once more we surged forward in an angry wave.

"Ab-Nadik," cried Mu-Lai to a dark slim handsome young Martian with black flashing eyes standing by his side, "not an Earthman crraat must live."

Red stabs of flame jetted from our guns in reply. Mu-Lai and Ab-Nadik, the betrothed of my Esta, dodged nimbly behind the golden altar, and blasted back at us from that shelter.

Around us scores of our comrades fell, but still we charged on. So fierce was our onslaught that the Mauros were forced to retreat into their chapel, even their great chief himself, and his handsome young lieutenant, Ab-Nadik. But, in spite of this retreat, snipers continued to pour atomic death upon us from all sides.

Still we came forward, scant scores of us, who had been hundreds before. With splintering swords we pried off the golden bands that bound our comrades on the altar. Weeping, sobbing, they gasped their gratitude. Captain Hammersmith clasped his brother in his arms for one brief moment. Then more blasts of force winged about us. Fast we retreated to the shelter of the col-umned passages, and from there we returned the fire of the Mauros.

But the enemy had reorganized, and now poured into the temple at all sides from many concealed entrances. The place swarmed with them. Swords and javelins flashed, atomic pistols barked, atomic rifles sizzled. We Earthmen had profaned the golden altar of Erlik. We must not be permitted to escape!

BACKING from pillar to pillar, the handful of us who were left, made our way slowly and painfully toward the main exit of the temple. But that way of escape we now found blocked by solid ranks of the enemy.

A black passage loomed to one side, and we slid into it, only about a hundred of us now, out of the fourteen hundred who had stormed the place, and the ten men whom we had rescued. Behind us, in the mazes of the temple, our wounded were putting up a fight as long as there was any life left in them. And we knew that they would never permit themselves or each other to fall alive into the hands of the Erlik-worshippers.

Along the sides of the corridor we found some movable stone benches, and with these we threw up a barricade at the entrance. Then our redheaded Captain called to me and Keating:

"Warren and Duke, come here. I want the two of you to take a dozen men and go down this passage to its other end. Duke, you guard the exit, and send back one man to report to me. Warren, if you can get out, take four or five fellows with you, fight your way to the lichen grove, and send in the reserves. We've given these Martian heathens so much hell, that with seven hundred reinforcements, we can cut our way to safety. Get going."

The Duke and I warmly shook our leader's hand, selected our squad of men, and felt our way down the dark corridor.

It turned and twisted, then gradually got lighter. Finally as we rounded a turn, we sighted a crouched figure in a white cape, sneaking toward us. Up came Keating's atomic rifle; but, as he pressed its button, I knocked the weapon aside. Just in time, too, for the skulking figure was that of Esta.

"Oh, my beloved," she cried in English, flinging herself into my arms.

"What ho! Eh, what?" the Duke exclaimed, edging forward. "I say, Warren, I didn't know that you had friends in this blasted heathen city. Introduce us, will you?" But his words, light as they sounded, had no humor in them. They were as cutting as cold steel.

"This is Miss Esta," I stammered, "the daughter of Mu-Lai."

"So!" came with a hiss from my squad. The Mauro chieftain had spared no women in his raid on Wacco. The Martian women had slit the throats of our wounded in today's battle. Then what hope for mercy could a woman of the household of Mu-Lai have, from even a British gentleman?

Up came a menacing row of atomic rifles. But I thrust Esta behind me, and drew my saber, and faced them. Knowing that it would do no good to appeal to their chivalry toward a woman of a race which had shown no chivalry to us, I appealed to their common sense.

"Don't be fools!" I cried. "Esta was educated in England. She has no stomach for this heathen slaughter. She has come to help us. Tell them so, Esta."

"Yes, oh, my beloved. What is it that you wish? Only command me, and Esta will obey."

A snort of contempt came from my men, but I cried triumphantly.

"There! What did I tell you!" Then to the girl I said, "Can you lead me safely out of this city?"

"Yes, beloved," was her reply.

"It looks fishy to me," the Duke gritted, his aristocratic eyes flashing cold. "Well, Warren, run along with your girl friend; but Heaven help you, if you double-cross us. And I'm sending four men to trail you."

"Someday you'll apologize to the lady for this. She's saving your worthless hide," I shouted, contemptuously. Then I turned and followed Esta.

The last that I heard behind me, as I rounded the next corner, was one of the squad anxiously asking.

" 'Adn't I better pot the blarsted blighter?"

And Keating's disdainful reply,

"Don't bother. If she takes him home with her, he'll end up on the golden altar of Erlik. So what's the bally difference?"

OUT through a door in the side of the temple, hidden by lichen-trees, she led me. This door opened upon a quiet peaceful sunlit court. Tied to a ring in the wall was a stately white slith, saddled and bridled.

"My brothers," she said simply. And, at the memory that those words kindled in her, her blue eyes flashed fire for a moment. God, but she was beautiful in her anger!

Then her face cleared, and she smiled up at me. I clasped her in my arms, and covered her face with kisses. For several minutes, she pressed close against me; then drew bashfully away. Suddenly she whipped off her white cape, and stood revealed to me in her blouse and pantaloons. Never had I seen such beauty! Her perfect features were lit with the light of service.

"Take this cape," she softly murmured. "With it wrapped around you, and riding my brother's slith, you can make a dash for safety."

"Safety?" I cried, though my heart was in my eyes, which were devouring Esta, rather than in my words. "Safety? Never! I shall bring back reinforcements, and we shall win!"

Alarmed, she clutched my arm, and her touch thrilled me.

"No, no!" she cried. "They will kill you all. Already your men are almost overpowered. Soon they will capture all of you, kill some, and throw the others into the dungeons. Then on each holy day many of you will be sacrificed to Erlik on the golden altar. Go, before it is too late, beloved."

"Never!" I cried. "I shall return to die here with the rest, if that be our fate. But I am grateful to you. I—I love you." My gaze burned into hers.

She hid her head. I thought I heard a sob. Then she straightened, and looked me squarely in the eye.

"My beloved is brave, as becomes the chosen of the daughter of Mu-Lai," said she. "Go, then, and bring back help to your comrades if you can. And may Erlik go with you. Esta will be waiting for you."

Once more I held her girlish form close to me. Then, as the hidden door in the side of the temple opened to disgorge the four Legionnaires whom the Duke had sent to follow me, I released my darling, untied the white slith, wrapped the cape about me, vaulted into the saddle, and clattered off out of the little courtyard.

As I turned the corner at the end of the alley, I twisted about in the saddle, and glanced back. The golden-haired Martian maiden stood waving one dainty hand at me. On each side of her stood two Legionnaires with jaws dropped open in stupefied surprise.

A strange exaltation thrilled through me. I felt that I could ride down any number of heathens. I filled my lungs with glorious thin morning Martian air, and drove my spurs into the sides of my splendid white mount.

SOON I had found the main thoroughfare of the city, and was winging down it, away from the temple, and toward the big fretwork gates of the main entrance. They stood slightly ajar, for we had smashed their locks and bars with our argan logs earlier that morning. To one side squatted two white-clad Mauros, their long atomic rifles leaning against the parapet.

"Ho, Ben-Stu," one of them shouted, recognizing the white slith as belonging to Esta's brother.

"It is not he!" cried the other, leaping up and reaching for his rifle.

I snatched out my atomic pistol, and sent a blast of pure force through his head. Then reining my mount, I shot down the other. Two dead Mauros. Two less enemies to meet our depleted forces.

Dismounting, I propped the two bodies up against the wall, so that they would look like the sleepy watchmen they had been but a moment before. Then vaulting once more into the saddle, I sped out of the city to the lichen grove on the hill.

Here I found the bullet-headed Hungarian, Kuswa, and his seven hundred men, fretting with inaction, and chafing over the delay. Briefly I sketched the situation. Then, with Kuswa and me at their head, the reinforcements filed quietly out of the grove and down to the city gates. No one showed up to oppose us. The two dead Mauros sat still as though dozing on guard, as we entered the city.

No time for concealment now! With a cheer, we charged down the central street toward the black-domed Temple of Erlik at the other end. The Martian cavalry heard us, and formed and met us just short of the temple. At their head rode Mu-Lai himself, slim, hawk-nosed, white-skinned, with thin sneering lips. I spurred to meet him.

But, as the two forces crashed together, I was swept slightly to one side, so that it was Kuswa, not I, who took on this chieftain of the enemy.

I sent atomic blasts from my pistol at Mauro after Mauro, until its force-chamber was exhausted; then drew my saber and laced out at the fiendish wide-hatted faces all around me. Two javelins lanced at my neck, and I could guard against only one.

My slith foundered, pulling me down with him. I ducked, and the blades flashed harmlessly above me. Then I was up and out of the saddle, fighting on foot, slashing the bellies of sliths, cutting at legs of Mauros, dodging the thrust of javelins.

It was not long before most of the combatants on both sides were off their sliths, struggling on the rubbled pavement. And gradually the tide of battle worked its way up to the wall of the temple, and through the garden gates, and to the temple steps beyond.

Down the steps to join us came our red-haired Captain and his mere handful of survivors.

SUDDENLY I found myself facing Mu-Lai in the press. We crossed blades, his javelin and my sword, and the Mauros and Legionnaires gave way to let us fight.

At first we fenced cautiously, until finally the Martian chieftain forced me back a pace, and drew back his javelin to spear me through. Putting both hands to my saber, I swung it around my head with such force that it swept his spear from his grasp. Caught off his balance, he crashed to his knees before me. He was at my mercy. I drew back my blade to pierce the heart of this slayer of women and children, this torturer of Christian men.

But the memory of a blue-eyed gold-framed face stayed me. I lowered my point.

"Rise, father of Esta," I mumbled in Martian. "I cannot kill you."

Mu-Lai glanced up at me, with surprise and perhaps gratitude in his cruel eyes. Then something struck my head from behind, and I pitched forward into black unconsciousness.

MY return to my senses was equally black, the blackness of night. Not a star flickered above. I lay on damp stones; and around me was a musty, foetid smell.

I sat up. I stood. I groped about. Stone walls on three sides of me, hemming me in. And on the fourth side iron bars. A prison cell!

I stumbled over something soft and yielding. A human body. It groaned. Kneeling, I felt of it. It wore a military uniform, the uniform of an officer of the Legion.

"Hammersmith!" I cried. "My Captain!"

"That—you—Warren?" he thickly replied.

"Yes. What happened?"

He sat up, and clasped my hand in the black darkness.

"They got us. All of us," he said. "I was the last to go down. Well, I guess we shall grace the golden altar of Erlik together, you and I. But it was a glorious fight while it lasted. There *were* three thousand of us. Now there are just you and I."

"We can kill ourselves—or each other," I suggested, feeling for my weapons. But they had been taken from me.

A flickering light appeared in the distance. I could now see a dimly lit corridor, stone walled, stretching away from the barred door of our cell, and two white-swathed figures coming toward us, one of whom was carrying a torch.

It was my Esta! And her father, Mu-Lai, the Mauro chief!

My darling looked sweet and worried and wholly desirable. And, strange to relate, the bloodthirsty old Martian did not seem at all fierce or wicked at the moment. Perhaps it was due to some strange effect of the flickering torchlight. But, as I stood there, clutching the bars of my cell, he looked to be a courteous kindly gentleman of my own Earth.

And why not? We of the Legion of Death were regular fellows when off duty—no better, no worse, than the average run of mankind. Yet to our Martian enemies, in the heat of battle, we doubtless seemed like fiends from the hell of their dark god. And so, by the same token, the Mauros were probably quite charming in the bosom of their own homes.

These thoughts flashed through my mind, as I stood there staring out through the bars at Esta and her hawk-faced father.

Mu-Lai advanced and held out his hand.

"My dear Sir," he said in perfect English, "you are a brave fighter, and a worthy foeman. Erlik loves such as you. And so, I am informed, does my daughter." He smiled at his little joke. "Furthermore, you spared my life in the battle. So I am prepared to offer you your freedom—if you will embrace the faith of the Dark Star, and will join the desert tribe of Mu-Lai."

I glanced from his aquiline face to the pleading eyes of the girl. Why not? It seemed my only chance for life; and perhaps, if I accepted, Esta might— Perhaps the unloved Ab-Nadik had perished in the battle.

And then I thought of Bill Hammersmith, lying behind me, wounded, in the cell.

"The Chief is very kind," I replied, "and the Chief's offer is most magnanimous. Set my Captain free likewise, and I will gladly accept."

"The *other* Earthman crraat must die on the golden altar of Erlik," he snapped.

"Even if he embraces the Dark Star faith like me?" I asked.

"I wouldn't trust the infidel."

"Sir," I said, "neither the Captain nor I can ever return to the Martian Foreign Legion. We would be shot for treason. So it will be safe for you to trust us."

Esta cut in with, "Oh, my be— Oh, Sir." She was speaking English, like her father and me. "You cannot save *him*, but you can save yourself. What is the use to throwaway two lives, when one can be saved? And I *want* you saved."

"I'm sorry, dear!" I replied with sad dignity. Then, turning to her implacable father, "Captain Hammersmith and I stand together, Sir!"

FOOTSTEPS sounded in the darkness, and the rattling of a scabbard. A tall dark handsome young Mauro came forward out of the gloom. It was Ab-Nadik!

Esta's face whitened. Fear leaped into her beautiful eyes.

"Ah, father of my betrothed," said Ab-Nadik in Martian, casting a respectful glance at Mu-Lai. "I see that you are preparing to pass sentence on the last two of the Earthman crraats. But what are *you* doing in this foul place, sweet Esta?"

Mu-Lai's eyes flashed a warning at his daughter.

"She came with me, to see the infidels who have killed so many of our men. She is a fearless girl, Ab-Nadik—a worthy bride for you."

Ab-Nadik showed two rows of white teeth in a self-satisfied grin.

"Yes, my chief, she is pure and steadfast. Now that the enemy has been repulsed, Sir, perhaps we can plan for an early wedding."

"There will be no wedding!" Esta spoke clearly, calmly, though her face was pale. She reached through the bars and took my rough hand in her smooth soft one. *This* is the man I love!"

My heart pounded at her words. Yet it all seemed so hopeless now.

Mu-Lai's face clouded with anger. Ab-Nadik stared at Esta, unbelieving; then rage and hate welled into his dark molten eyes. A sneer overspread his handsome face. He whirled savagely toward Mu-Lai.

"She, the daughter of a chief, marry an unbeliever?" he gasped. "She must be mad!"

Mu-Lai jerked his daughter away from me with one sinewy hand.

"Ab-Nadik," he gritted, "I did not tell you of this, for I thought the girl had but a passing fancy for this man from another world. Then, too, he had saved my life. But he slew our men, so many of them that my heart is now hardened against him. Esta shall be yours."

"No! No!" cried my beloved. "I shall kill myself first."

Ab-Nadik grinned with malice, his burning eyes filling with hate as he glowered at me.

"Then," said he to Mu-Lai, his voice like the hiss of a desert serpent, "the crraat shall die?"

Mu-Lai nodded.

"Yes, he shall die. *Both* of the Earthman crraats shall die!"

"On the golden altar of Erlik."

Once again Mu-Lai nodded, his eyes black slits of fanatic hate.

Esta, in a frenzy, flung herself upon Ab-Nadik and pounded his chest with small clenched hands.

"Oh, I hate you," she cried brokenly. "I love him, I tell you. I love only him."

Ab-Nadik laughed harshly and drew her within his arms.

"But you shall learn to love *me*, light of my heart," he exulted, "after *he* is dead!"

The young Martian tried to kiss Esta, but she twisted her face aside.

"Come, Ab-Nadik, let us go!" Mu-Lai said sternly. "Esta, I command you!"

THEN they dragged Esta away, kicking and squirming. With tense fingers I stood gripping those bars. Oh, that I were free to fight for her, to carry her with me, far from this heathen city of a strange planet.

Ab-Nadik turned, and cast a triumphant leering glance back at me. Helpless, raging, I shook my fist at him. How I longed to get my fingers around his throat. My Esta! Would I ever see her again?

Hammersmith patted my shoulder.

"The fortunes of war, my boy," he said comfortingly. "You passed up your chance. The old chief would have saved you, had you accepted his offer. You should have seized your freedom and let me die on the altar."

"Never!" I declared. "It was freedom for *both* of us or for *neither.*"

"Bosh!" he retorted. "You're just being quixotic. I'd have butted in while you were buzzing the old buzzard, but I hoped you might get away with it. Looked like you might, till that Ab-Nadik guy showed up."

"Skip it!" I snapped.

For a while we sat in the darkness, each busy with his own thoughts. Death was close at hand. It is one matter to face death in the heat of battle; it is another to face it in the quiet calm darkness of a stinking prison cell.

I knew that Hammersmith felt the same as I. He reached over and clasped my hand warmly in the dense darkness. No fear in that clasp—only an attempt to probe what lay ahead, that which has baffled men since time began. Weak and wounded, he awaited death—unafraid.

Suddenly, I released his hand. "Look!" I whispered.

His gaze followed mine down the corridor. Someone, carrying a torch, was coming toward the dungeon.

It was Esta, alone!

In one hand she carried the torch and in the other a large brass hoop strung with heavy iron keys.

A hurried word of greeting. Then the barred door of our cell was unlocked and swung open. Esta handed the torch to the pale Hammersmith; then I clasped her slim, warm body in my arms. It was a long, long embrace, filled with pent-up emotion. I could feel the rapid beating of her heart against my breast. Was there ever such a courageous girl as she?

"How did you get away, Esta, dear?"

"I slipped out while father and Ab-Nadik held council!"

Again I embraced her.

Finally she gently pushed away from me, and said, "Hurry, beloved. There is a secret passage out of this dungeon. There are sliths, saddled and awaiting, beneath the city wall."

"How many sliths?" I asked, scarce daring to hope.

"Three," she replied, with bashful downcast eyes.

A fierce wild joy surged through me.

I straightened my shoulders and drew a deep breath.

"Lead on!" I cried.

Down the dark corridor we followed the girl, until she paused at a heavy barred door at one side, and unlocked it.

"The treasure chamber of Daloss," she whispered.

And indeed it was! The light of the torch, held high by Captain Hammersmith, disclosed unnumbered bars of solid gold piled high about the walls. Brass-bound chests, containing who knows what wealth, filled the center of the room.

"Precious jewels," said Esta, noting the direction of my gaze.

One chest stood open, overflowing with the thin gold minted slabs that pass for coinage on Mars.

"Take!" the girl commanded. "We shall need them."

But I shook my head.

"I am robbing thy father of a more precious jewel than any of these," I said. "And that is enough to have on my conscience. I am no common thief."

She sighed. Then gazed at me with blue eyes full of approval.

Suddenly she stiffened, alert with listening.

"Someone comes," she said fearfully. "If he finds the cell empty, he will try this door, knowing it to be the only possible

166

means for your escape. Unfortunately it does not lock on the inside." She unsnapped the huge key-ring from the key in the lock, and handed the key-ring to me, as she continued breathlessly.

"Quick! That other door over there, across the treasure chamber, leads to the secret passage. I will lock the door through which we entered, and hold back whoever comes, until you have time to reach the sliths."

Brushing a kiss on my forehead, she snatched the torch from Hammersmith's hand, and darted from the chamber, shutting and locking the door behind her. We two Legionnaires were in darkness—alone.

It had all happened with such stupefying swiftness, that I had had no chance to remonstrate. And now she was gone—my Esta!

I crowded my ear to the door, in an effort to learn what was going on in the corridor outside. Esta was speaking.

"Oh, my father, do not ask me."

"So, it is you! Ab-Nadik was right. You did loose the Earthmen crraats from their cell," came Mu-Lai's voice. "You, my trusted daughter, descendant of the Dark Star himself! Where are the prisoners?"

"I—I will not say, Father. I—I love him so."

"Perhaps in the treasure room," suggested the savage voice of Ab-Nadik. "If she would cheat *me* of my love, she would not be above cheating *you* of your jewels."

"Ah—could it be?" Mu-Lai snarled. "We shall see. I have a key."

I heard a scuffle, evidently Esta trying to keep her father away from the door. Then came his voice.

"Aside, girl. You have vexed me enough today. If you are a traitor—"

Hammersmith spoke in my ear. "Warren—come. They'll be inside in a minute."

I dreaded to leave Esta to the savage mercy of her angry father, yet there was no other course. Free—perhaps I could come back to rescue her. Imprisoned—I would die, unable to help her.

I STUMBLED across the room. Once I bumped against a chest—an open one, filled with the slab-like coins. My hand clasped one, and I slid it into the pocket of my blouse—as a souvenir of Daloss. I have it still, an unbelievably ancient Martian coin, solid proof to me of my adventure, when sometimes even I doubt that it could have happened.

"Here." Hammersmith reached for my hand in the darkness. "I have the door open. There's a tunnel ahead."

Hurriedly we stepped into the tunnel, as a key grated in the lock of the main door of the treasure chamber behind us. Hammersmith closed our exit and locked it.

"They will be delayed getting *that* open," he said grimly. "Now, let's move for those sliths."

Rapidly we proceeded along the dark tunnel. Esta had said it led to freedom, and we knew that she would not betray us. Sliths were awaiting us, she had said. But how could I bear to leave Daloss without her?

Finally we saw faint light far ahead. We pushed forward, and came to a small barred iron grating hidden in a gully of shrubs. The grating was locked.

"One of these keys ought to do the trick," Hammersmith said grimly, lifting the huge key-ring. "I hope those fellows got detained in the treasure room."

With fumbling nervous fingers he tried one key after the other. At last a key slipped into place, and the lock mechanism turned. The grating gave way at our touch, and we stood in the silvery starlight of a Martian mountain night.

Three sliths, saddled and bridled, and slung with food and water, were tethered behind some bushes to our right.

"The girl did not lie," breathed Hammersmith. "Here are our mounts!"

But I shook my head. A mad desire for Esta surged within my veins.

"I must go back to get her," I said bitterly. "I cannot leave her behind."

"You are right!" spoke a guttural Martian voice nearby. "You cannot leave her behind, for you yourself shall never depart from here."

A tall figure in flowing cape rushed from the bushes, brandishing a javelin.

"Infidel, you die! I suspected you would try to escape this way."

It was Ab-Nadik. The man had evidently circled back alone, while Mu-Lai was following us through the treasure room passage.

DESPERATELY, I glanced about for some weapon of defense. I saw a long lichen branch lying in the bushes near me. It was about five feet long and several inches thick.

Hammersmith, though weak from his many wounds, also saw the stick and lunged for it just as I did. Faster, however, was I; and up I came with it clenched tightly in my right hand.

Ab-Nadik loomed above me. I saw the quick flash of moonlight on his downward-thrust blade; saw beyond it the triumphant leer of the white teeth in his copper-hued face.

With one despairing effort, I swung the stick forward and upward at the shaft of his spear with all the strength in my body.

Crash! Wood hit metal shaft, and sent it hurtling away out of Ab-Nadik's hands, to fall with a rattling clangor on a nearby rock. My soft lichen stick bucked under the impact. I cast it away.

"Now, you heathen murderer," I snarled, "it's my turn to crow!"

Like two madmen we met. A sinewy fist sent stars whirling before my eyes, but I did not fall. Instead my own fist bored into his ribs.

I heard the Martian grunt. His arms flayed blows at me, but I would not yield. Again my fist shot out. This time a louder grunt.

My dazed bloodshot eyes caught a glimpse of a sagging face before me. Quickly I shot still another blow at that vision, felt knuckles sting from the impact.

I looked again, and the vision was gone.

"Come on. You knocked him cold. Let's light out before any more come."

It was Hammersmith. Vaguely I could make out his swaying form on a slith.

Stumbling through a red haze, I groped my way to one of the sliths, and somehow managed to clamber astride it.

"But what about Esta?" I groaned. "We can't desert *her.*"

"Okay, Warren. I'm with you. I'll go back and fight the whole crowd for you. I'll—"

Hammersmith slumped forward on his slith's neck. Game to the end in spite of his wounds, he had at last fainted dead away.

I could not leave him, for I owed him a loyalty higher than love. Riding close to his mount, I lifted him across my saddle, grabbed his reins, and set out for the mountain pass that led to the red sands of the great desert of Mars.

The third slith whined softly, sending a pang through my heart, for *that* beast was to have carried my Esta.

In the pass, I revived Hammersmith with water from a small skin in one of the saddlebags. Then we dashed past the Mauro sentries at the outer defile, and were on the open desert, now lit by the full glare of both moons.

THE rest of our journey across the red sands is an uncertain nightmare to me. I have a vague recollection of hiding the keys in some rocks. I remember reaching our old encampment, only to find it abandoned. Then of pushing on to the canal city of Ricca, winter quarters of the Martian forces. Our water gave out. Hammersmith died—at least, I think so. At any rate, I remember burying his body. And I slid off my slith and dropped unconscious on the desert sands, within sight of the first Martian sentry at Ricca.

Of course, I was tried for treason and desertion. They could not make the first charge stick; for, after all, the Capital City *had* ordered the attack on Daloss. Furthermore, a conviction for treason must be reported to the higher-ups, and pig-eyed old Colonel Ak-Ak was afraid of the effect of such a report. But they did convict me of desertion.

My sentence was three long Martian years in the penal labor battalion. I have five more days to serve, and then I shall be free!

Three thousand of us, I say. There were three thousand of us, who rode like mad, with sabers held high and hell in our eyes, into Daloss, the City of Lost Souls—but only one returned.

And he, as soon as he is free, will not return to the Earth, but rather will struggle back across the red desert sands of Mars to the City of Lost Souls, where—he hopes and trusts—his Esta will be waiting for him.

THE END

The Winged Peril

By ROBERT MOORE WILLIAMS

*They came in flying saucers, and Mankind seemed powerless against them
until one man decided that merciless invaders are always equipped
with an Achilles' heel.*

"BUT WHAT the hell is it?" Quarter said irritably. Wading
boots and all, old Simon Pile pulled him out of Silver Creek before
he hardly had time to wet a line, insisting that the newspaper man
come up to his log house to look at something. Even after he saw
it, Quarter wasn't quite certain what it was.

"It's a bee!" Simon Pile breathed pure rapture; his lined old face
softened and grew warm from the inner ecstasy flowing through
him as he spoke. "It's a new species never known before. I shall
name it *apis pilensis*, in honor of myself, since I discovered it. Look
at its size, see how alert it is. Although it is larger than the biggest
queen I have ever seen, it is obviously not a queen, it is a worker.
And look at the colors! Have you ever seen anything like it?"

On Pile's face, the ecstasy deepened until he was practically
beside himself with excitement. He was a beekeeper, a bee-fancier,
a bee-raiser. He went to bed at night thinking about bees, he got
up in the morning thinking about them. Quarter, who felt he was
secretly honored by being one of the very few men Pile liked and
trusted, had always had the private opinion that the old bee keeper
probably dreamed about bees during his sleep. Quarter, even if he
was annoyed at the interrupted fishing, regarded the old man with
fond tenderness.

Sitting on the box in the living room was a box made of clear
plastic. The newspaper man bent down to examine its contents.

At the sight of the bee in the box, some of his irritation went
away. The insect was—*out of this world,* the words came into his
mind. He was a little annoyed at the triteness of the expression,
but the words did provide some kind of description, if not of the
bee, at least of the feeling in him. The insect was two inches long.

Illustration by
William Llewellyn

Panic reigned as the invader moved in

It glowed with gradations of gold interspersed with rings of black. The colors seemed to be vibrating with life itself, the kind of life that some men sometimes sense, but no man really understands.

THE WINGED PERIL

By Robert Moore Williams

Quarter had the impression that the bee was exceedingly angry—at Pile and at him, possibly also at itself, for allowing itself to be caught in a plastic box.

The anger of the insect, helpless as it was, brought up a little touch of fear in the newspaperman. With the fear came the nebulous ghost of an idea—something he had read or heard somewhere, something about bees. He tried to recall what it was. It eluded him. But there was a threat connected with it, a danger of some kind.

"Where did you get it?"'

"That's my bee trap," Pile answered. "I use it to trap wild bees. I bait it with honey. When the bee lights on the honey his weight is enough to trip a trigger, and the spring lid flies shut."

"You set it to catch a honey bee, but you caught an eagle bee instead," Quarter said. He thrust his finger toward the box to see what the bee would do. The insect roused up instantly, glared at the approaching finger. Quarter grinned. "He looks as if he'd like to bite my finger off. I—" He moved the finger closer. *"Yeeeooowww!"* The sound that broke from his lips was a full-bodied scream of mortal anguish. If he had touched a hot stove, he could not have jerked his hand back faster.

HIS FIRST dazed thought was that lightning had struck his arm. He glanced hastily at it, to reassure himself that he still had an arm. Pain like a red-hot needle was gouging a groove along his nerves.

"What is it, Bill? What—what—" Pile had apparently been startled to within an inch of his wits by the sudden scream. "What happened? Are—are you hurt?"

"Your damned bee stung me!" Quarter said, massaging his arm. The pain was already diminishing markedly. It seemed more like a sudden electric shock than a sting, a jolt that comes like lightning and goes as quickly as it comes.

"But he couldn't have stung you, Bill. He's in the box."

"I don't give a damn where he is, he stung me. Do you think I scream just to exercise my vocal chords?" Quarter stared at his finger. The skin was unbroken—there was no mark, and no swelling.

"Let me see it, Bill," Pile peered at the finger through thick-lensed glasses. "But there isn't anything." He blinked fearfully up at Quarter. "Are you feeling all right, Bill? I mean—" He caught himself as if to keep from saying what he had on his mind.

The look in his eyes said the words for him. "I'm not, out of my head," Quarter said vigorously. "I don't care whether you can see anything or not, that damned bee stung me."

"But Bill, it couldn't have stung you. It's inside the box. See."

Looking down, Quarter had the impression that the bee was still glaring at them. But mixed with the glare was an expression of gloating. "I'm projecting my own thoughts on to the bee," Quarter told himself firmly. The pain in his arm was dying down to manageable proportions. "Hey, what are you doing?" Pile had thrust his finger toward the box. The bee instantly faced the approaching finger.

Pile's sudden scream was one of the most satisfying sounds that Bill Quarter had ever heard. The agitated dance the old bee-keeper did around the room also pleased the newspaper man, not because he enjoyed seeing Pile suffer, but because Pile's scream and dance were proof that the bee had stung through the plastic box. The sight relieved Quarter's fears that he *had* suddenly taken leave of his mind.

The old bee-keeper stared at the box as if a favored and trusted pet had suddenly bitten him. In a sense, this had happened. Pile was one of those rare people who are *simpatico* with bees, whom bees never sting. But this one had stung him. The expression on his face was one of acute bewilderment.

"It couldn't have stung you, Simon," Quarter said maliciously. "It's in the box." The look on the old man's face made him instantly sorry he had spoken. "Are you hurt?"

"NO, NO, it's all right." Pile rubbed his arm. Quarter had the impression that if the arm had been torn from his shoulder, Pile would have cheerfully insisted that everything was all right in preference to admitting that a bee had harmed him.

"I don't like your bee," Quarter said. "How'd you get him in here?"

"I just carried the trap in my hands."

"And he didn't sting you?"

"No."

"Then it must have taken me to rouse him up to fighting pitch." Quarter was cheerful. If it was a forced cheerfulness, he would have been one of the last to admit it. He didn't like the idea of bees with electric stingers. There was something abhorrent about it, something foreign, alien, unearthly.

But at that moment the real nature of the problem had not been brought home to him. He had seen something very interesting, a bee with an electric sting possibly somewhat similar to the shocking ability of the electric eel, but he had not seen anything really astonishing or disconcerting. And there was the matter of the interrupted fishing. He turned to the door.

"Simon, it was nice of you to call me up here to look at this—" He opened the door.

BᵣᵣᵣᵣZZZZttt!

As he opened the door, something that buzzed like an angry hornet went past Quarter's head, moving into the room. He ducked.

BᵣᵣZZZZZttt!

The second buzz went past his head.

"Bees!" Quarter yelled. As he spoke, the third bee went past his head with a sound similar to a jet supercharger warming up.

175

Quarter's first wild inclination was to cut and run. Shame kept him from it. Pile wasn't running. The bee-keeper was standing in the middle of the room turning his head in all direction as he tried to locate the bees he could hear but could not see.

Since Pile wasn't running, Quarter couldn't. Standing in the doorway, he stared goggle-eyed at what happened next. There were at least four bees in the room, maybe more. One circled the box on the table as if it were taking up a sentry position there. The other three bees lit on the table.

The three of them pointed their heads toward the plastic box. Their bodies formed a triangle, their heads pointing inward. Their actions indicated concerted, directed, conscious effort. Their wings buzzed.

A TINY filament of smoke—or was it steam?—puffed out from the side of the box. The smoke seemed to flow in a circle. Inside the box, the trapped bee got hastily out of the way.

The three bees outside the box needed only seconds to complete their task. Quarter, staring paralyzed and entranced, could not see an electric discharge flowing from them to the side of the box, but when they had finished, they had cut a circular hole in the plastic. The segment they had cut out fell away.

The bee trapped inside the box scrambled through the hole and launched itself into the air. The three bees outside the box spun upward in movement almost too fast for the eye to follow.

All of this happened in seconds. Quarter stood in the open door, too stunned to close it. Later, he wondered what might have happened to him if he had shut it.

Bzzzzzt! Bzzzzzt! Bzzzzzt! Bzzzzzt! Four bees went past his head. Then the fifth one came. *BzzzzZZZZtttt!* The last one circled Quarter's head like a miniature jet plane. In that angry buzz he seemed to sense the warning, "Watch out for yourself, Bud. I've got my eye on you."

That fifth and final bee, Quarter was willing to bet, was the one from the box, the one that had been trapped.

"B-B-Bill!" The old man looked panic-stricken. The delighted happy look was gone from his face. His expression indicated he had taken a mortal blow. "Bill, it left me, it went away from me."

The bee he had captured and had loved, as he loved all bees, had fled from him. That was what was hurting him.

Something else was hurting Quarter, something, vastly different. Fear. Plain, simple, panic-inducing, soul-destroying fear.

Quarter was as broad-minded as the owner of a weekly country newspaper ever gets to be. He tried to keep his mind open to any new fact that came along, to any theory that any man cared to express. He had absorbed the atom bomb and the flying saucers in his stride. Prior to the events of this morning, he had thought he was able to meet the devil himself, complete with horns, hoofs, and a pointed tail, and take him in his stride.

HE DISCOVERED he was mistaken. There were some things he could not take. Standing in the doorway of that neat little log house, with the bright sunshine of the early morning pouring through the door, Silver Creek rippling in the sun at the bottom of the slope, the peaks of the mountains clear in the distance, Quarter found himself covered with sweat and trembling violently as his nervous system tried to soak up the shock it had taken.

He had seen, or heard, four bees come through the door. While one took up the circling position of a sentinel, three had burned a hole in the side of a plastic trap, releasing another bee held prisoner there. How had they communicated? Some form of radio, Quarter supposed. He furiously asked himself: *What am I thinking?* They didn't communicate. They didn't burn a hole in that box. It wasn't possible. They couldn't...

His eyes came to focus on the box itself. The hole was clearly visible, the circular piece of plastic that had been cut from the box was lying on the table top.

In the few seconds it had taken for the bees to burn a hole in the box and release the prisoner, Quarter's world had turned upside down. Order had left, his established ways of thinking had been upset, the habits of a life-time had been badly disarranged.

In the back of his mind a thought was trying to come to consciousness. It was the nebulous ghost of an idea, which had something to do with bees. He tried to place it, but it faded out before he could contact it.

"We'll have to find them," Pile was saying. His eyes were on the empty box. "They're hived up somewhere near here."

"No!" Quarter said violently.

They had an argument. Quarter lost it. Deep in his heart Quarter knew that he would help Pile hunt for those bees, if the old man insisted on it. He also knew that the beekeeper would insist. Pile would climb Pike's Peak on his hands and knees if he thought there was a new and different kind of bee to be found on top of it.

During the next two weeks, Quarter left his newspaper to run itself while he and Pile searched what seemed to the newspaperman to be a hundred thousand square miles of villainous mountain country. Pile thought the bees might be found in a hollow tree. They looked for hollow trees. The bee-keeper thought they might be found in a cave. They looked for caves. They found a skunk's den and an irritated black bear and several rattlesnakes, but they didn't find any bees. Pile set bee traps by the dozens. He caught plenty of ordinary honey bees, but he didn't catch any specimens of *apis pilensis*.

All the time they were searching, Quarter prayed they would not find the bees. He kept remembering the jolt he had gotten in his arm, and he began to wonder what would happen if that blast of fire had hit his eye. Would he have gone blind?

AFTER TWO weeks, they quit looking. Quarter was very happy to forget about *apis pilensis* and to get back to his fishing. He had never seen a trout burn a hole in the side of his creel or send a jolt of electric current up his arm.

Quarter was alone when he discovered the hideout of the bees.

He was fishing Silver Creek about a mile above Pile's place, and was moving along under an overhanging bluff when he saw a bee pass through the air above him. Automatically he followed the line of flight. The bee disappeared into a small cave barely visible under the lip of the overhanging cliff. He knew from the size that it was *apis pilensis*, Pile's bee. A smart scramble upward would be needed to reach the cave, but a moderately agile climber could make it.

Quarter made a mental resolution that he wasn't going to be the agile climber who scrambled up and stuck his head in that cave. Nor was he going to tell Pile where the cave was located. The beekeeper would insist on going into the cave himself, if he knew where it was.

Bzzzzzztt! Like a miniature jet plane, a big bee went past his head, startling Quarter so badly he almost dropped his fly rod.

Zzzzzzzppppttt! It went past his head again.

The swarms had sentinels out on guard.

With three bees zipping around him, Quarter beat a hasty retreat from Silver Creek. Again he had the feeling that he was about to remember something. He got into his car and drove back to town, fast. Lurking just under the surface of his mind was—fear. He didn't know whether he was afraid of the bee—or of something else. He parked his car in front of the garage beside his home and got out.

Something moved in the air above him. He caught a glimpse of it out of the corner of his eye. A bee!

It had followed him to town!

IN THE days that followed the panicky feeling grew in fever intensity. No matter where he went or what he did, he had a bee for company. Except possibly at night, and then he wasn't sure.

They were watching him as no hawk ever watched a rabbit.

One of the worst features of the whole situation was the fact that he couldn't talk to anyone about it. This was one of the things you don't tell your best friend, not unless you want him to look pityingly at you and hastily change the subject, and when you are gone quietly call a doctor. Quarter couldn't even confirm the fact that he was being shadowed by a bee, by asking someone else if he saw the insect. Half the time he wasn't sure the bee was there himself. It was so easy for a bee to hide. A big leaf was all he needed. He could light on the trunk of a tree and keep watch without being visible.

Along about this point Quarter began to wonder if a bee was actually shadowing him, or was he hallucinating?

The thought scared him out of a week's growth.

He was sitting at his desk trying to decide whether or not he was crazy when the door opened. A park ranger entered. "Got a little story for you, Mr. Quarter, if you want to print it. We're having some trouble up in the park."

"Trouble?" Quarter got himself under control and became the owner and editor of a weekly country newspaper on the alert for a news item. "What kind of trouble?"

"Something is killing game," the ranger explained. "I've found four elk, a couple of bears, and I don't know how many deer."

At the words a slight chill passed through Quarter. "Wolves?" he ventured.

"Wolves wouldn't tackle a bear or a bull elk at this time of the year," the ranger answered. "Anyhow, if wolves had killed the game, the carcasses would show teeth marks. These carcasses don't show anything." The ranger was a big man, jovial and friendly, but he was worried now.

"Hmmm," Quarter said. "Not illegal gunners then?"

"Not a chance. The game is just dying, so far as I can tell. There are no marks of any kind. It looks like poison, but there isn't any bloating, which rules out several common poisons."

"Where's all this happening?"

"Mostly in the Silver Creek neighborhood." The ranger laughed. "I talked to old Simon Pile about it and he said the bees are doing it. What's the matter, Mr. Quarter? You sick or something?"

"Just a sudden chill," the newspaperman answered hastily. "No, no. I'm all right. Thanks a lot for the item. Maybe I'll make a story out of it."

AFTER THE ranger had left, Quarter continued sitting at his desk. The chill passed, leaving sweat behind it. Bees killing animals. Quarter knew from experience how hard it is to kill a bull elk. Unless a bullet hits a vital spot, a bull elk will carry away half his weight in lead.

Bees killing animals. What if they were just practicing on animals before they got ready to start on human beings?

Again the chill came up in Quarter, rising from the deep marrow of his bones.

Then the thought that had been trying to reach his consciousness for days popped full-blown into his mind.

In the deep depths of his soul he wished he had never remembered it.

By itself, it was a simple thing, an article he had read about the so-called flying saucers. The writer had speculated that the saucers had originated on Mars and that they were manned by intelligent creatures engaged in inspecting Earth for purposes of their own. From the speed with which the disks traveled, and the sharpness of their turns, the writer had guessed that they must be manned by insects. Certainly no creature at all like a human being could stand the acceleration, the g's, created by the turns at terrific speeds. The writer had further speculated that the insects might be super bees.

The chill that came surging up from the depths of Quarter's soul as he remembered this article he had read was like nothing he had ever experienced before.

Suppose this fantastic speculation turned out to be true! Suppose super bees had actually landed on Earth and had begun to create their own civilization here!

Suppose Simon Pile had trapped one of them.

Back into Quarter's mind came the mental picture of the plastic bee trap, with the round hole neatly burned in one side of it.

Thoughts poured through his mind. *The human animal does not have too strong a foothold on this planet. We regard ourselves as lords of creation, masters of the universe, the end product for which all creation has aimed, the intended children of destiny. We think that Earth and heaven came into existence to provide a proper stage for our entry on the scene. No doubt the dinosaur, if it thought at all, thought the same thing. It is not necessarily true that we are the end-product of creation!*

The truth may be that even as a race we have only a thin and precarious foothold on existence, that all we have made for ourselves is a beachhead in the cosmos, that the forces arrayed against us may sweep us from this beachhead at any moment. The whole human race may be an accidental intruder into the scheme of creation, a by-product instead of an end-product, an accidental con-figuration resulting from the loose-jointedness in nature that goes under the name of Planck's constant h. It may be that we have slipped through this loose-jointedness in nature and have spread ourselves upon a stage that was never intended for us, that when our presence on this stage is detected by the rightful actor who properly is to perform here, we may be swept back into the oblivion from which we have daringly crept, while the real heir of creation, the creature for whom all the vast process of nature has moved, goes on to his destiny.

THE THOUGHTS boiling through William Quarter were not pleasant. They were fearful things, products of chaos and old night. They boiled through him at fever speed, tearing and twisting and gnawing at his vitals.

Maybe the real heir is here now, Quarter thought, *waiting in the wings to put in his appearance on the stage. During the time of the dinosaurs a small furry creature squeaked in the rushes at the edges of the swamps where the dinosaurs ruled as lords of creation—a small shrew. The dinosaurs were swept from the stage and that small shrew, geological ages later, became man.*

Where is the shrew squeaking at the edges of the marshes ruled by the human race?

Is he, perhaps, an insect?

Is he, perhaps, a multicolored bee who has solved the secret of space flight and is now building up his resources, establishing his strange cities here on Earth, staying out of sight among the forests and the mountains until he has become strong enough to emerge from hiding and sweep out of existence these distorted human creatures who have been masquerading as lords of creation in the absence of the rightful heir?

The super bees, which had been a personal matter concerning only Quarter and Pile, suddenly, in the feverish mind of William Quarter, became a matter which might concern the entire race.

Rising from his desk, Quarter headed for the nearest saloon, where he had three fast drinks. They helped a little, but not enough. His thoughts were still running at fever pace when he went home. His wife, sniffing his breath, gave him the silent treatment. He went into the bedroom and lay down. There was one crumb of comfort in being in the bedroom: the super bee that was watching him couldn't get in here.

There was another crumb of comfort in the fact that although animals had died, no human death had been reported.

Maybe the bees couldn't kill humans!

Quarter felt a lot better when that idea came to him. When he got up from the bed, he was almost happy.

Something about a pane of glass in the window caught his eye. Examining it, he saw what it was.

He had to sit back down on the bed, so great was the shock.

There was a hole in the glass exactly the same as the hole he had seen burned in the side of the bee trap.

They not only had him spotted, they had burned a hole in the window so they could get at him when they wanted to.

BEFORE HE had finished dinner that evening, he had decided what he was going to try to do, what had to be done. Until night fell, he puttered around in the garage, loading the garden hose into the trunk of the car and making other preparations. Even if a bee was watching him from the peaked roof of the garage, he made no effort to conceal what he was doing. They couldn't understand everything.

He didn't drive the car out of the garage until well after dark. When he returned again, it was after midnight.

Arising very early the next morning, Quarter announced that he was going fishing. When he went outside, he searched the air above him carefully. So far as he could tell, he was not being watched. Inside the garage, he picked up a piece of lath, which he put into the seat beside him.

Old Simon was already up when Quarter stopped his car in front of the beekeeper's place. Pile came trotting down to the car, pathetically glad to see him.

"Bill, have you seen anything?" were his words of greeting.

"I caught just a glimpse of something up on Silver Creek the other day," Quarter answered with elaborate unconcern. "If you want to ride with me, I'm going to fish up there this morning—"

Pile was in the car before he could finish speaking.

In the morning mist, Silver Creek was cool, but Quarter was wet with sweat before they reached the overhanging bluff. Old Simon, in spite of everything Quarter could do to stop it, bounded along like a mountain goat. Quarter, his piece of lath ready in his hand, went more slowly.

They reached the spot from which the entrance to the cave could be seen.

The air was quiet. No bees were visible. Or none that Quarter could see.

Pile was a little disappointed at that.

Quarter went forward with new eagerness. Deep down inside of him he felt like a man who has been lost in a horrible nightmare and now is beginning to reawaken. Had he dreamed all this, he wondered. Or had it actually happened?

PILE, THE big flashlight in his hand, scrambled up to the cave entrance. It was large enough to enter by stooping. As Quarter went through the opening, he heard Pile's exclamation of surprise ahead of him.

He took a look at what the rays of the flashlight revealed, and almost stopped breathing. This was the city of the super bees all right. But it was not like any hive ever seen on Earth. The whole structure had not been stuck to the ceiling with wax, the way ordinary bees attach a comb to the top of the cave; a space had been cleared out of solid rock for it, an opening at least two square yards in size. In this opening, the city had been in the process of construction.

A city was all it could be called.

There were no buildings as humans use the term, there were no streets—bees use air lanes instead of streets—but there was a complex structure the like of which neither of the two men had ever seen. It looked like a huge doll house, only it didn't have little chairs and tables and pianos, cook stoves, radios and TV sets, with a doll family engaged in using this structure.

It had structures, spheres, cones, pyramidal-shaped objects, all fitted together into a complex unit designed to serve some function. What was it supposed to do? Quarter did not know, but he had the impression that it was a system designed to generate some kind of energy—what kind was the secret of the super bees. It was constructed of plastic, not wax, synthetics of a hundred different kinds. The builders of this city had been masters of chemical synthesis.

Pile was moaning and pointing at the floor.

Covering almost every bare spot, piled in heaps in places, their bodies dull now, their wings stiff and still, were hundreds of super bees, all dead.

At the sight, William Quarter finally succeeded in waking from the horrible nightmare that he had been living. Life suddenly surged up in him again, whole, complete, and wonderful.

"They're dead, Bill, they're all dead," Simon Pile moaned.

"Maybe they got distemper," Quarter said gently. "You know how distemper will destroy a hive almost overnight."

Quarter had to coax Pile away. Old Simon came reluctantly, moaning softly to himself. "They're all dead, Bill. Why did they have to die?"

He didn't seem to notice the strangeness of the city they had been building, and the thought never seemed to enter his mind that they might have been anything other than an unusually large and new type of bee.

They reached the outside air.

B~~~ZZZZttt!

All the super bees weren't dead. At least one of them was very much alive. He came out of nowhere, like a streak of lightning. He struck like the lightning strikes—at Simon Pile.

Pile screamed, grabbed at his eyes, threw up his hands, and collapsed at Quarter's feet.

B~~~~ZZZrrrrt!

QUARTER KNEW the bee was after him. He had thought that, these bees, like the normal bees of Earth, could sting only once, but as he heard the angry sound charge toward him, he knew he had been mistaken. These bees didn't sting; they discharged some totally different kind of energy. And they could discharge it more than once.

Quarter struck with the lath he carried, directly in front of his eyes.

He heard the splat of an insect body meeting wood.

Crushed, the bee fell.

Quarter stood there crouched, ready, waiting, wondering if another bee would follow the first. He was the picture of an embattled cave man, face to face with the unknown, frightened—but standing his ground and ready to fight.

It seemed to him that an eternity passed while he waited. No sound of an angry bee came. Either there had been only one left, or if there were others, they were not attacking.

At his feet, Simon Pile moaned. Clawing at his eyes, Simon Pile moaned as he died. He was the one man who had loved bees, and they had killed him.

Eventually Quarter picked up Pile, carried him to his car.

"Heart failure," was the doctor's diagnosis of the cause of death. When Quarter called the doctor's attention to the slightly bloodshot right eye, the symptom was passed off as a minor hemorrhage going along with the coronary failure.

Quarter knew better, but he kept his knowledge to himself. He knew definitely and surely what had killed Simon Pile. But it was not knowledge that he could hope to communicate to any man without definite proof.

DURING THE months that followed, William Quarter slowly recovered his lost poise, his badly shaken emotional balance. It isn't good to think you may be the man who has discovered the next actor in the cosmic drama that is being played here on Earth, the solar system, even the universe—discovered the creature that perhaps destiny intended to succeed after your race has gone. This kind of knowledge is not healthy for any man to carry with him. But Quarter carries it. And carries it well.

So far as he has been able to discover, no super bee has ever kept watch over him since the day he and Simon Pile discovered the dead swarm. Nor have there been any reports of dead animals in the Park.

Quarter sometimes wonders if all the bees are dead. Of course, the western country is tremendously huge, and it is possible that at many places in it such swarms are coming into existence. Maybe the human race—except for a few individuals—will never know they exist until they come down from the mountains like a plague of locusts, destroying everything before them.

But, Quarter reasons, maybe these bees from Mars—or wherever they came from—maybe they're not the creatures that destiny intended to supplant the human species. If they didn't succeed in establishing their foothold here on this planet, maybe they're not as clever as they seemed to be.

This much is certain, they were not too clever.

They didn't know the effects of cyanide gas, when pumped through a long garden hose, the nozzle of which had been silently thrust through the entrance of the cave where they had been building their city. Any gopher could have told them how that gas works. But they didn't seem to know anything about it.

Quarter sweated blood getting the nozzle of the garden hose into the cave that night, but he got the job done.

William Quarter is a little man, unprepossessing in appearance, rather modest, quiet, intelligent. He never thinks of himself as a hero, an actor in a cosmic drama. But he's the man who killed the bees.

Maybe that means we humans are tough enough, strong enough, intelligent enough, to stick around this globe we think is ours a while longer. Maybe we're not. But one thing is certain— and William Quarter is living witness to it—we are not going to leave this globe without a fight.

THE END

A Home Among the Stars

By E. K. JARVIS

This drama—bitter and deadly, yet tenderly beautiful—was played against a backdrop of icy mountains by a race returned finally to Earth from—

HARDER was still a quarter of a mile away when the converted DC-3 took off.

He didn't stop running forward. Running was purely reflex now, and behind the reflex was the grim fact that Harder's life depended on reaching the plane before the jato take-off bottles sent it racing forward across the snow on its runners and up into the cold Antarctic sky.

Harder staggered to where the plane had been. He could smell the jato in the cold air, and at once he was engulfed by a swirling backlash of Antarctic snow as dry as confetti. For a while as Harder had covered the last few hundred yards, it had looked as if circumstances, for once, were on his side. He had come on foot across twenty miles of Antarctic wilderness to the U.S. Geophysical Year base where the last converted DC-3 of the expedition waited. He had no notion how long it had taken; time ceased to exist in a world of terrible cold, fierce winds and blinding flurries of ground-snow. Then, at last, he had seen the DC-3. Mather, he knew, would be the pilot; the last pilot of the last plane before Antarctica became snowy wilderness once more; waiting changelessly for the next expedition. And the plane seemed to stand still, as if it were going to wait for Harder. But the propellers were spinning and the jato bottles emitted exhaust plumes. For one long moment the DC-3's runners were stuck fast in the snow; then in a blinding, explosive roar, all the remaining jato bottles were fired simultaneously, the two-engined plane shuddered like a stricken animal, the runners broke free and the plane roared forward swiftly and was airborne in a few seconds. It streaked out of sight.

Harder waved frantically although he knew it was useless. They would never see him in the swirling backlash of snow.

He was marooned at the bottom of the world.

He stopped waving when the plane was a small dot against the immensity of Antarctic sky. With surprising objectivity he wondered how long he could survive alone. Cold, of course, would be his problem, for although the insulated Quonset huts hadn't been disassembled, there probably was no oil for the heaters. There was plenty of food that had been left, as it always was, for the next expedition. And water was no problem with five million square miles of snow all around him. But the next expedition wasn't coming for two years—and Harder thought with a wry smile, by then he would be quite dead and as perfectly preserved in the cold dry air as the sides of beef which had been left behind.

At least if I knew why, Harder thought, walking toward the nearest of the Quonsets. The door wasn't locked; there were no marauders to lock out in Antarctica. Harder went inside but did not remove his insulated parka. The dim interior of the Quonset— Harder saw that it was Major Mather's flight headquarters—was deceptively warm. But it was warm only by comparison with the minus fifty degrees outside. A thermometer on the inside wall, the line of mercury pale in the dim light, gave Harder his death sentence. The mercury stood at five degrees above zero, and it was going down.

Harder went to the oil heater first. The fuel chamber, as he expected, was dry. He spent a fruitless half hour searching for oil, but didn't find any.

So that's it, he thought. The end of Jim Harder, meteorologist. He sat down, wondering how long it would take for him to die. The big danger, of course, was sleeping. If he went to sleep he probably would never wake up, despite the insulated parka, because the insulation of the parka was designed to keep in body heat generated by activity. A day? A week maybe, with all the food he wanted? The strangest part of it was he didn't feel very cold. But he could explain that; he was a weather expert. He didn't feel cold because the humidity stood near zero—and dry cold can be killingly deceptive.

Yet he couldn't just surrender to the inevitable it wasn't his nature to do so. He spent several thorough hours searching the six other huts in the compound. There was plenty of food as he had expected. There was absolutely no oil. There was no point in leaving behind oil, which would become as sluggish as molasses in the fierce cold.

Harder sat down in Major Mather's flight hut. He should have been exhausted from his trek, but wasn't. Restlessly, he got up and prowled around from one corner to another.

Not expecting to, he was surprised when he found Mather's log. Then he decided it wasn't so unusual after all; Mather, probably, had sensibly made a copy, deciding to leave the log here in the event that anything it contained could be of value to the members of the next weather expedition two years from now.

Idly, Harder flipped the pages. The log was typed on loose-leaf. One entry toward the end stopped him cold. He read:

"Scoby came back from the weather station on Byrd Peak today. He wasn't very lucid. Exposure had nearly got him, but Doc says he will be all right. He told a grim story, and thank God he was lucid enough to tell it so we wouldn't have to send out a search party after Jim Harder. Poor Harder died in a snowfall.

It happened just under Byrd Peak, Scoby says. A word of warning to those who come after us: these snow avalanches are pretty nearly soundless and can fall without warning from the slopes of the steeper mountains.

"Funny, if I had to name one member of this expedition who seemed damn near indestructible, it would have been Jim Harder. There was something about the man—I don't know what." Harder smiled as he read; he had not realized Major Mather was so observant. He read on: "For one thing, Harder's of that vanishing breed, a loner. According to his Form 20 card, he doesn't have any relatives. And, while he isn't anti-social, he hasn't been as close as the other men. If he had one friend down here, it was Scoby, but even Scoby more than once told the base psychologist in the routine interviews that it was difficult to find anything under the surface in Harder. Anyhow, he was killed under Byrd Mountain, buried alive by snow. He was a strange sort of fellow, and lonely—but a good man. The world needs more of his type." The last pertinent entry on that page made Harder smile grimly. It said, "Scoby was quite broken up by his death."

There was one more relevant entry—on the final page of the log book. By then the letters of Major Mather's typewriter were faint, but since it was the last entry he hadn't bothered to change the ribbon. Harder read:

"…leave in about thirty minutes. I still can't stop thinking about Jim Harder's death. At least about the circumstances. It isn't Harder that bothers me. Harder's dead, and there's nothing more you can do for a dead man. It's Scoby. Harder's death affected him strangely. Scoby doesn't remember. Oh, it would be understandable enough if Scoby merely forgot the incidents of Harder's death, for Scoby, so he told us when he first came back, very nearly died out there himself.

"But—Scoby has forgotten Harder completely! It's as if, as far as Scoby's concerned, Harder never existed at all. He remembers taking a dogsled out to the weather station near Byrd, but he thinks he went alone. I asked him about Harder, and he said, 'Harder? Who is Harder?' I didn't press it. When we reach Tierra del Fuego, though, I'm going to ask the psychologist to have a look at Scoby. Poor guy, he must have some kind of repressed guilt feelings, or whatever terms the headshrinkers use. But of course neither Scoby nor anyone in the world could have helped Harder in a snow avalanche. The DC-3…"

Harder closed the book. His fingers were numb with cold. His smile was bleak; so that was Scoby's story, and, conveniently, Scoby had forgotten it.

What, actually, had been Scoby's motives? Harder couldn't answer that question, and since his life was already forfeit, the answer hardly mattered. If he had to guess, though, he would have said that Scoby just didn't have any motives. As Mather had written, Harder was a loner, the last of a dying breed. He liked Scoby as well as he liked any man, but he had never formed any close alliances. He was too busy searching.

Searching—all his life. He never knew for what. But he was restless, he couldn't remain long in one place, he wasn't happy unless he was constantly on the move and, instinctively, as soon as he reached a place he knew this wasn't the nameless thing he had been seeking. The searching, which dominated Harder's life and which finally had killed him because it had brought him down to Antarctica on the geophysical expedition and now he must surely die, was compulsive. If he had a specific goal it was in his unconscious mind, he had never been able to ferret it out. Yet he had had to go on. Looking, looking.

But Scoby's story amazed him as much as Scoby's behavior, for it hadn't happened that way at all—

But they had cleaned out the small weather station near Byrd without too much trouble. Scoby, a young New Englander, had seemed cheerful enough. It was hard to tell in the cold, for faces were reduced to eye-slits and breathing holes, but at least Scoby hadn't seemed sullen. Nor, certainly, had he reason for a grudge against Harder. It had all happened utterly without motivation.

"About finished, huh?" Scoby had said cheerfully inside the small weather-hut.

"Just about," Harder had replied. "Think the dogs're hungry?"

"Brother, aren't they always?"

"Okay. You check the gear on the sled, Scoby, and I'll go feed Fido."

Feeding Fido, as Harder had termed it, was a job. The frozen cakes of dog food that the huskies ate, for one thing, had a rotten-fish smell, which became apparent as soon as the cakes began to thaw. Also, Fido—a collective term standing for the team of fierce huskies that pulled their sled—could be mighty unpredictable during feeding.

Harder finished the job and went back to find Scoby, who had been busy at the unharnessed sled. The sled was packed and ready to go—but Scoby wasn't there.

Harder frowned. "Scoby?" he called. "Hey, Scoby, where are you?"

Then, instinctively, he looked up. He saw the ice-gleaming buttress of Byrd Mountain, the vane atop the small weather station, the dazzling white expanse of snow—and a shadow.

The shadow stretched out along the snow with the low slanting rays of the sun—this was the beginning of Antarctica's six month long summer, for the weather expedition had been a winter one—and then the shadow moved. Harder whirled and saw Scoby.

But he did not whirl fast enough.

If he lived another fifty years, which certainly didn't seem likely, he would never forget the look on Scoby's face. Almost, he wished it had been a look of hatred or malice. But it wasn't. There was a dreamlike look on Scoby's face, the vague, troubled, but not unhappy stare of the sleepwalker.

Then Scoby struck with the locking bar of the weather station door. The door was locked because it was exposed to ninety-mile-an-hour winds; the bar was ten inches of hard black steel.

For Harder the world exploded with the dazzling whiteness of eons of Antarctic snow.

When he regained consciousness, Scoby was with him. They were inside the small weather hut, and Harder was bound hand and foot. Scoby still looked dreamily happy.

"What the hell kind of crazy stunt was that?" Harder roared, straining at his bonds.

"I'm really sorry, Harder. It wasn't my idea."

"No? Then just who the hell's was it?"

"I don't know," Scoby said promptly and almost cheerfully.

"You're going to leave me here?"

"You'll be all right. You ought to be able to free yourself of those ropes in a few hours. But by the time you walk back to the base, we'll all be gone."

"You've gone Arctic-batty," Harder said. The snow and the isolation, he knew, could actually destroy a man's mind. But the expedition's psychologist, in his weekly checkups, was supposed to find and eliminate weak spots...

"Oh, no," Scoby contradicted him coolly, as if leaving Harder bound and helpless near Byrd Mountain didn't matter. "I'm not crazy. It isn't me doing this, you see. I've been ordered."

"Who by?" Harder asked sarcastically. "Major Mather?"

Scoby hadn't answered him. He got up, zipped his parka, and opened the door. The winds howled. "Well, this is goodbye, then," he said, extending his mittened hand as if he were going for a short vacation trip, and then withdrawing it stiffly, almost with embarrassment.

"At least tell me why," Harder had urged.

"It's—it's orders. I don't know why."

"Whose orders?"

"I don't know whose orders."

"Nor why?"

"No, nor why."

"Scoby, I feel sorry for you. You're sick."

"No. I'm not sick. I'm under order. I know that much."

Then the door had closed and faintly Harder heard Scoby giving his orders to the dog team. After that the Antarctic silence closed in. Except for the keening of the wind, there was nothing.

It took Harder six hours to release himself, and another hour to restore the circulation to his arms and legs. Then he started out in Scoby's tracks...

To arrive moments too late at the base, in time to see the final plane take off without him.

Now, in Major Mather's hut, Harder smiled bleakly. He was thirty-one years old, healthy, and strong, and he enjoyed life although—or perhaps *because*—his had been a strange one.

He had packed a great deal of living into his thirty-one years. He was an orphan and had absolutely no relatives that he knew of. He had never formed any attachments that could keep him from his strange quest—strange because although he was compelled to search, knew that the search, somehow, was the meaning of his life, he never knew what he was searching for. He knew this, though—when he found it, whatever it was, he would know. He would know.

For a moment he thought of Scoby. In a way, Scoby leaving him to die had been like that. Scoby had no motive, yet Scoby had acted from some strange inner-compulsion. Like the compulsion that had been driving Harder all his life...

194

He remembered it all now, as if this were the moment before death. World War II. The beaches at Guadalcanal. The Japanese prison camp. Then, after the war, the back pay he had put into a secondhand sloop and the months of labor which had made it seaworthy and the years spent in the South Seas, exploring, beachcombing, searching...Papeete, Santa Ana, Tahiti, Mau, New Caledonia, the tawny bare girls on glistening coral beaches, the whisper of the wind through palms, the incredibly clear tropic nights, the stars, the brief languid times which always preceded a renewal of the strange search...

And then Korea. He had volunteered, of course, almost as if the thing he had been searching for was death. But death didn't claim him and the war, like all wars, had ended.

Harder's quest hadn't. After Korea, he had wandered around the Orient. A year in Hong Kong and Macao, another in Japan, then finally the unexpected decision that it was time he settled down, at least to some kind of profession. For some reason he couldn't fathom, he had selected meteorology.

And once, six months ago, the reason had seemed clear. It had excited him. Meteorology was one of the few professions that could get him down to Antarctica. He might wander the world over and never see Antarctica otherwise; it was as if the lifelong search, incredibly, had been leading him there. He'd been assigned by the Government Weather Service to the Geophysical expedition, and for the first time in his strange life he had really been excited, thinking—and not knowing why—that the long, so far fruitless search would end at the bottom of the world.

But the six months with the expedition had been a fiasco. Antarctica was snow, cold, endless night, endless waiting. It had been, Harder admitted ruefully to himself, a mistake. He had been angry with himself, too. The long endless wait in Antarctica, the enforced inactivity for weeks on end, with only occasional jobs to do, had left him with too much time for thinking. His search, he decided, was an unconscious ruse; he wasn't searching for anything. He had spent his years seeing the world—and avoiding life. The search had ended in Antarctica, all right, and Harder thought he at last knew why he'd never been able to glimpse the goal. Why he couldn't even come close.

Because, ironically, there wasn't any. Harder had been avoiding responsibility, and that was all.

Now he thought: or was it? What about Scoby? Wasn't Scoby's motiveless action part of a bigger picture? Especially since Scoby really seemed to have forgotten, as if not an inside but an outside power had commanded him to do what he had done to make sure Harder remained in Antarctica...

But that was nonsense. Harder was going to die, and nothing he could do would change that. If the quest had been, anti-climatically, a quest for death, wasn't this the long way around?

Harder slept.

When he awoke, it was too numbing cold and the realization that sleep should have meant death, but hadn't.

The door was open.

Outside, the wind howled.

Harder didn't feel cold.

And he wasn't alone.

The thing was a glowing, radiant cone as tall as a man. Harder felt the hackles on the back of his neck rising in atavistic fear, as if knowledge of the radiant cone existed in racial memory.

A voice told him: "You have nothing to fear."

Harder didn't believe it. The cone glowed and waited. Patiently?

Harder made a break for the door.

The glowing cone didn't try to stop him. The door slammed behind him and the wind swept him along. He had never felt such unreasoning fear before; he even got the notion that the fear, like Scoby's strange attack on him, was directed from outside. But that didn't stop him from running.

He stumbled in the snow. There was no place to go, really, and certainly no place to hide. He looked back. He hadn't heard the door of Major Mather's hut opening, but the glowing cone was outside now, looking like gold against the white background. Harder got up, breathing hard, and kept running.

He stopped in his tracks. The glowing cone was now in front of him. He turned, doubling back, but the wind on the high Antarctic plateau suddenly swept down at him, and it was like running on a treadmill.

"Stop!" the voice called. Harder assumed—somehow—that it was the voice of the glowing cone. "You can't get away from me. I wanted to prove that. Actually, you don't want to try."

Harder's lungs were on fire—he couldn't run any more. He stopped, panting, reeling in the wind, and with a sudden odd detachment, wondering where the fear came from. It wasn't like him at all. His life had been spent searching out new things, so unreasoning fear wasn't part of his makeup.

"Is this better?" the glowing cone said.

Even as Harder stared at it, the cone was transformed into a parka-clad man. The man had no face that Harder could see, or perhaps the wind-whipped snow hid his face from view. But whatever the reason, fear drained from Harder with the transformation.

"Come. It isn't far."

"Where are we going?"

"Come. I will explain later."

"Who—what are you?"

"Come, I serve you. I only serve."

A rope was produced, and climbing equipment. The wind died down, as if the glowing cone—now a man—could control it.

Harder suddenly was aware of an ice-ax in his hand. He moved forward, and felt the tug of the stranger's weight behind him.

He could not understand what happened next. The Geophysical base had been constructed on the broad mid-Antarctic plateau. The only nearby mountain was Byrd, yet almost at once they began to climb. The going should have been difficult, but was not. Harder chopped foot-holds in the ice with his ax. They climbed rapidly.

The whiteness dissolved.

Cresting a rampart of ice, Harder saw a valley—green, humid, with mists rising from it. He had read about such things—the mysterious warm valleys in the Antarctic. No one could explain them. They were like oases in a desert, and the best theory was that hot springs kept them warm and humid.

In the center of the valley was a round globe as big as a house. Nearby, water trickled. Above the freezing point? It seemed likely. Harder began to sweat, and unzipped his parka.

"Wait," the other man on the rope said.

"What is it?"

"Wait. I can tell you now."

"Did you make Scoby do what he did?" Harder guessed.

"I had to. It was the only way I could be sure you'd stay."

"What for?"

"Because you've finished your work. Because you're going home."

"Home?"

"But there's something we have to do. Another has been— waiting. Come."

With reluctance, Harder left the warm valley of the mists.

They climbed again through a defile in the snowy mountains. Harder, in the lead, rounded a bluff of ice. And saw a vision.

No, it wasn't a vision. It was real. It was there. Harder ran forward.

Trapped in a block of transparent ice was a girl. Her eyes were open and she watched Harder as he approached. She was quite the most beautiful girl he had ever seen, and there was a serenely patient expression on her face, as if she had been waiting for him all his life and would have, if necessary, gone on waiting indefinitely.

In a frenzy, Harder began to hack at the block of ice with his ax. Ice chips flew, blinding him. Behind him he heard laughter. "She—she'll suffocate in there!" he protested.

"Really? Look at her clothing."

Harder looked. The lovely girl wore a gown that might have swept across the marble floor of a dancehall in Victorian times.

"She—"

"She's been there eighty years. We've been waiting for you. Can you control the fear this time?"

"What do you mean?"

"I'm going to turn into the cone of light again. The fear isn't your fault, you see. Although this was the most deserted spot on Earth, we didn't want anyone coming near it, finding us—or the ship. Well?"

"I'll try."

The man faded. The cone appeared, and Harder's hackles rose. With an effort he forced himself to stand still. Then he stepped back as the radiant cone bore down on the block of ice. The cone hit it apex first, and streams of water gushed away. The block of ice dissolved.

Almost, Harder acted too late. He didn't realize the radiant cone's mistake until the damage had been done. The block of ice split, the girl started to fall—where there had been solid ice there now was an abyss hundreds of feet deep beneath her feet.

Harder dove after her, at the same time seeking solid ice with his ax. The ax caught and held, but the torrents of water rushed over it and it would not hold for very long. With his free hand Harder caught the girl's arm before she could be swept down into the abyss. His own arm was wrenched almost from his socket. The ice ax slipped. The girl looked up at him with mute fear and hope mingled in her expression. This was no game the radiant cone was playing; the girl's life depended on what Harder did.

Slowly he raised his arm. If he moved it too quickly, he might lose his hold on the girl. If he was too slow, his ice ax might not hold. Yet as he looked down at her he knew wordlessly, as if time stood still and a music like the music of the spheres sang the message to him, that this girl was a part—a very large part—of what he had been searching for.

He felt his hand slipping, but the look of fear and hope on the girl's face had been replaced by one of trust—and love.

With his last remaining strength, Harder pulled her to safety. By then the radiant cone was a man again, and was waiting with his climbing rope to take them both to the valley of the mists.

There were others inside the round structure. It might have been, Harder thought with wonder, a fancy dress ball. For the people within the globe seemed to be wearing costumes from all the ages of human civilization. He saw a Greek wearing tunic and mantle; a beardless Roman in a toga; a glowering, fierce-bearded ancient Briton in blue paint; Islanders in almost nothing; Renaissance Italians in tight hose and fancy jackets and plumed hats; the whole gamut of human civilization.

The girl held his hand and smiled up at him. "You saved my life," she said.

His mouth was dry. His tongue felt swollen. "All my life I've been searching for—"

"This place. You found it. It is inevitable that you did. It was your mission, as it was all of ours."

"Who are you?"

She was still smiling. "Well, I am Marie and I am a lady of the Emperor's court in Vienna. I—disappeared—on an Alpine excursion in 1877. Or, if you prefer—"

"But who are you?"

The girl merely said, "We are going home."

The radiant cone entered the metal structure behind them. It floated to a bank of machinery on the far wall. None of the others seemed afraid. It touched the machinery, merged with it—and disappeared.

"It won't return," the girl said. "It had no sentience of its own. It was a robot—to help us find the way."

"But why?"

"I told you. We are going home."

"We...don't belong here?"

"No. Haven't you guessed what this structure is?"

"No. Tell me."

"We came—a long time ago. We each lived a life. We searched—and we will remember."

"What were we looking for?"

"Nothing. Or perhaps everything. There's a long journey ahead of us. You can get the details later. We came a long time ago, I said. We are human—as the inhabitants of this planet, this Earth, are human. An age ago, we planted them here. As we planted colonies—everywhere. We came to study them. Through the ages, we studied. That's why you seemed to be searching for something, always searching. So that you would get to see, and know, and later understand, so much of your world, your century. When we return home, when all our information is tabulated, considered, studied—an answer will be found."

"What answer, Marie? What answer?"

"We are a peaceful people. For some reason we can't fathom, the colonists on all the outworlds are not peaceful. They want war. They kill each other. When their science permits them to reach space—in the case of this planet, in another fifteen or twenty years—they must either seek the ways of peace, or they will bring the holocaust of war with them. It is hoped that with what we have found the mistake will be remedied, the error found, and one day soon one of us will return with the answer this world needs, the answer, inherent in its own qualities, that will bring it eternal peace. When that answer is found one of us will return with it."

"Who? Who will return?" But strangely, Harder already knew the answer.

"The only one who can. The one who knows this final century. You will return with it. But first, the trip home."

"Then, is it home for me? And where is it?"

"It is a world you never heard of. It is home for you, yes. But so is this Earth. You belong to this world too."

"When will I comeback?"

Her fingers returned the pressure of his hand. "No," she said softly. "Not alone."

There was a throbbing roar. With them and all the others from all the generations in it, all the searchers, the spaceship blasted off and sped toward its destination.

THE END

The Metal Martyr

By HENRY SLESAR

*Here was the strangest emergency operation ever performed in deep space.
It required the hand of a master surgeon, and in order to forestall disaster, the
patient had to die!*

ONCE *they named it Poseidon. Now, the planet spun like a black cinder
in the cosmos, and the colonists of the New World system wryly dubbed it
Ashes. It was a dead world, murdered by a wrathful god with a weapon called
cobalt. But now and then, Life flickered; faintly, feebly. And one day a voice
sounded in the radar-phones of the planet Quicksilver, calling pitifully for help.*

"Come kill me. Please, come kill me!"

The Space Ambulance was busy.

The internes, in their cool white smocks, moved briskly around
the loading platform. They snapped orders at the corpsmen
bearing the stretcher cases. They offered pat words of sympathy to
tearful relatives. They ministered briefly to critical patients,
assuaging their fears of what acceleration might do to their
overworked hearts, their broken bones, their tortured lungs.

"You—corpsman!"

The interne's hand fell on Russ Fairchild's shoulder. The
corpsman shrugged it off, trying to conceal his vexation.

"Check the g-straps in Section 3," said the interne, com-
mandingly. "And don't miss any!"

"Yes, sir!"

Fairchild strode off and went into the spaceship. At the
doorway, he almost collided with Wetzel. The other corpsman
gave him a rueful grin and jerked his head back in the direction of
the interior.

"Full house," he said. "Thirty pieces of meat already. One
patient more and we'll have to double 'em up."

"Then start doubling," said Fairchild curtly. "Control just told us to hold up for another victim."

Wetzel leered. "Well, there is a redhead in Section 3 I wouldn't mind doubling with. Take a look when you go in."

"I'm checking g-straps," said Fairchild. He brushed by Wetzel, who gave him a mock salute and stepped out on the platform.

Inside the ship, an old man with a bandaged rib cage reached out for Fairchild with a withered arm and stopped him in his path.

"Doctor," he said weakly, "Doctor, can I talk to you?"

Fairchild looked down at the wrinkled hand that clutched his gray sleeve. He noted the bulging veins, and the green discoloration of the fingernails. "Silicontoxis," he thought. "Green Fever," It was the fungoid killer of the planet Quicksilver.

He pushed the hand away. "Sorry," he said tersely. "I'm not a doctor. I'm a corpsman. Ask one of the men in white."

"It's the pain—" the old man gasped.

Fairchild hesitated. "Where does it hurt?" he asked.

The old man groaned and clutched his bandaged ribs. "In here! Bad. Can't you do something?"

Fairchild looked around him, then he put his strong brown fingers on the old man's ribs. With professional deftness, he examined the bandages.

"These are not tight enough," he said. "I'll get an interne to fix you up. Lie back and take it easy."

With a sigh, the old man relaxed. "All right, doctor," he said. "Thank you."

"I'm not a doctor!" Fairchild snapped. He grabbed a fold of his gray uniform and tugged. "See?" he said. "Gray. Gray!" But the old man had already closed his eyes.

The corpsman continued on his way. A young interne was reading fever charts in Section 3 when he got there, and Fairchild interrupted him.

"Silicontoxis in Section 1," he said. "Bandages coming loose. Maybe you can fix him up on your way back."

The interne looked up. "Russ!" he said. "I didn't know you were aboard." He looked embarrassed.

"Where else would I go? Fix him up, will you, Paul? The old man's in a lot of pain. I would have done it myself, but you know the rules—"

The young face flushed. "Sure, of course. I'll see him. Listen, Russ—"

"What?"

"I just wanted to tell you—"

"Tell me what?" said the corpsman. "How sorry you are?"

"Something like that." The interne swallowed hard. "Anyway, I'm glad you're aboard. Even if—"

"Even if I'm wearing gray instead of white," Fairchild finished, "I know."

"It was a tough operation. I don't think I could have done better, Russ. It was just the breaks."

"Save it, Paul." Fairchild touched him on the back familiarly. "You've got work to do, and so have I, Doctor," he added.

He walked off stiffly.

"Corpsman!"

It was a woman's voice, the kind that evoked a sultry image. Fairchild turned towards it, and remembered what Wetzel had said. Wetzel was a vulgar clod, but his appraisals of women were often reliable.

Her red hair was spilled on the pillow like a burst of flame. Her lips were equally fiery, and they were parted now in a smile that was much too seductive for an Ambulance patient.

"Corpsman, could I get something to drink?"

Fairchild's face relaxed for the first time that day. "I'll send a nurse around, Miss. I've got things to do."

"Can't it wait?" The woman stretched out a well-molded arm. "I thought the patients always came first." Her smugness was a bit annoying.

"They do." Without thinking, Fairchild picked up the chart at the end of her cot and examined it. Her temperature was on a normal plateau. The bottom sheet described her condition as "fatigue." He looked at her curiously.

"How do you feel?" he asked.

"Awful," she said. "I'm a complete wreck."

The corpsman looked at the first page again. The name read: ALLINGHAM, DEE. He hooked the chart back on the cot.

"Lie back and rest," he told her. "You'll get your water in a little while. We'll be blasting away in fifteen minutes."

"What's all the delay?" Her eyes met his, and said a few things. Fairchild looked away.

"Another patient coming," he said. "Be here any minute."

"How long will it take to get to Home?"

"Six, seven days," He started to go, but something compelled him to linger by the girl's bedside. He told himself that it was medical curiosity, and to justify it, he reached across the blanket and took her pulse. Her wrist was cool.

"How'm I doing?" she asked coyly.

"Fairchild!"

The corpsman dropped the wrist and wheeled around. A tall man with iron-gray hair, wearing a military uniform, was standing behind him. His face was leathered, and so deeply scarred around the mouth and brow that he seemed to be wearing a perpetual frown. But now, Captain Ball of the Ambulance was grimacing as well.

"What do you think you're doing?"

Fairchild straightened his back. "Nothing, sir," he said. "Taking a pulse."

"Maybe that was nothing last year," said the captain. "You know different now, don't you?"

"Yes, sir!"

"You know what corpsman duties are?"

"I do, sir."

"Then stick to them!" The captain looked stormily at the pretty girl. "Sorry, Miss Allingham," he said. "If you require medical attention, call the interne." He glared at Fairchild. "Since you don't seem to be busy," he said, "you can go up forward and help Wetzel. He's bringing in the last patient."

"Sir, I was supposed to check the g-straps—"

"Then why haven't you?" said the captain.

Fairchild's face darkened. "I was just about to."

"Do it on your way back, corpsman." The captain turned on his heel. "But bring that patient in first."

"Yes, sir."

Wetzel said, "Wait 'til you see this one!"

Fairchild, about to lift his end of the stretcher, paused. He looked more closely at the unconscious figure.

"Android!" he said.

"Now we're a bunch of mechanics," said Wetzel cheerfully. "Pretty soon we'll be ferrying sick computers and broken rockets."

Fairchild studied the placid, smooth-planed face in wonderment. It was blank, expressionless, without benefit of the color that pumping blood gave to the human countenance. He winced slightly, then he picked up the stretcher handles.

"That's not the whole story, either," said Wetzel. "Wait 'til you see his chart. I sneaked a look on the loading platform."

"What ails him?"

"I dunno." Wetzel grunted as they moved through the ship's narrow passageway. "But I know where he comes from. Guess."

"Let's not play games, Wetzel."

"Okay, professor!" Wetzel's tone was light, but there was a barbed edge. "Find out for yourself."

But as they entered Section 3 of the Space Ambulance, Wetzel couldn't keep the secret any longer.

"He's from Ashes!" he announced.

"What?"

"So help me. Says so on the chart. 'Patient removed from planet Poseidon in state of shock.'"

They strapped the android in the one remaining cot of Section 3, only two beds away from the red-headed "fatigue" case. Wetzel nudged the other corpsman when he spotted her.

"Did you see her?" he whispered. "How about that?"

Fairchild shrugged. "Very nice," he said dryly. "She's Dee Allingham. Mean anything to you?"

"Depends. That babe could mean *plenty* to me." He chuckled lasciviously.

"Allingham's a big man on Quicksilver. Head of a mining company."

Wetzel grinned. "Well," he said, "my Pop used to tell me, 'Leo, it's just as easy to love a rich girl as a poor girl.' " But he didn't say "love." "Listen to Pop I say!"

Fairchild tugged at the g-strap that secured the android into position. As the buckle tightened around the synthetic man's chest, he suddenly groaned and stirred. The perfectly-shaped head rolled from side to side, and the modeled lips parted.

"Our boy's moving," said Wetzel.

"I think he's trying to say something." Fairchild leaned over him.

"Corpsman!"

It was the girl again. Wetzel came to attention when she spoke, and dug Fairchild's side with his elbow. "Hey," he said. "Miss Millions wants us."

The other didn't budge. "Probably wants a cocktail," he said acidly. "You handle it."

"With pleasure!" Wetzel moved off rapidly.

The android had become still. Fairchild put his hand on its chest and then drew it away with something like squeamishness. There was no heartbeat; only the unpleasant murmur of some internal apparatus.

Then the android opened its eyes.

"Kill me," he said, staring at the corpsman. "Please. Please! KILL ME!"

The blast-off horn moaned throughout the ship. Captain Ball saluted the young interne, and gave his hand one peremptory shake. The two corpsmen and three nurses stood at attention as the leathery-faced man gave them final inspection. Finally he was satisfied, and went forward to the pilot's cabin.

The journey was under way.

Ten minutes after blast-off, the young interne made a hurried accounting of the effects of the acceleration on his passengers.

Three of them were short of breath, and needed an oxygen booster.

Two of them were bleeding badly from the nose, mouth, and ears.

One of them, an old man in Section 1, had been spared the misery of lingering silicontoxis. He was dead.

The crew had survived the blast without ill effects. But Wetzel still had a complaint.

"It makes me sick," he said to Fairchild. "Wet-nursing a machine! Now, I get a better idea. Maybe that little redhead in 3 could use a nice sponge-bath. That would be my idea of service."

"Sure," sneered Fairchild. "She's real sick. 'Fatigue.'"

"Oh, I know the poop on that," said the other confidentially. "Seems she wants to get to Home in the worst way. But the next spacer out of Quicksilver doesn't leave for at least two weeks."

"What?" said Fairchild, unbelievingly.

"It's straight," Wetzel assured him. "So she pulls the big sick act, and gets a berth on the Ambulance. Pretty clever, huh?"

Fairchild frowned. "Yeah. Clever, like robbing orphans. Doesn't that spoiled bitch know that beds are precious?"

"Come off it, professor! We had the room. We even had room enough for an android, didn't we?"

"But if we didn't," insisted Fairchild, "she'd have got on board anyway. Her old man could pull enough strings."

Wetzel stood up from the coffee-room table. His flush, red-cheeked face was set in displeasure.

"Still got stars in your eyes, huh, professor? Good, clean-living boy, huh? You weren't so clean when you got a face full of floating blood, were you? I'll bet you were a mess then!"

"Can it, Wetzel!"

Wetzel grinned humorlessly. "Sore spot, huh, Russ? You were gonna be a big-shot surgeon. But you couldn't handle a little zero-g operation, could you?"

Fairchild got up angrily, his hands clenched in two hard fists. "I said can it!" he shouted.

"You scare me!" Wetzel jeered. "You frighten me to death! I heard about you, professor. One little incision and you lost your head. Blubbered like a damn kid!"

Fairchild reached across and seized Wetzel's tunic by the chest. He shoved the corpsman backwards.

"Go on!" said Wetzel. "Take a poke! Let me have it, doc! I'm only a lousy corpsman remember? I got no right to push *you* around!"

Fairchild shook with his rage. Then he made a growling noise in his throat and let go. Wetzel brushed off his uniform, and grinned widely. He watched Fairchild re-seat himself and wrap his hands around a mug of coffee, staring into the black depths.

"That's it," said Wetzel. "Save your strength, professor. How long will it take to get another chance? Two years? Three? You got a lot of studying to do."

Fairchild wouldn't answer. Then Wetzel's good humor seemed to be restored. He clapped his hand on the other's back.

"Ah what the hell," he said. "No good us bein' at each other's throats. What do you say, Russ? Pals?"

Fairchild looked up at him blankly, "Okay, Wetzel. Let's forget it." But he didn't shake hands.

"Hi, doc!"

Fairchild looked around. Dee Allingham was standing at the foot of her cot, clutching the rail to keep from floating off.

"What are you doing?" he said. "Why are you out of bed?"

She smiled. "I got tired of staying in bed. And besides—I can't just lie here and listen to that—that Thing over there."

Fairchild looked in the direction of her eyes. The android was lying on his back, eyes opened.

"What's he been saying?"

"You know what. Same old business. He wants to die."

"You better get back to bed."

She ignored his admonition. "What's wrong with him, anyway? What kind of android do they make on Ashes?"

"How did you know about Ashes?" Fairchild said sharply. Then he realized that Wetzel must have been talking. "We don't know much about it," he told her. "They built their robots and androids for military purposes. The population was small."

"But fierce," said the girl, her eyes glowing. "Fierce and brave."

Fairchild felt disgust for the look of excitement on her face. "They were throwbacks," he said. "Hot-headed belligerents. They weren't smart enough or strong enough to make a peaceful existence, so they blew up their whole world."

"But they were *alive,*" said Dee. "You have to admit that!"

"And now they're dead," Fairchild replied abruptly. "All that's left are poor helpless things like that—" He gestured towards the synthetic man.

"Kill me!" it moaned.

"Why don't you *do* something for it? Why don't you put it out of its misery?"

"That's not my job. We'll let the Home doctors do it. And besides—*hey!*" He cried out as the girl suddenly vaulted herself away from the cot and drifted rapidly towards him with weightless speed.

"Catch me, corpsman!" she said.

Fairchild had no choice. His arms reached out and caught her in mid-flight, around her trim waist. She laughed loudly as he held her.

"You damned fool!" he said.

"Good catch, doc! Don't let me go!"

"Where do you think you are—?"

She giggled. "Don't you like it?"

Viciously, he carried her back to the cot and put her down. He fumbled with the g-strap, trying to hold her squirming figure on the cot.

"Kill me! Kill me!" said the android loudly.

At the sound of his flat, metallic, mournful voice, the girl ceased her struggling. She lay quietly as the corpsman completed the strapping job. Fairchild looked flustered, but she was no longer enjoying his confusion. "Behave yourself!" he said. "Quit acting like a spoiled child."

"Why can't you do something about that damned thing?" she said. "'Kill me! Kill me! It's driving, me crazy!"

"He has more right to be here than you do, Miss Allingham."

She pouted. "You're pretty high-and-mighty for a man who—" She stopped.

"Yes?" said Fairchild.

"Oh, nothing. Go away, corpsman." She turned her head to the wall. "You bore me to death."

"Kill me!" said the android.

On the fourth day in space, Fairchild got to know his passengers better.

There were two space-tug pilots, both with collapsed lungs resulting from a meteor strike on their ship.

There was a case of space blindness, and a sad one, because the victim was a child of nine.

There were three cases of Mott's Disease, the strange, strangling illness that the colonists had to fight on every planet in the New World system.

There were half a dozen radiation cases.

The rest were assorted, including old standby aliments that the settlers couldn't seem to leave behind them on Earth.

But as it turned out, the deadliest disease aboard wasn't even listed in standard pathological textbooks. It was the same pernicious disease that had plagued mankind since the first selfish act took place in the Garden of Eden.

"What do you think of our android?"

Paul, the young interne, sat back on his bunk and put a cold pipe between his teeth. Fairchild, who had reluctantly accepted the invitation to the interne's quarters, considered the question. All was quiet for a moment.

"I've got one theory," he said tentatively. "But no proof."

"What is it?"

"I don't think he wants to die out of pure misery."

The interne, thwarted by the No Smoking rule aboard the Ambulance, sucked on his empty pipe. "How do you mean, Russ?"

"I mean this. I think our android friend wants to die because he has to. I think he was *built* for suicide."

Paul shivered. "That's a horrible thought."

"Remember," the corpsman said. "The people on Ashes built androids for war. They were creating soldiers, to spare them from bloodshed."

"Yes, but android soldiers would *accept* death. They wouldn't *seek* it. That would be wasteful."

"Of course," Fairchild agreed. "But I think they resorted to building special-purpose androids, designed to do nothing but kill themselves for the cause."

"Like the Kamikazes of World War Two—"

"Exactly. Resembling humans as much as they do, these suicidal androids could infiltrate a position and then knock themselves off."

"But why?" Paul took the pipe out of his mouth. "What would they gain?"

"I haven't figured that out yet." Fairchild stood up and looked at the books strapped to the interne's cot. They were all medical volumes: *Space Medicine, Cosmic Radiation Pathology, Diseases of the Outer Planets.* He thumbed their bindings sadly.

"Well, maybe I'll figure it out before the trip's over." He started for the doorway, but froze when the unexpected happened.

BOOM!

"What was that?"

"Are we hit?" Paul jumped to his feet.

"It was an explosion! Aft, someplace."

"Let's go!"

They went through the doorway in a hurry. As they raced through the ship, those passengers who could lift their heads were doing so, curiously.

"What's happened?" one of the space-tug pilots called to Fairchild as he rushed past.

"Don't know!"

"Fairchild! Williams! Wetzel! What's happening back there?" It was Captain Ball, following closely on their heels.

"We're going to find out, sir," said Paul.

The three men continued down the length of the Ambulance. When they reached Section 3, Wetzel joined them. On first glance, everything looked normal. Then Fairchild's gaze went to the strange patient from the planet Ashes.

"The android!" he gasped.

They rushed to the cot. The synthetic man lay on his back, eyes still open. The even features were still placid and expressionless, but somehow, even more peaceful than before.

There was a gaping hole in its chest.

"Someone's shot him!" said Paul.

They looked in horror at the mock human mechanism, exposed by the still smoking chasm that a heat-bullet had created. The revelation was extraordinary.

Captain Ball exploded, "Wetzel! Fairchild! I hold you strictly accountable for this!"

Paul said, "Sir, Mr. Fairchild was off duty. He was in my cabin."

"You can't blame *me!*" Wetzel whined. "I didn't have anything to do with it."

Fairchild bent over the android.

"Is it—is he still alive?" Paul asked uneasily.

"I think so. Hard to tell, without a pulse or breathing. But I think his lips are moving."

"Who would want to *do* such a thing?" said Ball, looking around at the bed-ridden passengers helplessly. His mind filled with thoughts of triplicate forms, and investigations, and senatorial subpoenas.

"But he's not *human,*" Wetzel protested. "I mean, he's really just a machine. Does it even matter?"

"He was our responsibility," Paul said harshly.

"Quiet!" Fairchild bent closer to the moving lips. "I think he's going to say something."

They stared silently.

The android's mouth, trembled, its perfect lips struggling to form a word.

"Th—th—"

"What's he saying?" asked the captain.

"Quiet, you damn fool!" Fairchild forgot his rank for a moment, but fortunately, Ball did, too.

"Th—thanks..." the android said. "Thanks...mmm...Miss..."

Fairchild looked up.

"Did you hear that?" he said grimly.

The three men looked blank.

Fairchild got to his feet and pushed past them. He went over to the cot twice removed from the android's and said, "Where's the gun, Miss Allingham?"

The redhead stuck out her lower lip. "What gun?" she said.

"Don't give me that!" said Fairchild savagely. "The heat-gun you shot the android with!"

The pretty mouth opened in surprise. "What? Me?"

Fairchild moved quickly. He reached down and gripped the girl's shoulder. His strong hand pushed her head away from the pillow before she could prevent it. It came out with a small, jewel-encrusted revolver. The corpsman examined it. It bore the initials D. A., and had obviously been fired.

Tight-lipped, he turned to the commanding officer. "Captain Ball," he said, "I suggest that this woman be placed under arrest."

"Miss Allingham!" The captain looked unhappier than ever, thinking of her father's widespread influence. "Why did you do it?"

The girl glared at him and then began to sulk. "Don't look at me as if I were a *murderer*," she said. "It's only an android. It's not a real person. It's a machine!"

Paul said quietly, "But you still had no right…"

"No right?" Dee's nostrils dilated with wrath. "That thing *wanted* to die. It kept *begging* for it. It was driving me crazy!"

Fairchild went back to the android's cot.

"I did him a favor!" she shouted after him. "I did more for him than you could, you phony doctor! At least I had the *guts!*"

"He's still alive," said the corpsman.

Wetzel said, "What's that funny noise?"

The captain and the interne came over.

"Some piece of machinery's going," said Ball.

Fairchild looked at them.

"I've got a horrible idea," he said. "Paul—remember what we were talking about? About the android, and the suicide impulse?"

"Yes?" The interne looked puzzled.

"Well, there *could* be an advantage to such an android in war." Fairchild stood up, and stared down at the gaping wound.

"If he carried a bomb—" he said.

"A bomb?" The captain took a hesitant step backwards.

"Russ, you don't think—"

"Well, figure it out. The android wants to die. The men who made him wanted him to die. Because they knew that wherever he was would be destroyed with him."

Dee Allingham shrieked, "Oh, my God! My God! We'll all be killed!"

"Shut up!" Wetzel left the redhead's side and came over to the other corpsman. He was sweating. "Ross—we gotta do something!"

"If it's true," said Paul, "then we can't let him die. We can't!"

"How do we stop him?" Fairchild examined their faces, but no one seemed to have an answer.

Then Wetzel said, "We can throw him out! We can ditch him!"

"But he'll just follow the ship!" said Paul.

Captain Ball licked his lips. "We can strap a rocket exhaust to him. We can shoot him out into space!"

"But how far?" asked Fairchild. "If there's a bomb in his body, it's sure to be a cobalt. Even if we shot away a thousand miles, the concussion could rip us apart. Anyway," he said, turning his gaze once more to the dying synthetic man, "I don't think we'll have the time."

Talk! Talk!" the girl shrieked, and this time the other passengers broke their stunned silence and began to wail in fear. "Why don't you *do* something?" She began to sob hysterically.

"We will," said Fairchild. He spoke to Paul. "We can operate," he said.

"Operate?" Paul stared back. "But how—on what—"

"Can you do it, Williams?" asked the captain, his voice unsteady.

"No!" Paul shook his head violently. "I wouldn't know where to begin—" He clutched Fairchild's sleeve. "Russ! You do it! You've got a steadier hand! Please—"

They all turned to Fairchild. Suddenly, the corpsman seemed calm.

"I'll try it," he said. His tone seemed confident.

They put the android on the table.

With his bare hand, Fairchild explored the artificial rib cage.

"Be careful," Paul breathed. "Be careful, Russ."

"Quiet!"

His hand touched the sharp edge of some metallic box. It felt hot, as if it contained high-voltage current. He jerked his fingers away.

"Rubber glove!" he snapped.

Paul helped him on with it. Quickly, he returned to his exploration.

"Seems like ten thousand wires," he said. "All of them ripped apart by the bullet." His hand touched something else. "But there's some kind of cable—"

"I think it's hopeless," Paul said. "We don't know the mechanics of this thing—"

"Then we have to figure them out! We have to find out what's *unnecessary* in its body!"

"Unnecessary?"

"Don't you see? The android has parts resembling streamlined human organs. A lot of parts have been built out. But if we find something extra, something we can't explain—something that doesn't belong in the anatomical system—"

"Then it will be the bomb!"

Fairchild nodded. "The cable must correspond to the spine, or the ganglia. It's the nerve center of the android. The box probably performs a heart function, and—wait a minute!"

"What is it?"

"This box is thick. Much *too* thick."

"What do you mean, Russ?"

"They wouldn't require this much thickness for strength. There are plenty of alloys that would have done the job, and be a lot more practical."

Paul shook his head. "I don't get you, Russ."

"Don't you see? It's *lead*, Paul. They're *shielding* something in there, not just protecting it!"

"The bomb!"

"The cable must be attached to it. The trigger must react when the nerves of the android go dead."

"Then if he dies—"

"He will die, Paul." Fairchild yanked his hand out as the hot box began to burn through the glove. "Nothing can save him now."

Paul swallowed. "Then that's it. We're done for."

"Maybe not," said Fairchild. "If I can disconnect the box before the android dies, and substitute an electrical charge for the nerve impulses—" he looked hopefully at the interne.

He began to unpack the instruments from Paul's case.

"Call the ship's power man. Get him here right away, with a portable generator."

Captain Ball's face was as white as an official paper.

When Fairchild came out of the emergency operating room, he stared at him wordlessly.

Wetzel left the sobbing, red-haired woman and came up to the corpsman.

Paul came out of the room, his face drawn with the tension of the last few minutes.

"Well?" said the captain.

Fairchild smiled wanly. "The operation was a success," he said. "But the patient died."

Paul put his hand on the sleeve of Fairchild's gray uniform.

"Thanks, doc," he said.

THE END

If you've enjoyed this book, you will not want to miss these terrific titles…

ARMCHAIR SCI-FI & HORROR DOUBLE NOVELS, $12.95 each

D-181 **THE LADY OF LIGHT** by Jack Williamson
THE SWORDSMAN OF PIRA by Charles Recour

D-182 **A TWELVEMONTH AND A DAY** by Poul Anderson
PREFERRED RISK by Lester Del Rey & Frederik Pohl

D-183 **PLANET OF THE KNOB-HEADS** by Stanton A. Coblentz
OUT OF THE VOID by Leslie F. Stone

D-184 **DIVIDED WE FALL** by Raymond F. Jones
VASSALS OF THE LODE-STAR by Gardner F. Fox

D-185 **THE ANT WITH THE HUMAN SOUL** by Bob Olsen
NIGHT OF THE TROLLS by Keith Laumer

D-186 **GATEWAY TO INFINITY** Milton Lesser
AROUND THE UNIVERSE by Ray Cummings

D-187 **WEST POINT, 3000 A. D.** by Manly Wade Wellman
HOLY CITY OF MARS by Ralph Milne Farley

D-188 **M'BONG-AH** by Rog Phillips
MERCENARY by Mack Reynolds

D-189 **THE GREAT MIRROR** by Arthur J. Burks
TERROR FROM THE ABYSS by John Fletcher

D-190 **SINBAD: THROUGH TIME AND SPACE** by Chester S. Geier
THE ENORMOUS ROOM by H. L. Gold and Robert W. Krepps

ARMCHAIR SCIENCE FICTION CLASSICS, $12.95 each

C-71 **WORLD'S FAIR, 1992**
by Robert Silverberg

C-72 **THE PROFESSOR JAMESON SAGA, Book Three**
by Neil R. Jones

C-73 **THAT WORLDS MAY LIVE**
by Nelson S. Bond

ARMCHAIR SCI-FI & HORROR GEMS SERIES, $12.95 each

G-23 **SCIENCE FICTION GEMS, Vol. Twelve**
Theodore Sturgeon and others

G-24 **HORROR GEMS, Vol. Twelve**
Allison V. Harding and others

If you've enjoyed this book, you will not want to miss these terrific titles...

ARMCHAIR SCI-FI & HORROR DOUBLE NOVELS, $12.95 each

D-171 **REGAN'S PLANET** by Robert Silverberg
SOMEONE TO WATCH OVER ME by H. L. Gold and Floyd Gale

D-172 **PEOPLE MINUS X** by Raymond Z. Gallun
THE SAVAGE MACHINE by Randall Garrett

D-173 **THE FACE BEYOND THE VEIL** by Rog Phillips
REST IN AGONY by Paul W. Fairman

D-174 **VIRGIN OF VALKARION** by Poul Anderson
EARTH ALERT by Kris Neville

D-175 **WHEN THE ATOMS FAILED** by John W. Campbell, Jr.
DRAGONS OF SPACE by Aladra Septama

D-176 **THE TATTOOED MAN** by Edmond Hamilton
A RESCUE FROM JUPITER by Gawain Edwards

D-177 **THE FLYING THREAT** by David H. Keller, M. D.
THE FIFTH-DIMENSION TUBE by Murray Leinster

D-178 **LAST DAYS OF THRONAS** by S. J. Byrne
GODDESS OF WORLD 21 by Henry Slesar

D-179 **THE MOTHER WORLD** by B. Wallis & George C. Wallis
BEYOND THE VANISHING POINT by Ray Cummings

D-180 **DARK DESTINY** by Dwight V. Swain
SECRET OF PLANETOID 88 by Ed Earl Repp

ARMCHAIR SCIENCE FICTION CLASSICS, $12.95 each

C-69 **EXILES OF THE MOON**
by Nathan Schachner & Arthur Leo Zagut

C-70 **SKYLARK OF SPACE**
by E. E. "Doc' Smith

ARMCHAIR MYSTERY-CRIME DOUBLE NOVELS, $12.95 each

B-11 **THE BABY DOLL MURDERS** by James O. Causey
DEATH HITCHES A RIDE by Martin L. Weiss

B-12 **THE DOVE** by Milton Ozaki
THE GLASS LADDER by Paul W. Fairman

B-13 **THE NAKED STORM** by C. M. Kornbluth
THE MAN OUTSIDE by Alexander Blade

If you've enjoyed this book, you will not want to miss these terrific titles...

ARMCHAIR MYSTERY-CRIME DOUBLE NOVELS, $12.95 each

B-16 **KISS AND KILL** by Richard Deming
THE DEAD STAND-IN by Frank Kane

B-17 **DANGEROUS LADY** by Octavus Roy Cohen
ONE HOUR LATE by William O'Farrell

B-18 **LOVE ME AND DIE!** by Day Keene
YOU'LL GET YOURS by Thomas Wills

B-19 **EVERYBODY'S WATCHING ME** by Mickey Spillane
A BULLET FOR CINDERELLA by John D. MacDonald

B-20 **WILD OATS** by Harry Whittington
MAKE WAY FOR MURDER by A. A. Marcus

B-21 **THE ART STUDIO MURDERS** by Edward Ronns
THE CASE OF JENNIE BRICE by Mary Roberts Rinehart

B-22 **THE LUSTFUL APE** by Bruno Fisher
KISS THE BABE GOODBYE by Bob McKnight

B-23 **SARATOGA MANTRAP** by Dexter St. Claire
CLASSIFICATION: HOMICIDE by Jonathan Craig

ARMCHAIR SCI-FI & HORROR DOUBLE NOVELS, $12.95 each

E-5 **THE IDOLS OF WULD** by Milton Lesser
PLANET OF THE DAMNED by Harry Harrison

E-6 **BETWEEN WORLDS** by Garret Smith
PLANET OF THE DEAD by Rog Phillips

E-7 **DAUGHTER OF THOR** by Edmond Hamilton
TALENTS, INCORPORATED by Murray Leinster

E-8 **ALL ABOARD FOR THE MOON** by Harold M. Sherman
THE METAL EMPEROR by Raymond A. Palmer

E-9 **DEATH HUNT** by Robert Gilbert
THE BEST MADE PLANS by Everett B. Cole

E-10 **GIANT KILLER** by Dwight V. Swain
GOLDEN AMAZONS OF VENUS by John Murray Reynolds

ARMCHAIR SCI-FI & HORROR GEMS SERIES, $12.95 each

G-21 **SCIENCE FICTION GEMS, Vol. Eleven**
Rog Phillips and others

G-22 **HORROR GEMS, Vol. Eleven**
Thorp McClusky and others

If you've enjoyed this book, you will not want to miss these terrific titles...

ARMCHAIR SCI-FI & HORROR DOUBLE NOVELS, $12.95 each

D-1   **THE GALAXY RAIDERS** by William P. McGivern
        SPACE STATION #1 by Frank Belknap Long

D-2   **THE PROGRAMMED PEOPLE** by Jack Sharkey
        SLAVES OF THE CRYSTAL BRAIN by William Carter Sawtelle

D-3   **YOU'RE ALL ALONE** by Fritz Leiber
        THE LIQUID MAN by Bernard C. Gilford

D-4   **CITADEL OF THE STAR LORDS** by Edmond Hamilton
        VOYAGE TO ETERNITY by Milton Lesser

D-5   **IRON MEN OF VENUS** by Don Wilcox
        THE MAN WITH ABSOLUTE MOTION by Noel Loomis

D-6   **WHO SOWS THE WIND...** by Rog Phillips
        THE PUZZLE PLANET by Robert A. W. Lowndes

D-7   **PLANET OF DREAD** by Murray Leinster
        TWICE UPON A TIME by Charles L. Fontenay

D-8   **THE TERROR OUT OF SPACE** by Dwight V. Swain
        QUEST OF THE GOLDEN APE by Ivar Jorgensen and Adam Chase

D-9   **SECRET OF MARRACOTT DEEP** by Henry Slesar
        PAWN OF THE BLACK FLEET by Mark Clifton.

D-10   **BEYOND THE RINGS OF SATURN** by Robert Moore Williams
        A MAN OBSESSED by Alan E. Nourse

ARMCHAIR SCIENCE FICTION CLASSICS, $12.95 each

C-1   **THE GREEN MAN**
        by Harold M. Sherman

C-2   **A TRACE OF MEMORY**
        By Keith Laumer

C-3   **INTO PLUTONIAN DEPTHS**
        by Stanton A. Coblentz

ARMCHAIR MASTERS OF SCIENCE FICTION SERIES, $16.95 each

M-1   **MASTERS OF SCIENCE FICTION, Vol. One**
        Bryce Walton—"Dark of the Moon" and other tales

M-2   **MASTERS OF SCIENCE FICTION, Vol. Two**
        Jerome Bixby—"One Way Street" and other tales

If you've enjoyed this book, you will not want to miss these terrific titles…

ARMCHAIR SCI-FI & HORROR DOUBLE NOVELS, $12.95 each

D-11 **PERIL OF THE STARMEN** by Kris Neville
THE STRANGE INVASION by Murray Leinster

D-12 **THE STAR LORD** by Boyd Ellanby
CAPTIVES OF THE FLAME by Samuel R. Delany

D-13 **MEN OF THE MORNING STAR** by Edmond Hamilton
PLANET FOR PLUNDER by Hal Clement and Sam Merwin, Jr.

D-14 **ICE CITY OF THE GORGON** by Chester S. Geier and Richard Shaver
WHEN THE WORLD TOTTERED by Lester del Rey

D-15 **WORLDS WITHOUT END** by Clifford D. Simak
THE LAVENDER VINE OF DEATH by Don Wilcox

D-16 **SHADOW ON THE MOON** by Joe Gibson
ARMAGEDDON EARTH by Geoff St. Reynard

D-17 **THE GIRL WHO LOVED DEATH** by Paul W. Fairman
SLAVE PLANET by Laurence M. Janifer

D-18 **SECOND CHANCE** by J. F. Bone
MISSION TO A DISTANT STAR by Frank Belknap Long

D-19 **THE SYNDIC** by C. M. Kornbluth
FLIGHT TO FOREVER by Poul Anderson

D-20 **SOMEWHERE I'LL FIND YOU** by Milton Lesser
THE TIME ARMADA by Fox B. Holden

ARMCHAIR SCIENCE FICTION CLASSICS, $12.95 each

C-4 **CORPUS EARTHLING**
by Louis Charbonneau

C-5 **THE TIME DISSOLVER**
by Jerry Sohl

C-6 **WEST OF THE SUN**
by Edgar Pangborn

ARMCHAIR SCI-FI & HORROR GEMS SERIES, $12.95 each

G-1 **SCIENCE FICTION GEMS, Vol. One**
Isaac Asimov and others

G-2 **HORROR GEMS, Vol. One**
Carl Jacobi and others

If you've enjoyed this book, you will not want to miss these terrific titles…

ARMCHAIR SCI-FI & HORROR DOUBLE NOVELS, $12.95 each

D-21   **EMPIRE OF EVIL** by Robert Arnette
THE SIGN OF THE TIGER by Alan E. Nourse & J. A. Meyer

D-22   **OPERATION SQUARE PEG** by Frank Belknap Long
ENCHANTRESS OF VENUS by Leigh Brackett

D-23   **THE LIFE WATCH** by Lester del Rey
CREATURES OF THE ABYSS by Murray Leinster

D-24   **LEGION OF LAZARUS** by Edmond Hamilton
STAR HUNTER by Andre Norton

D-25   **EMPIRE OF WOMEN** by John Fletcher
ONE OF OUR CITIES IS MISSING by Irving Cox

D-26   **THE WRONG SIDE OF PARADISE** by Raymond F. Jones
THE INVOLUNTARY IMMORTALS by Rog Phillips

D-27   **EARTH QUARTER** by Damon Knight
ENVOY TO NEW WORLDS by Keith Laumer

D-28   **SLAVES TO THE METAL HORDE** by Milton Lesser
HUNTERS OUT OF TIME by Joseph E. Kelleam

D-29   **RX JUPITER SAVE US** by Ward Moore
BEWARE THE USURPERS by Geoff St. Reynard

D-30   **SECRET OF THE SERPENT** by Don Wilcox
CRUSADE ACROSS THE VOID by Dwight V. Swain

ARMCHAIR SCIENCE FICTION CLASSICS, $12.95 each

C-7   **THE SHAVER MYSTERY, Book One**
by Richard S. Shaver

C-8   **THE SHAVER MYSTERY, Book Two**
by Richard S. Shaver

C-9   **MURDER IN SPACE** by David V. Reed
by David V. Reed

ARMCHAIR MASTERS OF SCIENCE FICTION SERIES, $16.95 each

M-3   **MASTERS OF SCIENCE FICTION, Vol. Three**
Robert Sheckley, "The Perfect Woman" and other tales

M-4   **MASTERS OF SCIENCE FICTION, Vol. Four**
Mack Reynolds, "Stowaway" and other tales

If you've enjoyed this book, you will not want to miss these terrific titles…

ARMCHAIR SCI-FI & HORROR DOUBLE NOVELS, $12.95 each

D-31 **A HOAX IN TIME** by Keith Laumer
INSIDE EARTH by Poul Anderson

D-32 **TERROR STATION** by Dwight V. Swain
THE WEAPON FROM ETERNITY by Dwight V. Swain

D-33 **THE SHIP FROM INFINITY** by Edmond Hamilton
TAKEOFF by C. M. Kornbluth

D-34 **THE METAL DOOM** by David H. Keller
TWELVE TIMES ZERO by Howard Browne

D-35 **HUNTERS OUT OF SPACE** by Joseph Kelleam
INVASION FROM THE DEEP by Paul W. Fairman,

D-36 **THE BEES OF DEATH** by Robert Moore Williams
A PLAGUE OF PYTHONS by Frederik Pohl

D-37 **THE LORDS OF QUARMALL** by Fritz Leiber and Harry Fischer
BEACON TO ELSEWHERE by James H. Schmitz

D-38 **BEYOND PLUTO** by John S. Campbell
ARTERY OF FIRE by Thomas N. Scortia

D-39 **SPECIAL DELIVERY** by Kris Neville
NO TIME FOR TOFFEE by Charles F. Meyers

D-40 **RECALLED TO LIFE** by Robert Silverberg
JUNGLE IN THE SKY by Milton Lesser

ARMCHAIR SCIENCE FICTION CLASSICS, $12.95 each

C-10 **MARS IS MY DESTINATION**
by Frank Belknap Long

C-11 **SPACE PLAGUE**
by George O. Smith

C-12 **SO SHALL YE REAP**
by Rog Phillips

ARMCHAIR SCI-FI & HORROR GEMS SERIES, $12.95 each

G-3 **SCIENCE FICTION GEMS, Vol. Two**
James Blish and others

G-4 **HORROR GEMS, Vol. Two**
Joseph Payne Brennan and others

Made in the USA
Monee, IL
20 January 2023

25717437R00132